So
Close
to YOU

So Close to You

RACHEL CARTER

An Imprint of HarperCollinsPublishers

To my father, Phil Carter, for never doubting

CHAPTER 1

The bonfire in the clearing spits out flames and smoke. Red, yellow, orange sparks fly up into the night sky. My classmates cluster around it, everyone drinking out of red plastic cups. It's the seniors' unofficial end-of-the-year party, and this small open space in the woods is packed and pulsing with bodies.

I stand to the side and pretend to sip at the bitter, cheap beer. The forest rises behind me, the silhouettes of trees towering overhead. Shadows dip and blend as the wind rustles branches and sends the smoke of the bonfire in all different directions. Someone has hooked up a stereo to a car battery and I can feel the beat pounding through the crowd. The lyrics, something about mushrooms and dark corners, are muffled in the shouting and noise.

The fire gives off enough light to illuminate the clearing, but beyond this circle the woods are a black, impenetrable wall. I don't know why the seniors decided to throw this party at Camp Hero, a state park at the very eastern end of Montauk. I've been here a hundred times with my grandfather, walking along the sea cliffs that border the park, or hiking through the dense, sunlit forest. But it feels like a different place at night—the darkness creeps through the trees like a living thing.

On the other side of the fire, my best friend, Hannah, waits in line for the keg. She looks bored and a little lost in her long peasant skirt, her black hair parted down the middle. A tipsy girl in front of her stumbles, and beer splashes on the people nearby. Hannah scowls and steps away. She catches my eye across the clearing and raises her eyebrows in a *What have you gotten me into?* look.

I smile and turn to see Shannon Perkins approaching. "Hey, Lydia," she says. Her blond hair is straight and sleek, her bright dress tight. "I thought you said you weren't coming tonight." Her eyes are glassy and unfocused and she smiles widely in my general direction.

"How could I miss all this?" I wave my hand toward the keg, where a bunch of guys are lifting Dave Marcus, a senior, into a keg stand. "One, two, three, four . . ." everyone chants in unison as he sputters around the foaming beer. The crowd is roaring and the wind whips through the fire, making it crackle and spark.

"Yeah, Dave!" Shannon calls out, and her voice is immediately swallowed up in the rest of the noise. "Do you think he's gonna break his record?" she asks more quietly.

I give her a confused look. "I have no idea."

"Oh, right, Lydia. I forgot you never come to these things."

I shrug. I *don't* ever come to these things, and I'm still not sure what compelled me to tonight.

Shannon smiles at me again, slightly more focused this time. "I liked that article you did for the paper, the one about the squad. Let me know if you want any more quotes."

I smile back. "Sure. Thanks for helping out." Shannon and I both grew up in Montauk, and we've known each other since we were little kids. We're not exactly friends now—our social circles are different—but we're still friendly.

Shannon tugs at the spaghetti strap on her dress, forgetting that she's still holding her beer. It spills a little, and the tiny, amber-colored drops catch in her hair. "God, can you believe we're going to be seniors?"

I laugh, shaking my head. "No. Sometimes it feels like we're still in second grade, running around on the beach, building sand castles and stuff."

Hannah approaches us, her plastic cup empty. "I couldn't get any beer before the frat-boy routine started." She looks surprised when she sees me talking to Shannon, and they awkwardly nod at each other.

"Well, I'll see you around, Lydia." Shannon waves as she walks away.

Hannah steals the cup from my hand and takes a sip of the warm beer. She grimaces as she swallows. "What did the cheerleader want?" She wipes her hand across her mouth and shoves the drink back at me.

"Just to say hi. What's your problem with her, anyway?"

"I don't like cheerleaders on principle. It's for all of us artsy nerds that ever felt the sharp sting of a mean girl's wrath."

I roll my eyes. "You're delusional. Shannon's not like that."

"Whatever. All you Montauk kids are so weird. You're so . . . *nice* to each other. It's not natural."

I laugh at her scrunched-up expression. "It's a tiny town. You have to be nice to everyone. You're just mad you grew up in fancy East Hampton with all the celebrities."

"Hey, it's not all Barefoot Contessa and Burberry. Some of us are regular old middle class."

"You're so lucky I came along to save you from the pampered masses." I put my arm around her, squeezing her smaller figure up against mine. I'm not tall, but Hannah's practically miniature.

"Get off me." She twists away, laughing.

Hannah and I have been inseparable since eighth grade, when my small Montauk class started getting shipped over to East Hampton to attend the larger regional high school. Our lockers were next to each other, we were in all the "smart kid" classes together, and we both harbored a secret love of old musicals. Our friendship was basically inevitable.

There's a tall, lanky boy headed in our direction.

Hannah groans. "Don't look now, but your boyfriend's coming over."

"Stop," I whisper. "We're just friends."

"Yeah, right."

"Hi, Grant," I say, loud enough to drown out Hannah's giggling.

"Hey." He grins as he approaches. "Lydia. How's it going?"

"Good." I smile tightly. "How are you?"

"Awesome. I'm glad you came." He tries to catch my eye, but I avoid his gaze, concentrating on the cup in my hands.

"Awkward," I hear Hannah drawl under her breath. I resist the urge to elbow her.

It didn't used to be like this. Grant and I grew up next to each other on the same quiet, tree-lined street. But lately he's been watching me when he thinks I'm not looking, following me down the halls at school, and waiting for me after my classes. I'm dreading the day he tries to make a move.

"I didn't think I'd see you here." He sounds surprised.

I'm starting to get kind of offended. Sure, I don't come to parties often, but it's not like I'm a social pariah.

"Hannah and I decided to mix things up," I say, keeping my tone deliberately light. "You can only watch *Singin' in the Rain* so many times."

"That is *so* not true," Hannah mumbles.

Grant laughs. "I remember you used to make me watch that movie over and over. I think I still know it by heart."

I laugh with him, remembering the blanket forts we

would make in his living room that left only a tiny window to see the TV. Grant and I used to spend every minute together, just playing and laughing, and a part of me wishes we could go back to that time, before everything became so complicated.

"Do you want another drink?" Grant asks.

I shake my head. "I've had my fill of cheap beer for the night." To make my point I tip my cup over, and the last of the pale liquid splashes to the ground.

Hannah clutches my arm dramatically. "Not the precious beer. We can't possibly lose the beer!"

Grant laughs and plays at being offended. "You don't have to waste it."

Hannah straightens. "I dare you to tell me it accomplishes anything other than drunken hookups and hangovers."

"I don't know, what about a little liquid courage?" He holds my gaze before tipping his cup back and taking a sip. I look at Hannah helplessly. She shrugs, trying to contain a smile.

It's not that Grant isn't cute. He might have been painfully dorky when we were younger, with his love of *Battlestar Galactica* and anime, but lately he's cornered the whole sensitive guy thing. He wears Chucks and skinny jeans and he's the editor of our school's literary magazine. He's tall, so tall that I have to tip my head back to look at his face, and all long and lanky. The goth girls worship him.

"Well, I need a refill." He shakes his empty cup in my

direction. "Let me get you one." He gives me an intense look, tilting his head to one side and staring at me through a fall of shaggy black hair.

"No, thanks."

Hannah is quiet as he starts to move away from us. The music has shifted from pounding rap to some shrill popstar. The breeze picks up and I smell the sharp salt of the ocean, the beach only a few miles from here. It's a familiar smell for those of us who grew up in Montauk, a town so far out on the tip of Long Island it feels as though we're more connected to the water than the land.

"Is he why you wanted to come tonight?" The way Hannah asks it sounds like an accusation.

My mouth falls open. "Of course not! You know I don't like Grant like that."

"You keep saying that, but you don't seem to be doing anything to discourage him."

"I don't want to hurt him." I turn away, staring at where the fire burns in the middle of the clearing. A drunk guy is pretending to throw a freshman girl into the flames. The girl's shrieks echo through the night, so that it sounds like the screaming is coming from the woods behind us.

"But you'll have to, eventually," Hannah says. "He'll gather up his courage and then you'll break his little heart. He'll have to listen to so much Death Cab to get over the pain." She pats my shoulder, as though she's pretending to comfort Grant. "Even if you did like him, you two would never work. You have nothing in common."

I sigh. "I'm not going to date Grant. But it's not like we have *nothing* in common. We both like to write."

"He writes poetry that makes no sense and you want to be a serious journalist. Not the same thing." She suddenly straightens and snaps her fingers, pointing at me. "Though you *are* both hipsters."

I cross my arms and frown. "I am not a hipster!"

"Lydia, you've got bangs that hang in your eyes and you wear funky vintage dresses. I hate to break it to you, but that's pretty hipster for the Hamptons."

I look around the woods, at the girls in tight jeans and tank tops, in brightly colored jersey dresses. I do stand out in my red polka-dot dress, with its wide collar and pleated skirt. But I don't care; I buy almost all of my clothes at thrift stores and vintage shops.

Hannah puts her hands on her hips. "You're an Aries, Lydia. You're fiery and independent. He's a Cancer. A water sign. Sensitive. Meek. You'd squash his spirit."

I laugh. "Seriously?"

"Say what you want, but we both know there's truth to the signs."

I roll my eyes. Hannah, though cynical and sarcastic ninety percent of the time, claims that astrology is her bible. I blame it on her mother, who insists that Hannah call her Jet, owns a used record shop in South Hampton, and does tarot card readings on the side. Hannah's father is a Japanese artist who lives in Hawaii, where he's working on becoming a world-class surfer. Hannah says her parents are children she's sick of raising, and so she spends almost all her time at my house.

But even I can't get her to shake the astrology.

Hannah waves her hand toward the keg, where Grant is talking to one of his friends. "So if it wasn't for a boy, then why did you make me come to this stereotypical drunken grope-fest?"

I bite my lower lip, avoiding Hannah's gaze. "I just wanted to."

She leans forward and her hair spills over her shoulder. It's so dark, it's almost blue-black. "Out with it, Miss Bentley."

I fidget with my skirt, but Hannah won't stop staring at me, one eyebrow raised as she waits for my response. "Okay, *Miss Sasaki*," I say, mimicking her tone. "It was because of Camp Hero." I circle my finger in the air, pointing to the trees above our heads. "I heard they were throwing the party here, and I felt like I had to come."

"But you hate Camp Hero."

"I don't hate it, I just have a complicated relation-ship with it. My grandfather has been bringing me here for years, feeding me his conspiracy theories. I guess I wanted to prove this place doesn't have any power over me. That I can come here for something *normal*, like a party in the woods."

"As long as you don't start drinking the Kool-Aid . . ."

"Don't worry. I will never believe in the Montauk Project."

"Hey!" Grant exclaims as he joins us again, a beer clutched between his hands. "Who says the Montauk Project isn't true?"

I sigh under my breath.

"Please. Like there's some big, secret conspiracy happening out there." Hannah gestures to the dark forest behind us. "It's ridiculous. Montauk is too small a town to hide an underground government lab at one of the state parks. People would notice creepy army guys skulking around out here. There's no way they could get away with it."

"Secret. Government. Project," Grant enunciates. "As in, it's a secret. And this is the *government* we're talking about. The people behind this are like the CIA, only more elite and more dangerous. They're the most highly trained military personnel imaginable, partnered with the smartest scientists in the world, and they'll do anything to keep this a secret. The president probably doesn't even know what happens here."

Wanting a distraction, I grab Grant's drink from his hands and take a sip of beer. "Thanks." I shove it back at him. He looks surprised as he takes it from me.

"How could you possibly know that?" Hannah is clearly unwilling to let the subject go. "You have no idea if the Montauk Project even exists."

"Oh, it exists." Grant takes a long drink of his beer, his thin face stark in the dim light. "Trust me. Too many weird things happen around here for it to be a coincidence."

"Like what?"

"How about electronics suddenly not working for no apparent reason? Or fishermen seeing strange lights late at night?"

"That's easy," Hannah replies. "Everyone knows that the radar tower they built during the Cold War messes with communications sometimes. And those fishermen are drunk."

"That's what they want you to believe about the radar tower." Grant shakes his head, his messy hair flying from side to side. "But it's all part of the cover-up. To pretend that this place was just a harmless military base."

"But Camp Hero hasn't been used by the military in years. And it's a state park now. Why would the government open it up to the public if there's a secret research base out here?" Hannah steps closer to Grant. They're so focused on their argument, they've forgotten I'm here.

I look around the clearing impatiently. We've all had this conversation a million times before. I'm usually willing to get into it, but not tonight. Not when we're standing in the middle of Camp Hero, and I can practically feel my grandfather's presence around me.

"What better way to hide something than by trying to erase public suspicions? Face it. The Montauk Project is the East Coast Area Fifty-one." Grant's face is lit up, his brown eyes wide, almost feverish.

"Area Fifty-one?" Hannah rolls her eyes. "There are no aliens here. And please don't tell me you believe in those 'reptoids.' Alien creatures that look like giant lizards from another dimension are really coming down onto the beach to terrorize the surfers? Please."

"Why not? It's possible. The scientists study all kinds of stuff . . . like time tunnels. Which are really wormholes. Those holes could connect to anywhere. Even other planets."

"That's ridiculous," Hannah scoffs.

"Let's just drop it," I cut in, trying to lighten the mood. "It's like I'm hanging out with my grandpa or something."

The joke falls flat. "You shouldn't discount him." Grant reaches his arm out toward me, as if he can physically press his words, his belief, into me. "There are whole online message forums of people with evidence that the Montauk Project exists."

"Oh right"—Hannah laughs mockingly—"because conspiracy theorists on the *internet* are always trustworthy."

"Laugh all you want, Hannah. But this could be real. There are even reports that they kidnap people to use in their experiments. They especially like to snatch children. Easier to brainwash."

"If you believe that, then why are you even here right now?" I snap, starting to get fed up with both of them. "Aren't you afraid that men in lab coats are going to drag you down into their secret lair?"

"The government wouldn't risk that kind of exposure."

Grant seems unaware of my growing annoyance. "That's why they usually kidnap orphans, or people with no family ties. Can you imagine what would happen if people knew about what went on here? People would protest; it could even topple the government. Only a select few can know, and they're under the ground right now."

I stare down at my feet. The grass in the clearing has been worn away, and there's mud clinging to my sandals. I try not to think about people down there, in tunnels or tubes or hallways or whatever it is secret government projects are made out of.

I look back at Grant. "You know, I'm really sick of talking about the Montauk Project. I get enough of this conspiracy garbage at home." Grant opens his mouth, but I put my hand out to stop him from saying anything. "It's getting cold, and I left my sweater in the car. I'll be back in a while."

"Wait, I'll come with you," Grant says. Hannah is finally quiet, her gaze shifting between the two of us.

"No, don't. I just need some air."

Hannah's car is parked on one of the roads that winds through Camp Hero, almost a quarter of a mile away from the party. I walk through the dark, weaving slowly between the tree trunks, stubbing my toes on rocks and feeling the sharp sting of branches grab at my skin. Though I can still hear the music and the laughter behind me, the moon isn't very bright, and the trees cast deep shadows across my path.

A branch snaps in the wind, and I jerk my head up, straining to see into the darkness around me. Even though I know the Montauk Project isn't real, there's still something eerie about being here late at night. I can't help but think of the countless times I've walked through these woods with my grandfather, and worse, all of the years I spent believing in his theories.

I was seven years old when my grandfather brought me here for the first time. Camp Hero had only just been turned into a state park, and parts of it were still closed to the public. Before that it had been an abandoned military base with NO TRESPASSING signs scattered around the woods. Of course that never stopped my grandfather from exploring. He'd sneak in through holes in the fence and run whenever he heard dogs barking or the sound of a patrol car.

But by my first visit most of the fences were gone, and a parking lot sat near the cliffs. It was late July, and the air was heavy with the promise of a storm. As we parked the car, the sky already looked like a new bruise—blotches of purple, blue, and black. The trail leading to the bluffs was empty, the tourists scared off by the rising wind and the water crashing against the rocks below. Grandpa led me right to the edge of the cliffs, ignoring the signs that warned visitors to stay back at least twenty-five feet. Below us, rough waves broke against the sharp gray rocks. The Atlantic Ocean stretched out in front of us on all sides, so that the whole world seemed made of water.

That day, deterred by the rain, we didn't get past the parking lot, but it wasn't long before we came back again, and then again and again. In the early mornings we would leave my parents sleeping and drive through the small downtown center of Montauk, past the Fort Hill Cemetery, the Deep Hollow Ranch. When we were almost at the farthest eastern point of Long Island, we would make the turn into Camp Hero.

We'd spend the day hiking together looking for signs of the Montauk Project. My grandfather would point out manhole covers in the ground and tell me how they led to the underground facilities. We would inspect the concrete bunkers that were stuck into the sides of every hill—though they weren't natural hills, according to my grandfather, but top-secret government labs.

He told me about Nikola Tesla, a famous scientist he believed had faked his death to develop new psychological warfare tactics for the American government during World War II. The army base on Montauk Point became a cover for the experiments under the ground.

For years I believed all of his stories and theories about Camp Hero. Sometimes I'd even think I felt eyes on us, watching as we prowled the grounds of the camp, looking for proof that the underground lab was still active.

One cold day when I was ten, my grandfather took me to his favorite spot at Hero—a bunker hidden deep in the woods. It was late autumn, and the leaves were changing.

The bright reds and yellows obscured the concrete bunker as it receded into the side of a manmade hill. There was a cement door blocking the entrance, with a sign that read DO NOT ENTER. My grandfather told me that before they turned Camp Hero into a park, there was an apple-sized hole in the cement. If you looked through it at the right angle, you could see a large room filled with debris and a line of doors.

"Why would they have all of those doors if it was just for storage?" he asked. "Think about that." I did, but had no answers, so I stayed quiet, sitting on the damp grass. My grandfather is a tall man with a full head of steel-gray hair that was almost the same color as the concrete door of the bunker. "There are just too many questions. Not enough answers." He was mumbling to himself. Talking under his breath. "This is where they took my father," he whispered finally, so softly I could barely make out the words. He ran his hands almost reverently across the cement, tracing the grooves in the rough surface.

"What are you talking about, Grandpa?" I asked.

He turned to face me. He looked different, wide-eyed and manic, and I shrunk away from him as he came forward. He pulled something from his pocket and shoved it into my hands. It was an old leather-bound journal. I carefully opened it, not sure what I was looking at.

"This is my father's journal. This is the proof."

I knew his father had disappeared when he was a little boy, almost sixty-five years ago. But my grandfather never talked about it, and my father told me not to bring it up. This was the first time I had ever heard him mention it.

"Look. Look how he wrote the name Tesla in the margins. Look how he writes about a secret project he was working on."

I tried to skim the pages, but my grandfather kept flipping them over, faster and faster. My eyes started to blur. I wanted to be away from this person who seemed so different from my steady, strong grandfather.

"Don't you see, Lydia? My father was part of the Montauk Project. It's why he disappeared."

I nodded, though I knew, for the first time ever, that I didn't believe what he was saying. I could no longer deny the small voice of doubt that I had ignored for so long, the people in town who called my grandfather crazy, or the way my parents would roll their eyes whenever the Project was mentioned. Out of grief, my grandfather had allowed himself to get caught up in a story, a myth, and he had convinced me to believe in it too.

"You need to find the truth for yourself," he liked to say, but he never *found* any truth. Instead he paced the cliffs of Montauk searching for answers to questions that had long been buried, or had never existed at all.

It takes me longer than I thought to find Hannah's beat-up Toyota. She's parked off of the road, half hidden in the trees. Other cars are nearby, nestled in the woods, the thin moonlight reflecting off their metal bodies.

I open her passenger-side door and yank on my black cardigan, shivering in the cool air. Though it's early summer, the wind coming off the water is chilly and brisk. I look out toward where the ocean meets the cliffs. It's too dark to see anything but the shadow of the forest and the outline of the old radar tower jutting into the sky.

I close the car door, flinching at the sharp noise it makes, so loud out here in the empty darkness. Hopefully Grant and Hannah have finally stopped arguing and it's safe to head back to the party.

I step into the woods, but then I stop abruptly.

Someone is watching me.

CHAPTER 2

It starts as a prickly feeling, like something is hovering behind me. A shiver slides down my back. I stare into the black forest, but I can't see anything. "Hello?" I call out softly. No response. Maybe it's Grant following me out to the car. Maybe it's one of my classmates passed out in the woods. But why wouldn't they answer me? And why do I feel like something is crawling over my bare skin?

I take a deep breath. It's nothing. I'm overreacting. But I can't quite shake the feeling that someone is out there.

I step forward. Stop. It's silent, except for the distant noise of the party. I take two more steps. This time when I stop I hear something crack behind me. The sound of a branch underfoot. I whip my head around, expecting to see a man standing there, maybe with a knife, or a gun, or a chain saw. But there's nothing. I hold still, my heart lodged in my throat. Then, out of the corner of my eye, I see something move. Maybe it's a small tree blowing in the wind or some animal rustling the grass, but I start to run, panic clawing at me. I feel branches pull at my clothing, scratch at my face, but I don't stop. Something is right behind me, matching my steps. I can hear it getting closer.

The party is just up ahead, the bonfire flickering through the trees. I trip over an exposed root, falling to the ground. I scramble to my feet, ignoring the stinging in my palms, and I keep moving forward, aware that something is closing in on me. Then I run smack into a large object and fall onto my back. Hard.

"Whoa," Grant says, stumbling. He rights himself and leans down toward me, holding out his hand.

I stare up at him, one of my hands clutching a pile of wet leaves, one pressed against the top of my chest. My breathing slows and I blow my bangs out of my eyes. There's a sharp pain shooting up from my tailbone.

After a minute, I take Grant's hand and he pulls me to my feet.

"Lydia, are you okay? Why were you running?"

"I don't know. I thought . . . never mind. I'm an idiot." I rub my lower back. "What are you doing here?"

"I was looking for you."

Behind Grant I see light from the party streaming through the leaves and branches. People are dancing, vague figures that flow in and out of the trees.

I can barely make out Grant's face, just the shape of his long nose and thin, almost gaunt cheeks. He takes a step toward me.

"Don't be mad about the Hero stuff," he says. I stare at him in confusion before remembering the argument.

"I'm not mad. I just don't love talking about it."

"I get it. I wasn't spoon-fed conspiracy theories like you were." He takes another step toward me, until we're only inches apart. "It must be frustrating sometimes."

"It's not frustrating, exactly. Just sad." I think of my grandfather at the bunker, running his fingers over the concrete again and again. "I need proof before I can buy into something like the Montauk Project."

"Do you always need proof to believe in something?" His eyes are hidden, dark, and I wonder how my face appears to him. Am I like a ghostly version of myself? All deep hollows and shadows?

"Yes. I'm a journalist, remember? My job is to find the truth and then report it to the unsuspecting masses." I laugh nervously.

"You like being on the paper, huh?"

I love it. Interviewing people. Getting a tiny lead or suspicion and then chasing it down to figure out the truth. It's exciting. "Yeah, I do."

Grant smiles, the white of his teeth catching the moonlight. "Lydia. Do you want to . . . I mean, tomorrow I'm—"

"There you guys are!" Hannah's voice emerges from the black border of trees. The firelight is to her back, and she's nothing more than a shadow as she approaches. "You can't just leave me alone like that. I saw Brent Miller getting to second base with some freshman and now I need to scrub my eyes out with bleach." She stops and her long skirt makes a swishing noise as it settles around her. "So what are we talking about?"

I smile, a little too widely. "Nothing much."

Grant is staring down at the ground. "I was asking Lydia what she's doing tomorrow," he says quietly.

There's a strained silence.

"Why?" Hannah asks. "You want to hang out? I'm free in the afternoon."

"Actually," Grant starts, "I was thinking—"

"Tomorrow's Saturday, right? I'm busy all day," I quickly interrupt. "I promised my grandfather I'd come out here with him."

"Oh. Right." Grant's voice is flat. "Out here, you mean to Camp Hero?"

"Yeah, one of his clue-finding missions."

"Why do you keep agreeing to do that, since you're a nonbeliever?" Grant won't meet my eyes.

"Her grandfather thinks she still believes," Hannah says.

"Really?" Grant finally looks at me. "I wouldn't have thought you'd hide something like that, Lydia. It doesn't seem like you."

I shrug, uncomfortable. "It would really hurt him if he knew how I felt, or if I stopped coming out here to look for proof that the Montauk Project exists. Besides, I like spending time with him, even if I don't always like what we do." I glance out into the forest around me. Every shadow seems to be moving, every small noise twists through the trees. I turn to Hannah. "Look, can we get going? I've had enough of Camp Hero for now."

"I've been ready to go since we got here," she says.

Grant gestures at the party behind him. "I drove like four people so I should get back there. But are you free on Sunday?"

"I totally am," Hannah answers. She winks at me. Grant looks like he wants to strangle her.

I try not to laugh. "We can all do something. And sorry I can't hang tomorrow."

"Don't worry about it." Grant smiles. "I kind of wish I was coming, walking around here and looking for stuff. Who knows, maybe you'll find the truth this time."

"I doubt that," I say. "If there was anything weird going on at Camp Hero, my grandpa would have discovered it long ago."

The next morning I wake up late and lie in my bed, staring at the white ceiling of my room. The paint is starting to peel in one corner, and cracks spread out in thin, intersecting lines. My room is sparse and organized: a dresser, a brass bed, a bulletin board with my most recent stories attached in neat rows. I thrive on order. Hannah says it's because I'm an Aries, that I have a thing about control.

I tell her that she needs to get a new hobby.

As dust floats through the morning sunlight, I think about Grant standing in the dark woods, his face filled with hope. I like Grant, I always have, but the thought of kissing him fills me with a vague sense of revulsion. Not that I have much experience to go on. I've only kissed a total of three boys in my life and none ever blew me away. I'm still waiting for that perfect kiss, but I know that Grant isn't it. It would be like kissing my brother.

I sit up, pulling my long, tangled red hair over one shoulder. The heavy waves have knotted and I run my fingers through them as I slide my feet down to the floor.

"Lydia? Are you up?" I hear my mom yell from the kitchen.

"Yeah, I'm up!"

"What do you want for breakfast?"

"Why is everyone so goddamned loud in this house!" my dad calls out from the vicinity of the living room.

"Because we know you love it so much! Lydia, French toast or pancakes?"

"French toast!" I stand up, stretching my arms over my head, the hem of my old-fashioned silk slip riding up my legs. I don't bother getting dressed yet, just pull a robe around myself and wander out into the hall.

The stained-glass window at the end of the hallway

spills light and color onto the hardwood floor. I walk past my grandfather's bedroom on my way to the stairs. "Lydia," he says through the open door. "Come here."

"What's up, Grandpa?" I step into his room. It looks like it always does: cluttered and comfortable, with solid, dark wood furniture and a braided rug on the floor. He's sitting in a straight-backed chair facing his desk, papers strewn across the top. The warm scent of his pipe hits me as I cross the room.

I take a seat on the wide bed, the same one that's been in this room since he was a child. When I was a little girl, my family used to live in a condo near Amagansett, but my grandmother died when I was five and my grandpa didn't want to live alone. So we moved into this house, with its faded, blue-gray cedar shake siding, large windows, and wide front porch.

Grandpa still sleeps in his childhood bedroom, the same place where he listened to his mother crying through the walls after her husband disappeared in 1944, the same place he inherited after her death when he was only twenty. This house is in his bones, and I know that he will eventually die here, never having spent more than a few nights in another bed.

"Mom wants us downstairs for breakfast," I say. He turns his head to smile at me, his face pale and wrinkled, round glasses covering his green eyes—the same deep-sea color I inherited from him.

"I heard. We'll go down in a minute, but I wanted to talk about our trip today first." He taps the pipe out into an ashtray and starts sifting through the piles of papers on his desk.

I cross my legs, swinging my foot impatiently from side to side. I want to go eat French toast, but I try to give Grandpa my full attention. I might not believe his theories, I might even worry about him sometimes, but I'd never let him see that.

My small family is close in its own way, though it can sometimes feel distracted. Mom and Dad are always busy. They value their independence, and they've always encouraged me to do the same. I like to spend time alone, and the thought of having someone else in my space for too long makes me itchy and claustrophobic.

But if there's one person I rely on, it's my grandfather. He helps me with my school projects, drives me places when I don't have a ride, and still makes me dinner most nights. He's always supported me in my dream of becoming a journalist and has been helping me with my application to Northwestern, even though it means me moving halfway across the country to Chicago.

If exploring Camp Hero makes him happy, then I'll keep my mouth shut and pretend that I'm a believer.

"Look what I found." He hands me a wrinkled black-and-white photograph of a tall, slim man standing next to an old car. He's wearing an army uniform with a tucked-in shirt, high, almost baggy pants, and a cap that sits at an angle on his head. He's scowling at the camera, his face half hidden in shadow. "This is my father."

I finger the crumpled edges of the photo. I've never seen a picture of my great-grandfather before. "He looks serious."

Grandpa smiles and leans forward in his chair. "He *was* serious. But he was a good father and a good husband. He was a first lieutenant in the army, and he commanded a lot of men. He was stationed on the Western Front through the fall of forty-three. After the Allies invaded Sicily, he was sent to Camp Hero to work on a secret project. He writes about it in his journal, though he never says what it was."

His green eyes go cloudy and soft. "When he disappeared, we had no idea what happened. It was June fifth, nineteen forty-four. He went to the base that morning and never came back. His officers told us there was a training accident, that a gun went off by mistake and he died. But they wouldn't let us see the body, and we could never find any soldiers who were there when it happened. I knew, even then, that something wasn't right."

I nod. I've heard this story dozens of times before, and I know when to nod, when to murmur my agreement. My grandpa has a compulsive need to constantly rehash the details of what happened to his father, and I never have the heart to stop him.

"As I got older I started to investigate." He leans forward, and I recognize the excited look on his face. I stare down at the photo in my hands. I hate it when my grandfather gets this worked up—it reminds me of when I was ten, sitting outside the bunker, a sinking feeling growing in my stomach as Grandpa frantically shoved the journal at me.

"I realized that other people knew something wasn't right about Camp Hero too. People started coming forward about their experiences with the Montauk Project, and all the facts started to fit together like a puzzle. My father disappeared at Hero right as the Project was getting off the ground and was never seen again."

I avoid his gaze and turn the photo over, examining the writing on the back: *Dean Bentley at House, May 11th, 1944.* Only a few weeks before he disappeared.

"Everything changed after." Grandpa turns back to his desk and is still, his lined hands resting on the papers in front of him. "Mother got so quiet. It was my father's parents who really raised me. And my aunt Mary for a while. But she married young and moved away not long after my father disappeared."

I look up, startled. While my grandfather repeats the story of his father over and over, he rarely talks about the rest of the family. I know almost nothing about my great-aunt Mary or what his mother, my great-grandmother, was like.

"Mary painted the picture that's hanging in the hallway near the dining room, right?" It's a landscape of Montauk during fall, bright red and yellow splashes, the trees reaching out toward the edge of the canvas. Just looking at it makes me feel restless.

"Yep." Grandpa turns to face me. "She was a wild one. She eloped with a soldier from the base not long after my father left, and they moved back to his family farm as soon as the war was over. I think it was in South Carolina? Maybe Georgia. We didn't see much of her after that. It was so expensive to travel, and it's a hard life, farming, especially in those days. She came back a few times to visit, and we wrote letters. There was no email then." He chuckles softly.

"Do you have any photos of you from when you were a kid?" I hand the photograph back to him.

He carefully slips it into the pages of a notebook on his desk. "Most of the family photos were lost after the fire that took my grandparents' house in sixty-eight. I just found this one in my old treasure chest."

He picks up a battered red tin box from his desk and hands it to me. It's small and rusted, with a faded image of a bear on the top. I run my finger over the chipped paint.

"I used to put special knickknacks and things in there when I was little," he says.

I pry the lid off. It's warped with time, and the metal scrapes together before popping open. Inside are a bunch of random things: marbles, a small toy soldier, some string, an old bullet. "Why haven't you shown me this before?"

He takes the box back from my hands. "I had forgotten all about it. I hid it in a loose board underneath my bed decades ago. Yesterday I was down there looking for my slippers and the board came up in my hand. There was the box. After all those years."

"That's so cool."

"You're telling me. I never told anyone about my treasures. No wait, that's not true." His face falls as he clutches the box tightly in both hands. "I told my father. It was a few weeks before he disappeared. I remember he gave me the photo and told me to put it in a safe place. So I showed him my hiding spot. He was the only one who ever knew."

I lean forward and place my hands over his. "It's a good thing you found it." I squeeze his hands gently. "It's like there's a part of him still here."

The window is open. I hear a mourning dove outside, a short, staccato burst of song that repeats again and again. It blends in with the sound of my mother moving around in the kitchen below us, pans clanking together, the faucet turning on and off.

"You're right." He pulls away and clears his throat. He carefully puts the photo back into the box and sets it aside. "How did I get such a smart granddaughter, anyway?"

I smile and stand up. "Some people are just born lucky. Now can we please go eat French toast? I'm dying of hunger over here."

"Dramatic girl," he says as he rises to follow me from the room.

———

The kitchen smells like flour and eggs and maple syrup. It's a large, open space with windows that look out onto the garden. I take a seat at the round wooden table, pushing aside the newspaper and a mug that reads COME TO MONTAUK FOR FUN IN THE SUN! Grandpa sits down next to me and picks up a section of the paper and holds it in front of his face. Mom is at the stove, still wearing her workout clothes, sweats and a baggy T-shirt that hangs down to her knees. It's so different from her normal look—polished suits and shiny hair—that I hardly recognize her.

"Looking good, Mom," I say as I reach for a jug of orange juice.

"Don't be a smartass." She drops three thick slices of French toast onto my plate.

My mom is a self-proclaimed Weekend Mom. During the week she's busy working for a real estate office in town. When she's not showing houses, she's at meetings: for historical preservation, the Montauk Downtown Association, the PTA. Between her schedule and mine, we've perfected the art of the quick catch-up—a "hi" and "bye" in the mornings, a kiss good night. But on the weekends she's all about taking me shopping at the outlets or to the beach on warm days, and she always, always cooks breakfast on Saturday mornings.

I bite into the thick grilled bread, closing my eyes when the sweetness of the syrup hits my tongue. "Oh gawd, thish ish shoo goood."

"Don't talk with your mouth full."

I roll my eyes at her tone. "I'm seventeen, Mom. You don't need to scold me like I'm five." I hear Grandpa chuckling from behind the paper.

"Even seventeen-year-olds shouldn't talk with their mouths full. Plus, you'll always be my baby." She comes over and puts her hand on my head, smoothing down my sleep-messed hair. "You need to get this cut. It's all shaggy."

"That's the look." I pull away from her. "Stop, you're getting French toast in my hair."

"The look, huh? I guess I'm just an old lady now who doesn't know anything about style."

"I don't know, you're rockin' those sweats pretty hard."

"Watch it," she snaps, clearly trying not to laugh. "Where's your father?"

"Comatose in front of the TV."

"I heard that." My dad walks into the kitchen, sidling up to my mom as she stands next to the stove. He slips his arm around her, pressing his face into her neck, his dark hair a startling contrast to her pale gold. He's so tall he almost has to bend in half to reach her. She giggles, pushing him away with her spatula.

I almost gag on my orange juice. "Ew, get a room."

"We have a room," he says. "Actually, we have seven rooms. We just let you stay in one of them out of the goodness of our hearts."

"My dad the comedian."

He walks over to the table and sits down. He's in jeans and a flannel shirt, his regular work-wear.

"Are you going into the store today?" I ask.

He nods and fills a plate with food. My grandpa puts down the newspaper and picks up his fork. Mom sits down at the table. There's a moment of silence as we all concentrate on eating.

"How were your last days of school, Lydia?" Mom asks after a minute.

"Good. I'm glad it's over."

Dad points his fork in my direction. "Now you can start working for me full-time. Things are getting crazy down at the shop."

Dad owns and runs Bentley's Hardware, and there always seems to be some crisis happening that forces him to go in at all hours. But we all know he loves it—even though he complains, I think he would move into the stockroom if Mom let him.

"Maybe. I'm actually trying to get this internship. At the paper." I gesture at the *East Hampton Star* folded next to my grandfather's coffee mug.

Mom smiles. "Honey, that's great!"

"I don't know if I'll get it. I'm waiting to hear. But I sent them some of my clips from this year, and the editor said he liked them."

"Which clips?" Grandpa asks. "The one about the only female football player?"

I nod. "And the op-ed about gun violence."

"That's a good one. You'll be a shoo-in."

"Maybe you can still help out part-time," Dad says. "You've got to learn the business for that happy day when I'm sipping mai tais on the beach and plumbing equipment is but a distant memory."

"You'll never retire. We all know you love it."

"Don't say that. Your mom and I have our hearts set on a condo in Boca Raton."

"Yeah, right." I laugh, though the jokes put me slightly on edge. Dad is always talking about how I'll take over the store someday, and how his legacy will live on in me. I'm not sure he truly believes that I have no intention of sticking around Montauk forever.

"What time are you going in?" Mom asks him.

"In an hour or so. Stacy called in sick for her shift." He turns to me. "You gonna come help?"

I pause, pushing the last piece of French toast around in circles. "I can't today."

"Why not?"

Dad puts his fork down and watches me over steepled hands. He and I have the same high cheekbones, the same heavy-lashed green eyes. But instead of his almost-black hair, I somehow ended up with deep auburn. "If I wasn't in labor with you for two days, I'd wonder if you were mine," my blond, brown-eyed mother likes to say.

"We're going to Camp Hero today," Grandpa answers. I

stare down at my plate. There's a heavy silence, and I know my parents are exchanging a look.

"Hmmm." Mom stands up and starts carrying the dishes over to the sink. "Are you sure that's what you want to do today, Lydia?"

I glance at my parents. They're both waiting for my reaction. I know they think my grandfather is slightly unhinged—and sometimes I think the same thing. I also know that they're unwilling to play along and often wonder why I am. But they've never stood in the way of me making my own choices about anything, and that's one of the things I love the most about them.

My mom is giving me an out with her question. I could say no, call Hannah, and go hang out at the beach all day. But then I'd be disappointing my grandfather, and I can't bear to do that.

I turn to smile at him. "It's exactly what I want to do today."

CHAPTER 3

We drive down the hill near our house, past the red-and-white brick elementary school, around the pond in the middle of town, through the short downtown strip, and out onto the highway. I can see the beach and the water beyond the dunes. There are people walking the shore even though the air is thick and foggy. The weather reminds me of the first day I went to Camp Hero: the dark clouds forming circles above the water, the waves rough against the rocks.

"I saw some suspicious metal tubs that I want to check out near the north side. I want to see if they're still there." I'm driving Grandpa's old Honda while he sits in the passenger seat consulting a local map and his father's journal.

We pass the dunes and enter a thicker section of the

forest. The low, gnarled branches of the trees look like something out of a dark fairy tale. They reach and stretch their tangled arms out to us as we pass.

"Listen to this." Grandpa holds up the journal and peers at it through the bottom half of his glasses. "'May eighteenth, nineteen forty-four. As a soldier it is not my job to question why I'm ordered to do something. I've made a promise to serve my country, in any way I can, no matter the outcome. This new project is an order, and I have yet to decide if it's a moral one. I must remember that it's not my duty to judge it, but my duty to complete the task that is asked of me.' And above that he scribbled Tesla's name in the margins. It must be connected to the Montauk Project. Why else would he keep mentioning Nikola Tesla?"

"I don't know, Grandpa."

"It *has* to be significant." He grips the leather so hard his knuckles turn white. "The answers are out there. I just know it."

We are nearing the end of Long Island, and when we turn that final corner, the lighthouse looms white and red and quiet in the early afternoon. To the right is the sign for Camp Hero State Park.

This part of Montauk has become a tourist attraction. But during World War II, the army established Camp Hero and built lookout towers, barracks, a power plant, and huge guns to protect shipping lanes. All the buildings were designed to resemble a small fishing village, so that from the air the enemy saw white clapboard, a fake church, and what looked like scattered beach houses.

The history of the base is everywhere, but it's the rumors about the Montauk Project that give the camp its mysterious feeling, as though something dark and secret is always hiding out there in the trees. I like to think I'm immune to this feeling, though my mad dash through the woods last night might suggest otherwise. Nerves, I tell myself, as we drive straight through the gates until we reach a dirt parking lot that looks out over the bluffs. Grandpa quickly gets out of the car, waiting impatiently as I grab a sweater out of the backseat. I step out and pause to look down at the cliffs in front of us. The fog is thick, hiding the blue of the ocean, but I know it stretches in an endless arc, miles and miles of water.

I can hear waves crashing against the rocks below. It reminds me of a Walt Whitman poem I recently read in English class:

From Montauk Point
I stand as on some mighty eagle's beak,
Eastward the sea absorbing, viewing, (nothing but sea and sky,)
The tossing waves, the foam, the ships in the distance,
The wild unrest, the snowy, curling caps—that inbound urge
    and urge of waves,
Seeking the shores forever.

That line, *seeking the shores forever*, always makes me think of my grandfather. Though he looks and looks, he never seems to find his shore, his peace.

Behind me I hear him call out. He's standing near the trail that leads into the forest. I turn away from the ocean and trudge slowly up the dirt path until I reach his side. The radar tower hovers over our heads, the wire metal antenna partially hidden in the fog. Together we walk into the woods.

By four o'clock I am tired, sweaty, and sick of looking at trees. How my grandfather, a man in his midseventies, still has so much energy is a complete mystery. The *only* mystery in Camp Hero, as far as I'm concerned. Exhausted, I slump against a nearby picnic table.

Grandpa consults some papers he brought along. They are covered in black lines and rough notes: *Bunker. West forest near paved road. Possible entrance to Lab B.* I sigh and close my eyes. The clouds from earlier have turned into a light drizzle that makes the ground spongy and damp, the wet leaves glistening and heavy. The fog has lifted, but mist still curves in ribbons around the tree trunks.

"Maybe we should go home, Grandpa." I tilt my head back to feel the rain fall softly on my eyelids. "It's really starting to come down."

"Nonsense. It's barely raining. And we're not done yet. I need to go back to the southwest bunker."

"You've been there a million times before. Why would it be different this time?"

"It might be. We have to be thorough. I want to look at the door one more time. I think the concrete is starting to crack. We might be able to create another hole if we're lucky." He starts back through a narrow path in the woods, pushing aside branches as he walks. I straighten and reluctantly follow him.

The southwest bunker is a cement door that leads into the side of a small hill. It is eight feet tall and ten feet wide, with faded black lettering across the front: DO NOT ENTER. CLOSED TO PUBLIC. On either side of the door cement wings flare outward, two triangles that frame the hill. If you look at it from the side or the top, it appears to be a normal grass-covered mound. Only from the front can you see the cement structure set deep into the earth. There are bunkers like this scattered all over Camp Hero, some large and on the main road, some, like this one, hidden in the woods.

For some reason my grandfather keeps returning to this one spot. It's at the end of a long, rambling, tick-ridden path, a hike that only the most diehard conspiracy theorists would attempt to navigate. The bunker is almost concealed by the dense leaves and curving branches of nearby trees. The warning sign on the front is practically unreadable, and the cement is chipped, with a small chunk missing near the top.

These old bunkers were probably storage facilities used to house weapons or equipment during World War II, designed to look like hills to disguise them from enemy fire. Some of them were attached to long-range guns that jutted out over the ocean, ready to fire on German submarines. But according to my grandfather, they're actually secret doors that lead to an extensive underground network of labs and holding cells. Never mind that the cement looks less like a door and more like a permanent seal. Never mind that it is so overgrown that it clearly hasn't been opened in fifty years.

When we reach the bunker, I sit on the wet grass and lock my arms around my jeans. My grandfather starts bustling near the entrance, running his hands over the sealed edges of the door. What is he looking for? A break? A crack? A secret button that will slide it open and reveal all of its secrets? And if he finds it, then what? This seventy-five-year-old man will wander inside to fight a reptoid?

As I wait, I compulsively line up nearby sticks into neat, corresponding rows. One stick facing me, one away. Soon they are perfectly organized piles. Satisfied, I start to arrange the leaves that are scattered around my legs.

Time passes. The rain is a steady, falling mist that coats my button-down gingham shirt and the sweater I have draped over my shoulders. Tiny drops of water cling to my hair and face. The rain starts to get heavier. I stand up, my sweater falling onto the damp grass.

"Grandpa, I think it's time to go."

He still hasn't moved. He's soaked; his sweater looks heavy and uncomfortable, and his hair is plastered to the back of his head. "Not now, Lydia." He sounds distracted, absent.

I walk closer to him. We're so far in the woods that all I can hear are birds chirping in the trees. The air smells like wet earth and rotting leaves.

"Grandpa." I touch his shoulder gently. "We've been here for hours. It's time to go now." My voice is soft and coaxing.

"Just one more second, kiddo."

"No, Grandpa." I carefully grasp his hand. "Please, it's time to go now."

"If I could just get into this concrete. If I could just look inside."

"I know, but you can't. It's not going to open."

"There has to be a way."

I lightly tug at his hand. "You're not going to find it today."

"But I was so sure it would be different. I was so sure." His voice cracks.

"I know. But you saw the door. It's sealed shut. Nothing has changed from the last time we were here."

"But—"

"It's time to go now." I slowly lead him away from the bunker, his larger frame falling against mine. His manic energy from earlier is gone. This is always how we end up leaving Camp Hero—him dejected, me trying to hold him up and struggling against the weight.

We start through the path in the woods. "Lydia," he says softly, "I hope you never have to know what it feels like to lose someone you love. I know you must think I'm a crazy old man sometimes, but I think you'd be surprised at what you would do if it were you. At what you would feel you *have* to do."

I blink drops of water from my eyes. "I don't think you're crazy, Grandpa."

"I know there's something here. I know there is." The conviction in his voice sends a chill across my skin. As I shiver in the cold rain, I realize I've left my sweater at the bunker.

"Grandpa, we need to turn ar—" But I stop before I finish the sentence. If we both go back there, I'll never get him to leave again. "I forgot something. Can you go to the car? I'll meet you there soon."

He nods. I squeeze his arm before I let go. I stand watching as he shuffles down the path, a hunched gray figure fading into the trees. As soon as he's out of sight, I walk away, ducking under branches and wiping raindrops from my cheeks.

In just a minute, I'm stepping out and into the clearing, pushing my dripping bangs off my forehead. My sweater is on the ground near the tree trunk I was leaning against, the cream-colored fabric curled into a wet ball. I pick it up and turn back to the path. But something catches my eye. I freeze and drop the sweater back to the ground.

The bunker is still tucked into the side of the hill, half covered with leafy branches. It all looks the same, except for one major difference: The cement door is wide-open.

CHAPTER 4

"*Is* anyone there?"

My voice is loud in the empty clearing. There's no answer. I look around, searching for a park ranger, for anyone who can explain why this sealed concrete has suddenly opened. But I'm alone.

I inch closer. The cement has shifted, leaving a large, open space on the right side, as if it's an ordinary sliding glass door that someone pushed to the left.

I pause within arm's length. "Hello?" I call into the darkness of the open door. Shadows fall across the entrance, and I struggle to see into the space beyond. There are several black shapes, what looks like broken furniture spread across the floor.

Why is the seal open? And *how*? Goose bumps rise on

my arms, and I know they have nothing to do with the cold rain. I should go get camp security and notify someone that the bunker is open. I should get my grandfather, though I know he would go barreling inside without a second thought. I automatically reach for my cell phone before I remember that I left it in the car.

I turn away, ready to find help, when I hear a low humming noise. I cock my head, concentrating on the sound. It's a faint buzzing that echoes through the cement, and it sounds like it's coming from somewhere far away. I take a step toward the bunker, and another one, until I'm standing in the entrance, framed by the concrete. The large, open space is shaped in a half circle, with a wide, curved back wall. The floor is littered with broken pieces of wood and layers of dust. The smell hits me. It's musty and acidic, like old batteries.

There are metal doors all along the wall, some nailed shut, some boarded up, some falling off their hinges. I follow the low humming sound to the second one from the right. The door is a dull silver, the knob loose and hanging. I push at it but it doesn't budge. I push harder, and it opens a crack.

Behind the door, stairs lead down into blackness. The strange noise is louder here, a long, drawn out beeping. I hesitate, glancing back over my shoulder toward the clearing. I shouldn't go down the stairs. I should get help. But what if my grandfather is on to something, even if it's not what he thinks it is? What if there really is something down there? For his sake, shouldn't I keep going?

I take a step into the darkness and stop, my heart pounding in my ears. The constant sound is like a beacon calling me forward even as my common sense is telling me to get out of here. But I can't walk away because of fear—this might be my only chance to ever see what's inside one of these bunkers. If I leave now I'll never know the truth of what's at the bottom of this staircase.

I take another step down and put my hand on the wall, feeling something sticky and wet. I step down again, then push my foot forward as I search for the next step. Over and over I do this, descending into the black. The rhythm of my steps is broken only by the unevenness of my own breathing. I try to stay calm, but the farther I get from the light at the top of the stairs the more my heart races, the tighter my lungs feel.

The low, beeping becomes a wail, a steady stream of noise, louder and louder the deeper I go. When I'm halfway down, I start to see a blinking light. I move toward it, down and down and down. The air is getting colder, and the flashing light is red, perfectly timed with the relentless, piercing noise.

I stumble slightly at the bottom of the stairs. The red pulse is the only source of light. Through the hazy flashes I see that I'm in a wide, dingy hallway that leads to several scarred, metal doors. Most of them look sealed shut and have keypads next to the handles. I pause as I realize that the doors are new, not some relic from the past. People must have been here recently. Fear chokes at my throat, and I have to force myself to keep moving forward. With my hands stretched out in front of me I pull on each door as I pass. Nothing opens. Finally, at the very end of the short hallway, there's a door ajar.

I peer around the doorway, then step through into a long, wide hallway. Even through the red flashing light, I can see that the corridor is white—white walls, ceiling, floors. The alarm is louder now, and the acidic smell is even stronger here. It burns my nose and makes my chest hurt.

I press back into the wall. Camp Hero is not just a state park. I turn my head to look at the door behind me. It's still partially open, and this time the darkness beyond it looks more inviting than scary. It would be so easy to walk back up those stairs, to show my grandfather what I've found.

But when will I have this opportunity again? By the time I find my grandfather and hike back through the woods, the concrete bunker will probably be sealed shut. Then I'd never find out the truth of what's happening down here. I'd be just another conspiracy theorist who saw an unbelievable "clue." What if my grandfather is right? What if Grant is right? What if the Montauk Project has always been real?

I take a deep breath. I'm a journalist. My job is to find and report the truth. And I can't let my grandfather down. He's spent his whole life trying to answer this question, and I may have stumbled upon the answer by accident.

I inch along the hallway. It bisects in a T shape with another long corridor. When I reach it, I peer around one side. I'm about to choose which way I go next when I hear new noises mixed in with the piercing siren: shouting. Footsteps. I stagger back, pressing myself tightly against the wall behind me. Men run along the opposite hallway, their boots heavy on the tiled floor. Through the throbbing red light, I catch a flash of black clothing, metal gleaming at the men's shoulders. And then they're gone.

I rest my head against the wall, breathing hard. *What was that?* What were they doing down here? And what will happen if they find me?

The reality of what I'm doing slams into me. This isn't an article for the high school newspaper—this is something huge and possibly deadly. I don't know if those men are a part of the Montauk Project, but I'm not willing to die to find out.

I turn to make my way back to the staircase when I hear a thud from the half-open door. The door that leads to the bunker. The door that leads to safety. I watch in horror as it starts to slide farther open with a long creak.

Before someone—or some*thing*—can emerge from behind it, I dash forward and sprint as fast as I can down the opposite hallway. It dead-ends at a trio of doors. I randomly pick the one on the right and shove it open. It leads to a new hallway. I run down it, then turn another corner.

Where am I? I lean against another white wall, trying to

think over the constant shriek of the alarm. My palms are slick, and I quickly wipe them on my jeans. I need to keep moving, though I have no idea where I am and no idea how to get out of here. Fighting the panic that's rising in my chest, I try to focus: I need an exit, which means retracing my steps or trying to find a different way out. Either way is dangerous, but it makes the most sense to go back to the hallway I know leads out of here. Praying that whatever was coming through that door is long gone, I turn back the way I came.

I move slowly down the hallway and round a corner. Then I jerk to a stop, swallowing a gasp. A soldier is standing there with his back to me. He's wearing a black uniform and carrying a gun, and he's starting to turn—

Barely conscious of what I'm doing, I grab hold of the nearest door handle and shove.

I fall forward into a large room. The pulsing light is even brighter here. I regain my balance and stand up, then freeze. There's a dark figure in the room and he's coming right for me.

I jerk back, searching for the door handle. My fingers brush it, but the figure is suddenly upon me, pushing me against the door. He turns my body around and cold metal slams into my back. I see a flash of light as I struggle against the hands that settle on my shoulders. The grip is painfully tight, clamping me in place. Stunned, I look up into the face of my attacker.

The first thing I notice is that he's a boy, not much older than I am. He's tall and lean, with dark, dark hair. His face is shadowed, distorted by the red light, but I can see the sharp lines of his jaw and nose. The curve of his mouth. He's frowning at me.

"Let me go." My whisper is hardly loud enough to hear over the noise of the alarm.

He's silent, his gaze intent on mine. His eyes are black in the dim light. Fear catches up with me, and I gulp air quickly. The action pushes my chest against his. He jerks back, giving me a strange, puzzled look. I twist under his hands. His grasp tightens and then relaxes. Slowly, he peels his fingers from my shoulders. There's something deliberate about the way he does it, as though he has to force himself to let go of me. His dark eyes never move from my face.

As soon as his hands fall, I lunge to the side to put distance between us. He stands so still that I wonder if he's breathing. He's dressed in all black: a long-sleeved shirt tucked into slim black pants, and no embellishment unless you count the gun tucked casually into his waistband.

I keep one eye on him as I frantically scan the room, looking for an escape. The wall next to us is packed with computers mounted onto metal tables. The back wall is covered with what look like built-in flat screens and charts and graphs. All of the screens, all of the monitors are blank.

My gaze is drawn to the middle of the room, where a

gleaming chamber stretches twenty feet up to the ceiling. It's shaped like a wide tube, with smooth, round sides. The bottom half of the tube is metal, although halfway up it changes to clear glass. The door is open, and the inside is a darker metal, all in shadow. I have no idea what this strange contraption could be used for, but I don't have time to dwell on it. I need to get out of here.

There are no other doors in the room; the final wall is one long, two-way mirror. Maybe someone is in there, and that's why the boy let me go. He's probably waiting for the guards to show up and torture me for knowing too much. The puzzled expression never leaves his face, but I'm not fooled. He could attack at any moment.

Quickly I break his gaze and whip around. The only way out is past the boy, but the room is large. I just need to get him away from the door so I can make a run for it. I sprint forward, aiming for the back of the machine. I hear the boy move behind me, his heavy footsteps approaching. I abruptly shift directions, but the rubber soles of my sandals skid across the slick white tile. Reaching out, my hand slides across cold metal. With no way to stop myself, I fall forward and land on my hands and knees inside the tube.

I scramble to my feet. The boy has almost reached me. I frantically run my hands over the metal walls, looking for some kind of escape. A panel next to the door lights up. It's some kind of touch screen, with buttons and numbers. I glance at the approaching boy, then back at the screen.

There's no other way out of this strange hollow space, but I need to do something before he catches me. With my heart in my throat, I push my fist into a random button.

A metal door shoots out of the tube's entrance. It slams shut. The last thing I see is the boy's shocked face.

CHAPTER 5

The blackness around me is so thick it feels alive, crawling over my skin. I press my hands out to the sides, but all I feel is smooth metal. The silence in this hollow place is somehow more frightening than the sirens and the pulsing light.

Inside is a tomb, outside is a secret military operation waiting to kill me. I'm trapped.

I fight back the tears that threaten to fall and wonder which option is the lesser of two evils. Stay in here waiting to die, or go outside to face whatever's out there?

Something flickers underneath me. The round floor starts to light up—a harsh white. In another flicker, the fluorescent light spreads up the sides of the metal walls in long, narrow strips. I spin around. I'm still trapped, but at least I'm no longer in the dark.

The touch screen panel near the door starts to glow. There's a flashing series of numbers that look almost like coordinates on a map, then a series of unmarked buttons running along the bottom screen. I can't make sense of what it means. As I'm trying to decipher the code, the light around me begins to fade. Then everything goes black again. I punch at the darkened panel, but nothing happens.

I wrap my arms around myself. It's cold in here and getting colder. I'm only wearing my button-down shirt; my sweater is still on the ground outside the bunker. I rub my arms, trying to stop the shaking that seems to be spreading through my body.

There's a flash of light so bright that spots dance in front of my eyes after it disappears. I hear a humming noise. It starts out soft but slowly grows louder and louder. Soon it's a roar, like the sound of the ocean during a storm. The light flashes again, even brighter. I squeeze my eyes shut, but I still feel it sear across my skin.

Another flash and the noise screams and it shakes all through my body. Then I realize that it's the machine that's shaking: the walls, the floor, everything around me. My eyes snap open. The light steadily grows brighter and brighter. I put my hands out as I try to catch my balance but then snatch them back—the metal walls are burning.

What's happening? I tilt my head back and look at the ceiling—except it isn't a ceiling but a swirling mass of color. The center opens to a hole that gets larger and larger, and the noise is growing louder, the light brighter, and the whirlpool closer—until suddenly my body breaks apart and I float out into something I cannot see or feel or hear. For one moment I feel solid but not whole, awake but not conscious, and then everything dips, dims, and is gone.

I come back into my body with a rush of vertigo so strong my stomach feels like it flips over, and I fall to my knees gagging. When I think I can move without being sick, I sit up in the quiet darkness.

I pull myself to my feet and grasp at the smooth metal of the walls. My head spins so much that I can barely tell which way is up, or where my body stops and the walls begin.

There's a grinding noise when the door slides open. Light pours into the dark tube. I launch myself out of the machine and fall into a large room. The lights overhead are stark fluorescent white and the sirens have stopped. I scan the room, searching for the boy who was just here. Everything looks the same as it did before: white walls, tiled floors, large two-way mirror, and computer consoles pressed into metal desks—but no boy in black. I'm alone.

The door slides shut behind me. I turn to stare at it closing. I feel nauseous. I don't know what just happened in that tube, but right now I need to get out of here. I run to the only door in the room and twist the handle hard. It opens easily and I glance into the empty hallway.

I hear footsteps approaching, then the sound of men

speaking. I jump back into the room, frantically searching for a place to hide. I duck under one of the desks and notice a small crawl space behind a set of cabinets. I work my way into it, curling myself around the wires and dust that twist together on the floor.

The door opens. "There's no one here," a man with a deep voice says.

"Doctor Faust said there was activity. We have to check," a second voice says.

"Maybe it was a glitch. This thing never seems to work right." I hear the sound of a hand slapping against metal.

I hear footsteps coming closer, closer, and try to make myself as small as possible. The tip of a brown boot slides into my field of vision as one of the men approaches the desk. There's the sound of fingers tapping a keyboard, and I struggle to keep my breathing quiet.

"Something happened here. The energy levels sky-rocketed two minutes ago."

"Wait, do you hear that?"

There's a pause. I hear nothing but my own heartbeat throbbing in my chest, my throat, my fingertips.

"Nope. There's no one here. Let's take this to the general."

"Maybe one of us should stay in case something else happens."

"No need. These energy readings have to be a mistake. Let's go."

Footsteps fade away. The door shuts.

I wait a few seconds, then slide out from behind the cabinets, my heart still pounding. The guards could come back and realize their mistake at any moment. It's time to get out of this room, out of this underground lab, and back outside, where my grandfather is waiting for me.

I slip out into the white hallway and mentally retrace my steps. Was it left after the first hallway, then right through the doorway, then left into the room? Am I forgetting a turn? Everything looks the same down here. It's impossible to find any landmarks. Taking a chance, I turn left and sprint until I reach a door. I listen carefully but can't hear any guards, so I push through it. Another white hallway.

I follow it as it curves to the left. The fluorescent lights lining the ceiling in two long rows burn bright above my head. I press my hand onto the concrete wall as I walk slowly. It's shockingly quiet down here. Where have the guards gone?

And what about the boy from before? He's the only one who saw me, and he had to have told his superiors by now. They must be down here somewhere, looking for me in this maze of hallways and strange rooms.

I pick up my pace as much as I dare. I come to another door and open it. It should lead toward the staircase in the bunker. But instead it's some kind of maintenance closet filled with folded cloth and cleaning supplies. The smell of bleach is heavy in the air. I swear under my breath.

As I wonder where I could have made a wrong turn,

I hear the distant sound of footsteps echoing on the tile. I slip into the dark, cramped room and shut the door softly. It's pitch-black. I press my hand over my mouth as I hear someone walk past, their footsteps slowly fading.

I count two minutes before I step out into the hall again. As quickly as I can, I retrace my steps and this time take a right after the second hallway. It comes to a T. I remember this. I'm almost out.

I turn a corner and there's the familiar door at the end of the corridor. I dash forward and push through it. The narrow space that seemed dirty before now looks slightly different— cleaner and brighter. Are the lights different, too? I run for the stairs at the end, but I freeze halfway there. This hall *definitely* looks different. It's almost brand-new, not rotting and covered in black gunk. I touch the clean white concrete wall as a sinking feeling grows in my stomach. How can it have changed this much in only an hour?

What happened in that machine?

Grant's words from the other night spin through my head: *Time tunnels. Time machines. Wormholes.*

My grandfather told me that the government selected the east end of Long Island as the site of the Montauk Project because of the naturally high levels of magnetic energy in the air. According to him, that's how the time machines run, using alternating waves of magnetic energy. I was just in a strange . . . vessel, and I felt—was—ripped apart, a larger force that I couldn't see or identify or explain pulling me in different directions.

Could I have . . . ?

I scramble up the stairs. I need to get out of this bunker. I need to find my grandfather. Only then can I prove that everything is normal, that nothing impossible has happened.

This time the door at the top opens easily and I tumble into the large open space of the bunker. It looks the same as it did before, with broken furniture scattered around and dirt covering the cement floor. *Thank God.*

The concrete doors are sealed shut from the inside. I sprint across the bunker and push at the rough surface. Nothing happens. I pry at the edge of the door. It won't budge. *No.*

There's a sound behind me. I whip around.

The boy I was trying to escape stands in the doorway, silently. Watching me.

I shrink back against the concrete wall behind me. But I let go of some of the panic twisting in my chest. If he's still here, then I *couldn't* have traveled to another time. Nothing has changed. My grandfather is waiting for me out there in the park. But my relief is short-lived: This boy stands between me and freedom.

"What do you want?" My voice echoes in the empty space.

He has that stricken, confused look on his face, as though he's not sure what he's doing here. He says nothing but takes a small step closer to me. I crawl along the wall, looking for something I can use as a weapon. I've almost made it out—I won't let him take me back down into those labs.

He sees my expression and stops. "I won't hurt you." His voice is soft. I look at him warily. Can I believe him? He did let me go once before, but maybe he realized he shouldn't have? Maybe now that I've gone through . . . whatever I just went through in that machine, things are different.

"Stay back." I slide until I'm pressed against the corner of the door. The curved wall behind the boy is filled with metal doors that lead to the underground labs. Even if I could get to one, I'd be stuck in the bowels of Camp Hero again, running for my life.

A part of me would prefer running for my life rather than stand here under this boy's still gaze—but I can't force myself to move.

"I won't hurt you," he repeats. There's something quiet in his voice that makes me pause. "But you can't stay here. It's only a matter of time before the guards come to investigate the noise from the stairs."

I dig my fingers into the concrete at my back, not sure if I can trust what he says.

"Where should I go?"

"With me." He points to one of the doors along the back wall of doors. "I'll help you hide until it's safe."

I scoff. "You're crazy if you think I'm going in there with you."

"The guards are coming. If they find you here, they'll kill you."

I study his face. His jaw is clenched and his mouth is tight. It should probably intimidate me, but his eyes are soft, almost pleading. I can see that he badly wants me to trust him. I just don't know why.

If I try to run away from him, I'll be further from escaping than I am now. If I stay here, the guards will find me. Kill me, according to this boy. My best option is to believe what he's telling me. But I *really* don't want to go back there.

I cross my arms over my chest. "If you want to help me, then get me out of here. And not back through the bunker. Open the door."

He hesitates, still watching me. I can't tell what he's thinking. After a long moment, he finally nods.

He steps forward and I instinctually jerk back. The edges of his mouth rise so slightly I barely see them move. He lifts his hand in a gesture of peace. Everything he does and says seems measured and deliberate. "If I'm going to open the door, I need to get to the lock. It's behind you."

"Okay. Okay." I don't take my eyes off him, but I step away from the concrete. He walks toward the door. I watch as he pulls something from his pocket. It's a long, thin metal rectangle with random shapes carved into it. He reaches forward and slides the metal into an almost invisible opening. The concrete seems to groan, then begins to shift and open.

The second there's a large enough space for me to fit through I push myself out of the bunker and into the woods. I have to shut my eyes against the sudden brightness. I had gotten so used to the artificial light in the underground labs that the sun momentarily blinds me.

Squinting and blinking, I stumble across the open area of grass until I reach the tree line. Something touches my upper arm and I yank away. The boy freezes, his hand outstretched.

I back up quickly. "Why did you just help me get out of there? Why didn't you turn me in?"

His face is expressionless, but his eyes are watchful. I notice his features: sharp cheekbones, strong jaw, a slightly crooked nose, as though he's broken it more than once. Black eyes. Black hair.

He's beautiful. Thinking it shocks me a little. I've been so busy being afraid of him that I hadn't really noticed him.

He interrupts my thoughts when he tells me, "If they found you, they would have killed you."

I step away from him, retreating into the trees. "Why do you care?"

He doesn't answer.

"Who are you?"

"Elev—" He pauses. "Wes. I'm Wes."

"But who *are* you?"

He frowns, making his jaw look even harder. "We shouldn't talk here. They'll see us. We're too exposed."

I look behind him. The concrete door, now wide-open,

begins to groan shut again. We're standing just inside the circle of trees, barely out of sight. He's right. We need to get out of here.

He steps toward me cautiously, waiting to see how I'll react. I turn around and begin to walk into the woods. He quickly overtakes me and leads us deeper into the trees.

"Be careful," he says over his shoulder. "You're not wearing any shoes."

I glance down at my feet with surprise. Somewhere along the way I lost my sandals, and I never even noticed.

We move quickly through the underbrush. Leaves crunch under my feet. The sun is hazy, and I sense that it's late afternoon, maybe even early evening. I wonder when it stopped raining. I also wonder where my grandfather is and if he's looking for me.

I'm so distracted that I step on the pointed edge of a stick. Pain shoots up my leg and I hiss out loud.

Wes stops abruptly and turns to look at me. "Are you okay?"

I jump up and down on one foot as I try to assess the damage. "I'm fine. I think I'm fine."

"Sit." He points to a large boulder between two trees. "We can stop here. We're far enough from the facility. Their guards can't comb the forest around the base. It would be too suspicious. They'll send out scouts, but not for a while."

I limp over to the boulder and sit. Wes's gaze is trained on the woods around me, behind me. I can't stop staring at him. Who is he? If he works for the Montauk Project, why is he helping me?

Clearly something huge is happening underground at Camp Hero. It may be the Montauk Project or it may be something else entirely. Wes is obviously caught up in whatever it is. He should be dragging me back to the underground labs, not helping me escape.

"What happened in there? I fell in that machine, and I pushed a button, and everything went . . ." I shudder, unable to finish.

He looks at me, then down at the ground.

"The less you know, the safer you'll be," he responds.

I sit up straighter. "What does that mean?"

"Listen to me." He takes a step closer. "I will make sure you live, but we have to go back into the facility."

"I don't understand. Tell me what that means."

"There are things I can't tell you." His voice is even and soothing, but his mouth is a hard, tight line. "You need to trust me. We wait here until we're certain that the scouts have come and gone. Then we'll go back in."

"I don't even know who you are! How can I trust you?" I stand up, barely feeling the pain in my foot. "I'm not going back in there." I spit the words at him.

Wes goes still, his black eyes combing the trees again.

I open my mouth, but he puts his hand up before I can get a word out. "Someone's coming. Get down." His voice is so quiet I can hardly hear him.

I duck behind the large rock and sit in a tight ball. He

stares in the direction of the bunker and then looks back at me. Our eyes lock. "Stay here. Stay down."

He waits for me to nod before he disappears into the woods.

I listen for strange noises. All I hear are the ordinary sounds of the forest in the state park—birds calling to one another in the trees, a cricket chirping. Five minutes pass. Wes seems to have vanished into thin air.

I peer over the top of the rock. There's nothing out there but trees. I clench my hands into fists, suddenly feeling like an idiot. Why am I waiting in the woods for someone who *might* be connected to a deadly government conspiracy and who *definitely* wants to lead me back into a death trap? My grandfather is probably waiting for me in the parking lot. As soon as I find him, this will all be over.

I stand up and stare at the point where Wes slipped into the trees. I hesitate for a second, then pivot and run in the opposite direction.

I run through the woods as quickly as I can without shoes. After a few minutes, I slow to a jog, searching for a way out of the woods. Everything seems strangely unfamiliar.

I listen for sounds of the ocean. If I can find the cliffs, then I can find the parking lot and my grandfather. But before I hear any waves, I come across a road. It's little more than a wide dirt path, covered in tire marks. In the distance, dogs are barking, a man is shouting, and a car motor turns over.

I walk hesitantly toward the noise. I round a corner and the woods recede, the sky opening up over a large clearing. I recognize this place. I think . . .

In front of me are men standing in rows, holding huge guns. Another man is yelling at them. A bunch of old trucks are clustered nearby.

I can't take my eyes off the buildings that circle the men. The buildings I've passed a thousand times with my grandfather. The buildings that were abandoned and covered in graffiti only hours before. They look brand-new, gleaming with fresh paint. The old gymnasium, a white clapboard building, has a tall steeple on the top. A steeple that was built in World War II to trick enemies into thinking the building was a harmless church. A steeple that fell down over two decades ago.

I whip my head around. And then I fall to my knees in the dirt, staring wide-eyed into the empty sky. There's no radar tower. It's approaching twilight, the light is starting to fade, but you can see the rusted, wire tower from *anywhere* in Camp Hero. It was built years and years and years before my birth. Now it's gone. Like it was never there. Like it hasn't been built yet.

I hear a distant shout, and one of the men breaks away and walks toward me. "Miss? Are you all right, miss?"

I shake my head from side to side, unable to answer. Fear rises in my throat, so fast that I'm afraid it will come pouring out of my mouth if I open it.

The man comes closer. He has blond hair cropped short. He's wearing an olive-colored uniform: a khaki shirt with boxy shoulders tucked into high-waisted pants, three black stripes on his sleeves. I see the warm golden color of his skin before I close my eyes tight. "What is today?" I whisper to him.

"Sorry?" I hear leaves crunch as he comes closer. "What did you say, miss?" His voice drawls over the words like warm honey.

"The date." My eyes are still closed, and I press my hands to them. "What is it?"

"It's Tuesday. The thirtieth of May."

"And . . . the year?"

"Nineteen forty-four." He sounds concerned.

Nineteen forty-four. Fifty years before I'm born. I gasp. My lungs feel tight, aching, closing.

"Miss, are you all right?"

I grasp at my chest with both hands. "I—think—no—"

He squats down beside me. "Put your head between your knees." He cups the back of my neck with his hand and pushes me forward gently until my forehead is almost touching the ground. "Try to breathe through your nose."

I breathe in and out, trying to concentrate on getting air even as my thoughts come faster, faster. *Everything they say is true. That vessel was a . . . time machine. I'm in the past. I'm in 1944. 1944. 1944.*

I keep my head pressed into the dirt, hoping that if I

squeeze my eyes hard enough that maybe this will all go away. That I'll wake up and it will be hours earlier, and I'll be leaning against a tree while my grandfather searches the woods for nothing.

But no amount of hoping makes the soldier kneeling beside me go away.

My breathing finally steadies, and I sit up slowly.

"Okay now?"

I nod. I'm not okay, but this guy doesn't need to think I'm any more of a lunatic.

He straightens and reaches his hand out. I carefully rise to my feet next to him. He's several inches taller than me, almost six feet tall, though slightly shorter and broader than Wes.

Wes.

I push him out of my mind and look at the man standing in front of me. His cheeks are round and full, boyish. Some part of me notices that he has pale eyes, an even gray-blue, with light, almost invisible eyelashes.

Oh. He's more boy than man. He looks only a little older than the seniors that just graduated from my school. The seniors I was supposed to be celebrating with the night before.

"What's your name? What are you doing here?" he asks.

The men nearby are shouting in unison, "One, two, left, right." What *am* I doing here?

I have no idea how to answer. My mind is cloudy, fuzzy. I do know who I am, though. "I'm Lydia. Who are you?"

"I'm Sergeant Lucas Clarke, stationed at Camp Hero for the past year." Some of the men in the clearing are watching us now. I turn away from their eyes. "Why are you here? Camp Hero is closed to civilians."

"I don't know." I look at the ground. Stare at my feet. "I'm bleeding," I say dumbly.

He looks down to see little rivers of blood slide across the tops of my feet.

"You need a doctor. I'm taking you to the field hospital."

"No." I gaze into the woods and wonder if Wes is out there searching for me. He knew that I had gone back in time. He must have followed me here. Why?

Why didn't he tell me the truth?

What am I supposed to do now?

"Yes. You're bleeding." I look up at Lucas, startled out of my thoughts. "And you're disoriented. Let me take you to the hospital."

"No. I'm . . . I shouldn't be here." I try to step backward but I stagger and start to fall. Lucas grabs my arms, catching me.

"Come on." He pulls me against his side. "It's not far."

I make one more effort to pull away, one more effort to stand on my own, but the adrenaline has worn off and I barely have the strength to keep my eyes open. Lucas guides me forward and I move with him, the warmth of his body seeping into my own. As we slowly walk toward the white buildings, one thought runs over and over through my head, a song I can't turn off.

I've gone back in time.

I've gone back in time.

I've gone back in time.

CHAPTER 6

"Miss?"

I shift my body. My feet sting, and I rub them together under the blanket.

"Lydia?"

I open my eyes slowly. There's a man leaning over me, his green eyes inches from mine.

"Oh good, you're awake." He stands up and consults a chart in his hands. I sit up carefully and glance around the room. There are six other cots lined against the walls, though all of them are bare, with folded white sheets resting on top. The room has pale peach-colored walls and two windows that look out onto the forest. One of the windows is open, and a strong breeze tugs at the yellow curtains.

"Hello." My voice is rough with sleep. I'm wearing a white cotton nightgown two sizes too big, and it billows around me like a sail in the wind. "Who are you?"

"I'm your doctor."

My doctor has a short beard and dark hair sprinkled with gray. I notice his white coat is open, and I can see suspenders and blue shirt sleeves rolled up. "How are you feeling this morning?"

I stretch. My muscles ache, but otherwise I'm not in any pain. "Good. I feel good."

I hear voices outside. We must be near the mess hall, or the barracks. Bits of conversation and the acrid scent of cigarette smoke float in through the window.

"Do you know where you are?" The doctor looks down at me over his square, wire glasses. There's something familiar about his eyes and the full shape of his mouth. I nod. "The field hospital."

The doctor smiles, and I wonder if I just passed some sort of test.

Sunlight streams through the open window. "What time is it?" I ask. I've been here since last night, when Lucas handed me over to the Red Cross nurse on duty. She cleaned the cuts on my feet and helped me into bed, even though it was only early evening. Despite the sick feeling I couldn't shake, I fell asleep as soon as my head hit the pillow.

"A little after ten." The doctor sits down on a chair next to the bed. A heavy stethoscope swings against his chest.

"Do you mind if I look at your feet?"

I shake my head and he peels back the edge of my blanket. I have a small scrape on my right heel and tiny puncture marks scattered on both soles.

The doctor picks up a cloth and wets it with alcohol. I stay still as he cleans the cuts. He picks up one foot, then the other, prodding each scrape with his finger. Finally he straightens, pulling the blanket back over me. "These will heal in a few days."

"Thanks, Doctor . . . I'm sorry, what did you say your name was?"

"I didn't." He stands and places the used cloth onto a tray. "It's Dr. Bentley."

Oh my god.

"Did you say *Bentley*?" My voice sounds unnaturally high and piercing.

He tilts his head and looks at me oddly. "Yes. Are you all right?"

"I'm . . . I thought you said something else." I stare at him. We have the same green eyes, and the way he stands so straight and tall reminds me of my grandfather. We have to be related somehow.

I'm pretty sure my grandfather told me that *his* grandfather had been a doctor, and that he was still working during World War II. Could Dr. Bentley be Dean Bentley's father?

I try to sound casual when I ask, "Do you have any children?"

"I have a daughter and a son." He sits back down next to the bed and studies my face. I squirm under his strong gaze. "But I'd like to talk about *your* family, Lydia, and how you got into Camp Hero. Can you give me your full name for our records?"

"I—" My mind races. I didn't think that I'd have to come up with some kind of cover story. "You said you have a daughter. What's her name?"

He leans forward with his elbows on his knees and watches me. Finally he says, "Her name is Mary. She's about your age."

"Mary?" I whisper. Without thinking, I ask, "Is your son Dean?"

"Yes." He raises an eyebrow. "How did you know that?"

I stare at him, my mouth half open. It takes a minute for me to realize that Dr. Bentley just asked me a question. *Think, Lydia.* "I thought I heard one of the soldiers mention a Dean Bentley last night. I took a guess."

Dr. Bentley smiles and looks a little less curious. "Yes, Dean is an officer stationed here at Camp Hero. He's part of the reason I volunteer when they need a doctor. Mary's also here today. She's downstairs right now nursing a soldier who was knocked out during training."

Dean. Mary. I fall back against the pillows, staring at the tall, dark-haired man in front of me. Dr. Bentley is my great-great-grandfather.

I close my eyes. Meeting my ancestor has shifted

something inside me. I'm no longer disoriented, no longer in shock. I can't pretend that yesterday was a dream or a nightmare or anything but the *truth*.

I traveled in time. It's 1944.

I feel the bed move and I open my eyes to see Dr. Bentley leaning over me. "You look pale," he says, placing one hand on my forehead, the other against my wrist. "Are you sure—" He's interrupted by the door opening.

"Hiya, Dad!" A girl with curly, dark red hair bounces into the room. "Nurse Linny says she needs your help. . . . Is *this* the girl everyone's been talking about?"

"Mary, this is Lydia." Dr. Bentley straightens.

"Lydia!" Mary smiles at me widely. Her teeth are startlingly white against bright red lipstick.

Dr. Bentley looks from me to Mary. "I need to go downstairs to see to a patient. Will you stay with Lydia until I come back?"

Mary skirts her father, skips over to me, and plops down on the bed. I lean back, pulling my nightgown quickly out of the way. "Don't worry, Daddy. We have so much to talk about."

Dr. Bentley smiles at her and turns to me. His eyes narrow slightly. "When I get back I'd like to hear that story of yours, Lydia."

I nod and bite my lower lip.

Dr. Bentley shuts the door behind him as he goes.

Before I have time to start inventing a story, Mary leans

in close. She has deep Bentley-green eyes and full, arched eyebrows. Her face is heart-shaped, with high cheekbones and full lips. I stare at her for a minute, startled. She and I have the same hair color, the same high cheekbones. We could be sisters.

"So." She pats my hand. "Tell me everything. We're all *so* curious."

I start with the truth. "My name's Lydia . . ."

"Well, I know that. They've been talking about you all morning. Lucas had to tell the story a hundred times—finding the poor, lost-looking girl wandering around Camp Hero in factory clothes and no shoes."

"Factory clothes?"

"The dungarees, silly. So are you a factory girl?"

"I don't—"

"Are you some kind of spy? That's what my brother, Dean, thinks. He says we should interrogate you! That you might be working for the Germans or something. Isn't that crazy? He's flipped his wig. You're only a girl!"

"I'm not a spy," I gasp, though I guess I shouldn't be so shocked. In school we read about the four Nazi spies who landed on the beach in Amagansett in 1942. They were carrying explosives and American money and caught the train to New York City before they could be apprehended. Thankfully one of them confessed before they carried out their mission—to destroy key military factories on the East Coast. The remaining spies were executed.

Remembering the real spies sends a cold shiver down my spine. I can't forget that this is wartime. People are afraid, spies could be anywhere, and I'm a stranger with no proof of my identity who just popped up on a military base wearing bizarre clothes and missing my shoes. I should be grateful they didn't shoot me on sight.

"Of course Lucas told Dean that's a crazy theory. He said you were really upset when he found you, and does that sound like how a spy would act? And Dean said 'Maybe that's her cover,' and then Lucas got mad and stormed out."

I smile, surprised but grateful that Lucas defended me.

"Which is odd, because they never fight. They've always been great friends, even though Dean outranks Lucas. He's a first lieutenant, you know, and Lucas is a sergeant. They met at the base and now Lucas is always around Dean's house and our house, too. He comes over for dinner at least once a week." She leans forward again. "So why were you out there all alone in the woods?"

I try to process everything she's just said. It's 1944, World War II is happening *right now*, and I'm talking to my seventeen-year-old great-great-aunt. Somewhere out there, my great-grandfather, Dean, is still alive, and my grandfather is only a little boy.

I press my hand to my forehead.

First I need to come up with a story.

As if on cue, the door opens again to Dr. Bentley.

"I was just finding out all about Lydia, Daddy!" Mary

jumps up from the bed. For the first time I notice that she's wearing a nurse's uniform: a gray, button-down shirtwaist dress with a red cross stitched on the sleeve.

"No doubt she found out more about you, my dear. Our Mary could talk an ear off a chicken."

"That doesn't even make sense." Mary flips her hair to the side and it floats around her shoulders. It looks soft and romantic, even with her short and tightly curled bangs.

Dr. Bentley chuckles under his breath before sitting in the chair near the bed. "How are you feeling, Lydia?"

"Better."

"Are you ready to talk now?"

A vague story starts to form in my mind. I press my hands together on top of the blanket as I frantically think of the details.

"Yes, I think so."

"What's your full name?" Dr. Bentley pulls a fountain pen from his pocket and picks my chart up from a small table near the bed.

"It's Lydia Ben—net. Lydia Bennet."

Mary squeals. "Like in *Pride & Prejudice*! That's my favorite book."

Why didn't I put that together first?

"Yes, my parents loved *Pride & Prejudice*." I shift from side to side, already uncomfortable with the conversation.

"How did you end up in Camp Hero?" Dr. Bentley's voice is kind, but I know I need to have a good answer before they *all* start to think I'm a spy.

I stare down at my hands. I really don't like to lie. As a journalist, it's my job to report the truth. I guess it's time to put aside those convictions.

I get a sudden flash of Wes in the woods, saying there were things he couldn't tell me. Maybe I'm starting to realize what he meant.

"My mom died," I hear myself say. "My dad was killed last year fighting in the Pacific and it was just the two of us."

Mary makes a small squeaking noise, and she grabs my hand, squeezing it tight.

"We were living in New York City . . . but she caught a fever and died." The lies tumble out of me. "I couldn't pay the bills and I was evicted from our apartment. I had nowhere to go, but then I found the name of a distant relative in my mom's things. A great-aunt. Her name is . . ." My mind goes blank. A random name pops into my head and I grasp at it. "Julia Roberts." I wince, but they're both unfazed, waiting for me to continue. "Julia Roberts is my great-aunt."

I have an out-of-body feeling, and it's as if I'm floating on the ceiling, no longer connected to the words that are coming out of my mouth. "I found an address for her in Montauk. When I got off the train, I asked someone where it was and they said it didn't exist."

"What was the address?" Dr. Bentley asks.

"Oh, um, behind the Deep Hollow Ranch?" I give

them the vague location, knowing that it's not too far from Camp Hero.

"But there are no other houses over there!" Mary exclaims.

"That was the only address I had, so when I realized there was nothing there, I just started walking. It must have been the . . . grief that led me out here. It hit me all at once . . . that my mom is gone. I don't remember much after that. Then I had no shoes, and . . . Lucas was there."

Dr. Bentley's face is soft and sympathetic. If I ever make it out of here I am definitely joining the drama club.

"But why were you in those clothes?" Mary wrinkles her nose at the thought of wearing jeans.

Good question. I get a sudden flash of the Rosie the Riveter poster, with her fist curled up and her bandanna pulled tight.

"I *was* a factory worker. In the city. For the war effort. I was a riveter." Not that I have any idea what a riveter does, but luckily they don't push it. "I quit to come here."

"Don't you go to school?" Dr. Bentley asks.

Should I tell him I'm about to be a senior? Or will that just complicate things? "Not anymore. I'm seventeen, but I graduated early so I could work in the factory."

"What are your plans for when you leave here?"

"I . . . honestly don't know." They feel like the only true words I've said all day.

Mary clasps her hands together, her eyes shining. "You're

like a character out of a novel!"

"Mary, hush." Dr. Bentley stands up. "It sounds like this has been a very trying time for you. Is there anything else you need right now, Lydia?"

Access to a time machine?

"No thank you, you've been so kind already."

He smiles. "We'll leave you to rest then."

"But—" Mary starts.

"We both have patients. Rest now, Lydia." He gently takes Mary's arm and pulls her out of the room.

As soon as they leave, I flop back onto the bed and stare up at the ceiling. It's made of interlocking wooden beams. A spiderweb covers one corner, the silver strands glistening in the sunlight. Was it just yesterday I was looking up at the ceiling of my own bedroom? It feels like a lifetime ago.

I think about Mary's question—*What are your plans for when you leave here?*

I wish I had a good answer.

The only way to get home is to find the time machine. But the idea of going back into the underground labs fills me with dread. Am I ready to face those white corridors, those pounding footsteps again? Guards who would kill me if I was found?

And what about Wes? *Who is he?* He moved so quickly and so deliberately, like a soldier. Normal people don't move like that. He had training. And he also had a key to the concrete door.

So why did he help me? And where is he now?

My mind stops on another missing person: my grandfather's father, Dean Bentley. Only he's *not* missing in this time. He's somewhere in Montauk right now, alive and well. He might even be at Camp Hero. I might meet him. The realization is startling. What will he be like?

A knock at the door interrupts my thoughts. "Come in!" I call out.

It's Lucas. His eyes are soft and concerned, and he holds his cap in his hands.

I sit up and pull the blankets closer around my body, painfully aware that I'm only in a thin nightgown.

"I just saw Mary." He fidgets with the brim of the cap. "She told me what happened." He comes closer to the bed but stops a few feet away. "Why didn't you tell me when I found you?"

I fold my arms over my chest, tucking the blanket against my side. "I was disoriented, like you said. I just lost my mother. I was confused and sad."

"I know. I understand." He looks down, but not before I see his jaw tighten. "I lost my father in the Pacific."

"Oh. I'm so sorry."

I'm a terrible person.

"Where was your father stationed?" Lucas asks softly.

There's only one attack in the Pacific I can remember from American History. "Pearl Harbor. It was a while ago."

"My pa died in the Battle of Midway. Japanese fleet got him. Actually, it was Pearl Harbor that made him enlist in the first place."

"I'm sorry," I repeat. "He must have been really brave."

"He was. He used to run the farm where I grew up. I joined up right after he died, as soon as I turned eighteen."

"How old are you now?" I study Lucas in the sunlight. His skin is lightly tanned and freckles dot the bridge of his nose. He has the kind of complexion that makes his cheeks look rosy all the time.

"Twenty years old, miss."

"You don't have to call me 'miss.'"

"Well, what should I call you?"

There's something about the way he looks up at me through his eyelashes that makes me think of Wes. I don't know why. Wes's gaze was so different—more intense and probing, as though he was trying to read my thoughts. Lucas is lighter, easier, and being around him feels comfortable.

"Lydia. Call me Lydia."

"Then you can call me Lucas." He smiles. His teeth are slightly crooked on the bottom.

He takes a step closer so he stands at the foot of my bed, inches from my toes. "What are you going to do now?" His voice is serious. "Where will you go?"

"I don't know yet." I look up at him. Behind his head, there's a poster on the wall of an eagle soaring across the flag. AMERICA CALLING, it says. "No one really thinks I'm a spy, do they? Is someone going to interrogate me?"

"No, I'll tell the officers your story. You're a girl, they won't press it. But I wouldn't come back here again . . . especially without shoes on."

"I won't."

He twists the brim of his cap again. "I understand how hard it is to lose someone. It makes you do things you wouldn't normally do. And to lose both your parents . . . at least I still have my mother. I don't know what I would do without her or my sisters."

"Was it hard when your dad died?" I ask, steering the conversation away from my "loss."

"It was, but it feels a little better to talk about him. Everyone's lost someone in the war, and all that sadness starts to blend together. You learn not to talk about losing someone, that it's not special. But I don't want to forget what happened. I don't want to forget him."

"You should be able to talk about it." I grip the blanket in my hands, almost as hard as Lucas is holding on to his cap. "I don't know how long I'll be around but—I'll listen, if you want to talk."

He smiles a little and raises his face to mine. I notice that his pale blue eyes have flecks of gray in them, the exact color of the ocean in the early morning when the fog is still hovering over the water.

The door bangs open. I jump and break our eye contact. Mary is standing just inside the room, practically quivering with excitement.

"Lydia! I have the best news." She sees Lucas and stops. "Oh, hi, Lucas. I didn't know you were in here." She blushes slightly.

"Lucas is the soldier who found me yesterday." I smile at her, but she doesn't notice; her eyes are trained on Lucas. He breaks her gaze and stares down at the floor. I glance between them, not sure what to make of the odd undercurrent in the room.

Lucas must feel it too, because he starts to back out of the room. "I'll leave you girls alone," he says.

"No, it's all right." Mary steps forward and puts her hand on his arm. "Stay, I have wonderful news." She turns to me. "It took some finagling, and Dean is still worried you're a secret German spy, but I finally convinced Daddy to let you come home with us! We called Ma on the telephone and she's getting Dean's old room ready for you. Isn't it so exciting?" She hops up and down a little, shaking Lucas's arm.

"I don't know. . . ." I let go of the blanket, smoothing it out as I consider my options. If I stay with the Bentleys, it's a guaranteed roof over my head tonight. But unless I find the time machine again, I won't be able to go home tonight.

I need to get back to my own time. But I'm not eager to face those underground tunnels again, and I'm more than a little curious about my family and what they were like during World War II. I could meet my grandfather as a little boy. I could meet Dean.

A small idea starts to spark inside of me. I'm in 1944, the same year my great-grandfather disappeared. Today is May 31. Dean vanishes on June 5, less than one week from now. If I stay with Mary, I might be able to find out why.

Now that I know time travel is real, it's entirely possible that *everything* my grandpa believed about Camp Hero is real. Dean might be connected to the Montauk Project. It could have led to his disappearance. I don't know how I'll find out the truth—maybe he *did* die in a simple training accident—but I won't know unless I go to the Bentleys' house. Don't I owe it to my grandfather to at least try to solve his life's mystery: What really happened to his father on June 5, 1944?

"Oh please, you have to stay!" Mary rushes over and bounces down next to me. "Please, please! It will be killer-diller, like having a sister! We'll go to the movies, and to the beach, and you can meet all my friends. Suze—she's my best friend—she'll just love you, I know it."

Lucas smiles at me. "I don't think you have much of a choice, Lydia."

I picture Wes's face, his eyes intent on mine as he told me we needed to return to the underground labs. Now I know why he wanted to take me back immediately. I wonder what he would think of me staying in the past for a little while. Nothing good, probably.

Then I stop and shake my head. Why am I even

considering his opinion? I can't make my decision based on a relative stranger, even if he did save my life yesterday. I need to do this for me and for my family.

"Okay." I smile at them both. "I'll stay."

CHAPTER 7

A few hours later, Mary and I are pressed together in the backseat of Dr. Bentley's car. It's straight out of an old gangster movie: rounded body, pointed hood, gleaming black finish. I run my hand over the soft leather seat. "What kind of car is this?" The motor is louder than I'm used to, causing the seat to vibrate.

"Nineteen-forty Plymouth," Dr. Bentley says as he pulls away from the hospital. "One of the last models you could buy before they stopped making them."

"They stopped making this car?"

"They stopped making all cars," Mary says. "You must know that." She giggles at my confused expression. "They needed the factories for the war effort? You do remember there's a war happening, right, Lydia?"

"Of course I remember." I turn to look out the window, running my hands nervously over my jean-covered legs. I'm wearing my own clothes again, a black-and-white checked button-down shirt that I tucked into cuffed jeans. Dr. Bentley found me a pair of castoff black leather shoes to wear. They're too tight and they pinch my toes.

I pay close attention as we drive out of Camp Hero. There are two checkpoints. The first one is at a small gate that leads into the clearing where the barracks and hospital are. The one soldier at the gate waves us through as he recognizes Dr. Bentley. The second checkpoint is at a large gate near the camp's entrance. Two soldiers step out of a small gatehouse, guns slung over their shoulders. They speak quietly with Dr. Bentley before letting us pass.

We drive out onto a bigger road and I turn to look back at Camp Hero. There's a tall fence around the outside of the camp, and I can see a huge stone lookout tower near the lighthouse. It's all so different from the welcoming state park I'm used to.

"Is it always this heavily guarded?" I ask.

"Usually. They patrol the perimeter, too," Dr. Bentley answers. "We're all a little puzzled as to how you managed to get in here without being noticed."

"I think I walked through the woods a lot." I hedge.

"You must have come up through the forest on the west side. The main base is in the eastern area. There are only a few bunkers with long-range guns, and storage facilities farther west. It's much more heavily wooded."

Except, of course, for a secret underground compound.

We turn onto the main highway, and I'm surprised to see that it looks like it does in my time—uneven pavement framed by the forest and the sand dunes. I see the beach out the window on Mary's side, a constant stretch of blue.

Mary chatters next to me about a USO dance and soldiers stationed in town. I nod along, but I'm glued to the window as we start to approach the center of town. Even in my time, Montauk is considered small, with just one main drag of restaurants and shops. Now, it's even smaller—a general store with a wide porch, a taller brick building that appears to serve as a post office and a town hall, a feed store, a few blue-gray shingled fishing huts.

"The town is so tiny." I interrupt something Mary's saying about a dance.

"We're simple folk," Dr. Bentley replies. "A lot different from your city slicker life. You might find it a bit dull out here."

"You'd be surprised," I say drily. "Still, I guess I was expecting something else."

Dr. Bentley turns right at the fork in front of the pond and starts to drive around it. The late afternoon sun reflects on the water. There are almost no houses, just a small wooden cabin tucked here and there.

"There are more buildings on the north side of town,"

Mary explains. "Though the navy is stationed up there now. They even test torpedoes on Lake Montauk!"

"And then I fix the soldiers up afterward." Dr. Bentley chuckles.

"I thought you were a doctor in the army?"

He shakes his head. "I'm not an army man. I just volunteer where I'm needed. Sometimes it's for the army, sometimes the navy."

"Are you a volunteer too?" I ask Mary.

"With the Red Cross. I've had nurse's training and everything. As soon as I graduate, I'm going to enlist into the Army Nurse Corps."

"Oh." I try to follow the conversation, but I grow more distracted as I turn to watch the town recede through the back window. This *is* my hometown. I can see the structure of it in the way the land dips and curves, but it has become something new entirely. Gone are the neatly paved roads, the tourist restaurants, the bars, and the knickknack shops. There isn't even a town green.

Mary follows my gaze. "The town was bigger before the Depression. This man Fisher came in and built a bunch of fancy buildings—the Yacht Club, the Tennis Auditorium. He wanted to make it a high-class resort town. But he lost all his money when the stock market crashed and everyone stopped coming. We don't even have a soda fountain anymore."

I nod. The story, about how the industrialist Carl Fisher

bought up land in the late 1920s to try to turn the town into the "Miami Beach of the North," is a local legend. He had to abandon everything when he lost his fortune.

I see Montauk Manor rising over Signal Hill. It looks mostly the same as it does in my time—a grand Tudor-style castle, with its massive white stone body and brown wooden framework edged against the large gables. It has been a resort for as long as I can remember, but my dad likes to tell stories about how he and his friends would sneak in when it was empty and abandoned, wandering through the dusty ballroom, the long empty pools, the vacant rooms.

We turn right onto a road not far from my own house, then pull into a dirt driveway. My great-great-grandparents' house is two stories, painted white. It feels private—trees isolate it from the few neighbors down the street, and I can see that the backyard is surrounded by forest. The Bentleys must be fairly wealthy, especially in the small fishing community of Montauk in 1944.

I've never seen this house before, and I remember my grandfather telling me that it burns down in the '60s. It's a strange feeling, knowing the future. I find myself staring through the trees in the direction of my own home. My grandfather lives there now, with his family. I try to picture my grandfather as a little boy but I can't. Everything is so different in this time. I wonder if I would even recognize my bedroom, painted in another color and decorated differently. Perhaps it would be like the town—a ghostly outline, a shadow of a place I've always taken for granted.

Mary tugs me toward the bright red front door. Before we reach it, it opens to reveal a petite woman with dark red hair, identical to mine and Mary's. She's wearing a green button-down dress, with a short cardigan perched around her shoulders.

"This must be Lydia." Her face is soft, with small lines around her eyes and mouth. She looks genuinely welcoming, not at all suspicious, and I am instantly at ease. "I'm Harriet Bentley." My great-great-grandmother.

"It's nice to meet you."

She smiles. I notice that we have the same curve to our upper lip, the same high cheekbones. And now I know where I got my red hair from.

"Come in, dear, you must be exhausted." She steps back and I walk into the entryway. It's a long hallway, with hardwood stairs that lead up to a shadowy second floor. There's a formal parlor to the left, with stuffy-looking couches and an antique wooden coffee table. A grand piano sits near the front windows, which are covered in heavy black fabric.

"You have to see my room!" Mary grabs my arm. "And I bet you want to take a bath. You can borrow one of my dresses. We need to get you out of those strange clothes."

I glance helplessly at Mrs. Bentley, but she just smiles as Mary tugs me up the stairs.

—

A half hour later I am clean again and holding up what looks like a corset with straps attached to the bottom. We're in Mary's small bedroom, which is nothing like my neat, simple room at home. There are two twin ruffled pink beds and framed pictures of flowers on the walls. Clothes and shoes and makeup cover every available surface.

Mary is stretched out on one of the beds, flipping through a magazine. She catches my expression and laughs. "Have you never seen a girdle before?"

"I guess . . . but what are the straps for?"

She rolls her eyes at the question. "To hold up your stockings, though lord knows I have none of those left. When Ma gave her old bras to the war effort, she made me give up almost all of my nylon stockings. Can you believe that? What are the boys gonna do, wear bras into combat? I know we're not supposed to complain and all, but sometimes this war makes life so hard." She swings her legs in the air behind her as she flips through the pages of her magazine.

"Handing over your underwear? That sounds rough." The girdle is lower than a corset, and it's supposed to pull across my stomach and hips. It reminds me of the shape-wear my mom is always buying.

"Do I really have to wear this?"

Her eyes go wide and her mouth falls open. "Lydia, what kind of question is that? What would people think?"

I sigh and pull on the girdle. It sucks in my stomach and creates a smooth line over my hips. I turn in the mirror, inspecting my new hourglass shape.

"Where'd you get that scar?" Mary points at my right shoulder. I glance down at the white, raised circle, noticeably bright against my pale skin.

"I don't know." I run my fingers over the slight bump. "I've had it for as long as I can remember."

"I have a scar on my knee. See?" Mary flips over and lifts one leg. "Fell off my bike when I was nine." She sits up and jumps off the bed. "Here, I'll get you a dress to wear. I'd give you stockings too, but this war!"

She throws her hands up and then turns, sticking out her leg. "Look at all the holes I've mended in these already. And they were just hand-me-downs from my mother."

Her stockings are covered in small, carefully sewn lines.

"Sometimes I even have Suze draw a line up the back of my leg so at least it looks like I'm wearing them. I just got some leg makeup, though. Once it dries it looks exactly like stockings, and I saved up a ration so I can buy a new girdle this summer. I had to make the one you're wearing out of parachute silk."

My grandfather once told me about the rationing during World War II, how everyone was allotted only a marginal amount of materials like sugar, meat, tea, tinned goods, and even clothes, but I never really thought much about it. I certainly never imagined I would experience it too.

Mary rifles through her open closet. She tosses a thin green dress at me, and I pull it on over my head. It has a high neckline, boxy short sleeves, a small, tucked-in waist, and a swingy skirt. I admire the smooth, emerald fabric. Vintage dresses from the '40s are always covered in holes or smell like mothballs. I've never worn something *new* like this.

Mary hands me a pair of wedged cork sandals and I pull them on.

"You look swell, Lydia, but let me pin up your hair." She sits me down at a small vanity. I face the mirror as she stands behind me and plays with my hair. "I can't believe we both have red hair. What are the odds?" I shrug and avoid her eyes in the mirror. "We're the same age, you know. I just turned seventeen a few months ago. There was a USO dance that weekend and all the soldiers were there and everyone danced with me because it was my birthday."

"What is a USO dance, anyway?"

Mary's jaw falls open again, and her hands still in my hair. "How can you not know what a USO dance is? Did you hit your head out there in the woods?"

"Well, I mean, I know it's a dance for the troops."

She nods, obviously in some kind of daze.

"What does USO stand for?"

"United Service Organization. How can you not know this, Lydia?"

I shrug again.

Mary sighs and puts one hand on her hip. "The USO

entertains the troops in all sorts of ways. They put on dances, and they get big stars to travel all over to sing and tell jokes. Rita Hayworth goes to all the training camps and the soldiers just love her." She grabs a brush off the vanity and starts to run it through my hair. "I volunteer at the USO center in town at least once a week. We serve donuts and play music and sometimes just talk with the soldiers for hours. They get bored and homesick, and it's our job to keep them entertained."

Mary puts down the brush and picks up a few long metal hairpins and a pink plastic comb. "Maybe you can come help me next time I go to the USO center. It's easy. You just smile and flirt and dance with anyone who asks."

"Sounds like fun." I look at Mary in the mirror, but she pushes my head back down.

"You simply cannot move, Lydia! Or I will poke your eye out with this comb. You know, you should consider cutting your bangs shorter. It would soften your face. Like mine." She fluffs the curls on her forehead, then runs her fingers through a small section of my hair. I haven't had anyone play with my hair since I was a little girl. It feels nice. "What was your high school like?"

"It was pretty normal. I spent a lot of time with Hannah, my best friend."

"Tell me about her."

"She's really blunt and funny. Stubborn. She can be kind of intense."

Mary squeezes my shoulder. "Do you miss her terribly? She can always come visit, if you want."

"It would be hard for her to visit, trust me." I smile at the thought of Mary and Hannah meeting. The girly-girl and the cynic. Though there is something similar about them: they're both honest and confident in their own ways.

"So, did you have a special someone?" Mary grins at me in the mirror.

I shake my head.

"Oh well, I bet you were real popular. I bet you're a gadabout girl and everything."

"Gadabout?"

"You know, someone who gads about town." Mary swishes her hips from side to side and purses her lips. "So what do you think of Lucas?" She leans down and lowers her voice. "Isn't he so drooly?"

"What?"

"Don't move, I said! Drooly, dreamy. You know, handsome."

Lucas is definitely cute, but when I think *handsome*, I think of someone untouchable—the kind of guy you never meet in real life.

"There. You're all done." Mary's voice pulls me from my thoughts.

I stare at myself in the mirror. She has twisted my hair up into two swirls on either side of my head. The rest falls gently down around my shoulders. I look older, a different version of myself.

"It'd be better if we could curl it." Mary reaches up to touch the ends, which fall to the middle of my back. "And it's so long. Tonight I'll put it in pins. Or maybe rag rollers, since you just washed it."

I catch her eye in the mirror. "Thank you, Mary."

She bends down and presses her cheek next to mine. "Oh Lydia, you don't need to thank me. I can tell we're going to be great friends."

Mary and I sit on opposite sides of the dining room table. Heavy white china and thick cotton napkins rest next to each plate. It's so formal and different from my family's meals together. I think of all of us sitting around our kitchen table on breakfast-Saturdays, the loud conversation, the teasing, and a small ache settles into my chest.

"There's been a rumor that some of the wounded soldiers over in Europe might be sent to Hero," Dr. Bentley tells us. "If that happens we'll need more volunteers." He looks at me pointedly.

"I don't really know much about nursing." I push a piece of Spam casserole around my plate.

Mrs. Bentley smiles. "There are lots of ways to help out that don't involve nursing."

"Ma volunteers with the Red Cross too." Mary is wolfing down the food on her plate. "She makes food for the barracks, or organizes clothing drives. Stuff like that."

"There's a fundraiser at the church tomorrow. My women's group is hosting a clothing drive in support of the Red Cross," Mrs. Bentley says. "We'll send boxes of clothes and towels and things to victims of war all across Europe. Why don't you girls come by and help us sort?"

"Sure," I say. Mrs. Bentley offers me more food and I hold out my plate.

"See, there are lots of ways to help." She ladles out the casserole. "But if you want any medical training, my church group also meets with Red Cross nurses once a week. We learn simple procedures so we can help if there's an emergency."

"Like, when the wounded soldiers come home?"

"Or if there's an attack on our shores."

"But there aren't . . ." I trail off, remembering myself.

"Billy McDonald told me his dad saw a submarine in the bay last winter. He's a member of the Home Guard. They walk the beaches looking for enemy ships. We even have air raid drills at night sometimes."

Mary's voice is hushed, but excited. She leans forward and the soft light of the room makes her red lipstick look even darker and more dramatic. "And every night we have to put up the blackout curtains. Montauk is on constant blackout—no streetlights or house lights once it gets dark. It's because we're so far out on the coast, we don't want the U-boats to see the lights of the town. But I bet we'd be pretty safe here if the Germans did attack. There are soldiers everywhere, with the base at Hero and the navy up by the bay."

"The army and navy took over a lot of land to set up their bases," Dr. Bentley cuts in, his tone serious. "The Killing family was forced to sell their home to the navy and move down near the new town center. And the Parker boys lost part of their fishing business when they had to leave their storefront behind. A lot of families were affected."

"We all have to make sacrifices during wartime." Mrs. Bentley stands up, moving to a sideboard to get dessert. It's a brown, lumpy cake that smells of burnt molasses. "Have some war cake, Lydia." She cuts it quickly and sets a plate down in front of me.

"What about Camp Hero?" I take a bite and almost gag as the dry, bitter cake breaks apart in my mouth. It tastes like it's missing butter and sugar.

"What about it?" Dr. Bentley asks.

I swallow with effort. "I mean, what happens out there? Is it just a training camp? And a lookout?"

"Oh, no," Mary mumbles around the cake in her mouth. "They have watch towers near the ocean and these big guns and a few barracks. But it's not exciting at all, no dances or shows or anything. The navy lets us have our USO dances over at Montauk Manor."

"Dean is stationed at Camp Hero. And so is Lucas. In the officers' barracks. Lucas helps with training," Mrs. Bentley says as she sits back down at the table. The heavy blackout curtains stir behind her as a breeze comes through the covered window. It's an eerie effect—like someone is hiding behind the black material, pushing it along the wood floor.

"What about Dean? What does he do?"

"He recently came back from the European theater," Dr. Bentley explains. "As he tells it, his commanding officers pulled him from his troops in Italy and brought him back home. He was somehow selected to be involved in intelligence training at Camp Hero."

"He's always been a smart boy." Mrs. Bentley smiles proudly. "His officers saw that. He'll have an important role to play one day."

Mary scoffs loudly. "*What* role? We don't know *what* Dean does!" She sits back in her seat. "It's all *top secret*."

"Mary!" Mrs. Bentley says sharply. "Loose lips sink ships, remember."

Mary throws her fork down and it clatters against her plate. "We don't know anything, just that Dean is always off doing secret training and he won't tell us a thing, not even if I beg him! It's all very dull." She rolls her eyes at me.

I nod absently. Grandpa was right about one thing: Dean is working on something that he can't tell his family about, and it forces him to spend time at Camp Hero. But is it connected to the Montauk Project?

Intelligence training can mean anything. Dean could be training to become a mission specialist. The government could be grooming him to become a spy. Or the whole thing could be a cover for the work he's doing for the Montauk Project.

If I'm going to find out what really happened to Dean, I have to start searching for the answers.

Later that night, I rest on Dean's bed, wrapped in a white cotton nightgown. My hair is twisted around pieces of rags—something Mary had insisted on doing after dinner. The tight curls pull at my scalp.

Dean's room is all blue in the soft lamplight: blue-and-white-striped wallpaper, a blue quilt spread out over the narrow bed. Model airplanes hang from the ceiling on wires and dull gold trophies sit neatly on a tall bookshelf.

I spent my whole life hearing stories about my great-grandfather's disappearance, but I never really thought about what he was like. What did he care about? What were his hobbies? How old was he when he fell in love for the first time?

If I stay in the past long enough, I'll discover the answers to these questions. I'll spend time with Dean, and I'll learn about him and his family. My grandfather's memories of his father are blurred by age and sorrow. But my memories will be new and clear. I can share those experiences with him, but it won't ever be the same as being here. I might end up knowing more about Dean than my grandfather ever did. It's a disconcerting thought, and I almost wish it was my grandfather who had gone back in time, so he'd get to relive this through fresh eyes. But would he ever be objective enough to see his father for who he really is, and not as a larger-than-life tragic hero?

Will I?

I walk over to the low, wide bureau and open the drawers one by one. Socks, crisp T-shirts, folded slacks. I run my hand under the clothes in the top drawer and touch the crackled edges of a piece of paper. I pull it out. It's an old letter, brittle with age. "My darling," it starts, "you are my everything." I read to the end. It's from a girl named Elizabeth—the name of my great-grandmother—and dated 1940. I put it back into the drawer, feeling like a trespasser.

I trace my fingers over the dusty lettering on a basketball trophy. STATE CHAMPIONS, 1935. A stamp collection and a few comic books vie for space with novels—John Steinbeck's *The Grapes of Wrath*, Ernest Hemingway's *A Farewell to Arms*.

I pull out Virginia Woolf's *A Room of One's Own*. I carry it over to the bed and sit down, flipping through the pages. A quote jumps out at me: "I thought how unpleasant it is to be locked out; and I thought how it is worse, perhaps, to be locked in." I snap the book shut. Am I locked in or locked out by being here?

I turn to the window, where the black fabric hides the night sky. Wes is out there somewhere. He followed me to the past. He helped me escape. I need to find him again.

He's the only one who can tell me about the Montauk Project. And, for some reason, he might want to help me.

I wonder if he's furious that I left him in the woods. I wonder if he's looking for me, and if he wants to take me back into the underground labs. I look away from the window. While I'm not exactly glad that I'm temporarily trapped in 1944, I can't deny that it's exciting—and feels important—to meet my relatives, to see the past, and to get more answers about what will happen to my great-grandfather in the coming days.

I always thought going off to college and becoming a journalist would be my big adventure. But this feels bigger.

Maybe I am supposed to do more than just figure out the truth of what really happened to Dean. This might be my chance to make a difference, and to help my family. Dean will disappear in just a few days *unless* I can figure out a way to stop it. But should I try to fix the past instead of just learning its secrets?

It's one thing to look for answers; it's another thing entirely to change the question.

Overwhelmed, I lie back on the bed. The model airplanes stir in the empty air above my head, suspended forever, flying nowhere.

CHAPTER 8

I wake to the sound of raised voices. The dress Mary gave me yesterday is draped over the back of a chair. I pull it over my head and quickly yank out the rag rollers in my hair. Heavy curls fall in ropes down my back. I slip out of the room and creep down the stairs, stopping at the bottom step.

Dr. and Mrs. Bentley are in the parlor, perched on the overstuffed cream and yellow couches. A tall, dark-haired man about ten years older than me paces in front of the fireplace. I immediately recognize him from my grandfather's photograph: it's Dean Bentley, my great-grandfather.

"What were you thinking? How could you just let a *stranger* into the house?"

Someone clears his throat, and I notice that Lucas is sitting on a chair by the window. Both he and Dean are wearing fitted dark olive jackets over their uniforms.

"It wasn't like that, Dean." Lucas's voice is firm.

Dean scowls at him. He's squeezing a light brown cap tightly in one hand. It has a visor and a gold metal eagle attached to the top. "Don't you dare talk to me right now, Clarke. Mary told me it was your idea for that girl to stay here. How could you put my family in this position?"

Lucas stands up. "Lydia needed help." His face is harsh, with only his words suggesting the warmth I saw yesterday.

"You could have passed her on to the Red Cross, or one of the women's organizations. You didn't need to bring my family into it."

The two men square off across the parlor. Dr. Bentley stands, stepping between them. "We're happy to take Lydia in—"

Dean cuts him off harshly. "She's a stranger."

"Stop this." Mrs. Bentley holds up her hands. Her voice is filled with a quiet authority. "Arguing isn't helping. Lydia has nowhere to go. We need to help our neighbors during wartime."

Both Dean and Lucas look at her and step away from each other. Dean faces the mantel and rests his arm on it heavily. He lowers his head, visibly collecting himself. Lucas turns to the window, his shoulders tense.

"Find out anything good?" I hear a voice say quietly

behind me. I spin around on the steps to see Mary leaning over the stair railing.

"Not really," I whisper back.

She laughs and skips down the stairs, her blue dress fluttering around her legs. It has a pattern of all white roses, and a matching ribbon is threaded through her curly hair.

"Come on. It's time you met Dean."

The conversation stops when we reach the parlor. I hover near the doorway, gripping the fabric of my skirt with both hands.

"Just look, Daddy! Isn't Lydia such a dilly?"

Dr. Bentley smiles, so I assume being a dilly is a good thing.

"Hi, Lucas. When did you get here? Has Dean been talking your ears off? I bet he has." Mary pulls me into the room.

Lucas's eyes slowly scan my dress and my clean, curled hair. He opens his mouth, then shuts it.

"Mary, could you stop talking for two minutes?" Dean snaps. "We need to figure out what to do about . . . this situation." He waves in my direction.

"What's there to figure out? Lydia's staying with us. And she isn't a spy. Just look at her!"

"Putting her in a pretty dress doesn't make her any less of a spy." Dean glares at me. I glance around the room in an effort to avoid his stare. Framed black-and-white photos are propped on the fireplace mantel. Mary and Dean with their arms around each other, standing in front of the house. A small, dark-haired boy standing with Dean and a blond lady. A family portrait, taken in this parlor, everyone smiling into the camera.

"Oh, phooey." Mary drops my arm and stalks across the floor toward Dean. "You don't know anything."

He leans down to look her in the eye. "Mary, we're a country at war. You'd think that would teach you to be careful around strangers."

She scowls at him, her hands on her hips. "I trust Lydia."

"Why? Because you want a new friend?"

Lucas turns to me, ignoring the siblings. "How are you feeling, Lydia? You look . . ." He pauses, clearing his throat. "Well. Better. I mean, good." He's standing by the window, and the morning light streams across his face and turns his hair to gold.

"I'm fine." I smile at Lucas, but I can't stop staring at Dean. He's so different from what I expected. Younger. Tougher. Harsher.

"Listen to her!" Mary yells at Dean. The two of them are facing each other, only a foot apart. "She doesn't even have a little bit of a German accent!"

Dr. Bentley picks up a pipe from a nearby table and lights it. He seems unconcerned by the shouting match between Dean and Mary. I suspect it's a regular occurrence.

Mary turns to me. Her nose is scrunched up and her hands are clenched at her sides. "Lydia, tell him. Tell him you're not a spy!"

I look at Dean, his long face, sharp jaw, and heavy brows, his frown. I certainly never thought my great-grandfather would hate me on sight. The thought is disappointing and, somehow, I'm a little hurt.

"I'm not a spy." My voice is softer and quieter than I'd intended.

Mrs. Bentley gives Dean a look. "No one thinks you are, dear."

Dean runs a hand over his short dark hair. He avoids everyone's stares and looks out the front window. "If I really thought she was a spy, do you think I would have let her leave the base? Do you think any of the officers at Hero would have?"

I let out a breath, but he isn't finished yet.

"That doesn't mean she's a trustworthy person, or that my family should be taking in strangers off the street."

The smoke from Dr. Bentley's pipe floats into the air, and the spicy scent reminds me of my grandfather. Thinking of him makes me feel instantly stronger. He's the reason I'm here. I can face anything for him.

I turn to Dr. and Mrs. Bentley. "I know I'm a stranger. It means a lot to me that you'd take me in and help me when I have no other options. I promise I won't overstay my welcome."

The lines of Dean's face are severe in the sunlit room. "What if you already have?"

Mary throws herself down onto the couch next to her

father. "Gee whiz, Dean, leave her alone! You never know when to stop." She crosses her arms, clearly finished with the topic.

Lucas frowns as he watches the scene. He looks like he wants to say something, but whatever it is, he holds his tongue. He catches me looking at him and his face smooths into a slight smile. I give him an identical look, grateful that I'm not the only non–family member here.

As far as they know.

"Dean." Mrs. Bentley stands up. The room falls silent. She steps forward until she's right next to me. I smell her perfume, rose water and mint. "Lydia needs our help, and our family helps those in need. Now we'll ask around town to see if anyone has heard of her aunt. What did you say her name was, dear?"

"Julia Roberts," I mumble.

"Of course. Julia Roberts. But until then, Lydia is a welcome guest in our home."

I scan the room, stopping at Dean's scowling face. "I promise I won't be a burden."

As I say the words, I wonder if it's a promise I'll be able to keep.

A little while later, I sit outside on the front steps and watch as Dean's jeep disappears down the dusty driveway. He's heading back to Camp Hero to work on his mysterious project—a project I'm no closer to figuring out. I turn away and stare out at the Bentleys' yard. The grass is short and neat and there are flower beds tucked around the side of the house. In the far corner is a large vegetable garden with pale green sprouts rising from the ground. Mrs. Bentley calls it a Victory Garden, where she grows food for the family so they don't have to live only on rations.

The door opens behind me and I look up. Lucas is standing there. He stares down at me. "How are you?"

I take a deep breath. "I wanted to thank you. Without your help, I'd still be wandering around the camp right now."

"Oh, it's nothing." He comes forward and sits on the step, close enough that the fabric of my dress grazes his leg. "Everything will be just dandy, you'll see."

"Just dandy?" I repeat, smiling.

"Are you teasing me?" When he smiles the corners of his eyes crinkle slightly.

"I thought only old ladies used that word."

"You shouldn't make fun of an old country boy."

"Where are you from, anyway?"

"White Plains, Georgia. A tiny town in the middle of nowhere."

There's a slight breeze in the air that ruffles my skirt. I lift my face into the wind and close my eyes, breathing in the early summer smell of Montauk: fresh earth and the sharp scent of the ocean.

I open my eyes to find Lucas watching me. "So how did you end up at Camp Hero?" I ask.

He clasps his hands between his knees. "I was sent to the Western Front after training. Bomb went off nearby one day. I was fine but lost my hearing for a few weeks. I was classified as injured. They sent me back here to help train new recruits over at Hero. I'm lucky, really. Not to be on the front lines." He smiles, but there's disappointment hidden behind his expression.

I narrow my eyes at him. "Lucky maybe, but you're not happy about it, are you?"

He tilts his head, surprised. "No, not happy exactly. I'd rather be back in Europe. I'm not much help over here."

"That's not true. You're training soldiers, aren't you? That's a huge job."

"You're right." He laughs softly. "And someone has to find lost girls wandering around the base."

"You're my hero." I mean to say it sarcastically, but somehow it comes out sounding sincere. He looks at me strangely. "Anyway," I say quickly, trying to cover up the awkward moment. "Thanks again. I don't know what came over me."

His smile falls. "Grief makes you do things you wouldn't normally."

The front door swings wide-open. "There you two are!" Mary exclaims. "I've been looking everywhere for you. It's time to go. Are you coming to the fundraiser, Lucas?"

I turn to look up at Mary. She's beaming down at me, sneaking little glimpses at Lucas.

"I might stop by later, but I need to check on some supplies at the base first." He stands up without looking at me and starts walking backward toward a green army truck in the driveway. "Bye, y'all."

"Bye, Lucas! I'll see you soon," Mary calls out, waving her hand. As he pulls out of the dirt driveway, she slumps down next to me on the step and clutches my arm. "Isn't he so dreamy?"

"He's fine," I say.

"Oh Lydia, admit it!"

For some reason I think of Wes again, his eyes so dark they're almost black, his lips soft over the strong line of his jaw. I shake my head, pushing the image away.

"Lucas isn't really my type." I stand up, running a hand over my hair, smoothing out the scattered strands. "C'mon, let's go help your mom."

The fundraiser is at one of the local churches, a few miles from the Bentleys' house. I want to walk so I can see more of the town, and Mary grudgingly agrees to go with me.

It's a hot, muggy day for early June. Once we leave the circle of trees surrounding the house, we're on a dirt road with only a few single-level homes scattered along it.

I wipe at the sweat on my forehead, wishing I wasn't wearing a heavy girdle under my dress. "It's hot."

"You're the one who wanted to walk." Mary pouts. Her dress is already sticking to her skin. She turns her head at the low rumbling sound of an approaching car. "Wait, I'll fix it."

An army truck passes and Mary sticks out her thumb. The truck honks but keeps moving, obviously in a hurry.

"Rats," Mary says, trudging along beside me. She lifts her hair away from her neck. "We'll melt out here if we have to walk all the way."

"Did you just . . . try to *hitchhike*?"

"What?" Mary gives me a look. "Doesn't everyone?"

"It's dangerous," I hiss. "You could be *murdered*."

She laughs. "Are you kidding? No one has ever been murdered because of hitchhiking."

I gape at her but don't say anything else.

We walk around Fort Pond on a dirt road that leads into the center of town. Mary chatters about the USO dance that's coming up, but my thoughts drift to Camp Hero, to Wes, to Dean's approaching disappearance. I glance over at Mary, suddenly aware that her family will change forever in just a few short days.

Mary's cheeks are flushed as she waves her arms around. "It's this Saturday, June third, at the old tennis auditorium. All the soldiers will be there. Oh! We'll have to get something for you to wear. Maybe my blue dress."

Will Mary still be so carefree after Dean disappears? Will she think so much about clothes and boys and dances?

My grandfather told me so little about Mary and what her life was like after she eloped. I know she leaves Montauk, but I don't know if she was ever happy again. I don't even know who she's going to marry.

I force myself to smile at her. "That sounds like fun."

"Then why do you look like you're about to cry, silly?" She giggles. "I hope Suze comes today. I cannot wait for you two to meet!"

She starts to skip down the road, her black-and-white saddle shoes kicking up the dirt. Dust hovers around her in a heavy cloud.

When we arrive downtown, Mary pulls me in the direction of the general store. "Let's get some root beer before we go to the fundraiser," she says. The store is in a small, shabby wooden building. Two old men sit on the sagging front porch. There's a large radio resting on a table between them, the cord disappearing into the open window of the store. *"The frontlines are expanding as British soldiers in the three hundred fifty-sixth Infantry Division march on Italy . . ."*

Mary waves as she pushes open the screen door. The old men nod but don't take their eyes off the empty highway in front of them. "Tommy Sullivan's family owns the store," she says as we step inside.

It smells of dry wood, spices, and raw meat. A counter stretches along the left side of the shop, displaying sodas, beers, meats, and cheeses. The rest of the room is filled with wooden shelves.

Mary drops her voice, though we're the only people

in the store. "Tommy was my old beau. He was drafted last year before he even finished school. Now he's in the Marines. I write him whenever I get the chance."

Cans and tins of brands I've never seen before line the simple, mostly empty shelves—Brer Rabbit Gold Label Molasses, Van Camp's Chili Con Carne, Armour Treet, Dromedary Gingerbread Mix. The walls are cluttered with brightly colored ads and local notices. Handwritten signs ask citizens to turn in any scrap metal or steel to the Montauk war effort. In an ad for Nestlé's, a soldier bites into a bar of chocolate under the slogan CHOCOLATE IS FIGHTING FOOD! There are even propaganda posters. The words DELIVER US FROM EVIL: BUY WAR BONDS loom over a sad-looking little girl in front of a swastika. Another shows the lighthouse on Montauk Point: THIS IS AMERICA— FOR THIS WE FIGHT: MAY ITS RADIANCE LIGHT SAFELY THE WAY TO PORTS OF FREEDOM.

Mary heads toward the side of the counter and stops at a white, rectangular metal box with ICE printed on the side. She reaches inside and takes out two glass bottles, handing me one. I open my bottle and sniff at the brown contents. "Mr. Sullivan makes the root beer himself in their bathtub," she says.

I sip at the liquid, surprised by the tangy, bittersweet taste. It's nothing like the root beer I've had before, but it's good.

I take a step toward the door, still holding the bottle,

but Mary stops me. "Wait. We have to drink it here. Mr. Sullivan reuses the bottles."

When we finish, she drops the empty bottles on the counter, then reaches into her pocket and places a nickel and a penny next to the register. "Have a nice day!" Mary smiles at the two old men sitting outside.

A car with a square black top drives past. It honks, a high, cartoonish sound. The old men wave in response as the tinny voice on the radio speaks of soldiers on the move.

CHAPTER 9

*W*e enter the Montauk Associated Church through the back door. Women and girls crowd around tables piled with clothing and towels and blankets. Mrs. Bentley stands in the middle of the room, directing the other volunteers.

Her face lights up when she sees us. "Oh, girls, thank the good lord you're here. There's so much to do. Go over to a table and start folding. Clothes in one pile, sheets, towels, and blankets in another. When you're done you can put them into a box. We're trying to have everything ready by the end of the day."

Mary and I find a table in the corner that's piled high with fabric. I'm grateful to have something to do, and I like organizing the clothes into neat piles. Mary is less charmed by the project and gets bored after a few minutes. "I'm gonna find Suze," she says, tossing a child's shirt onto the table. "You'll be okay alone?"

"Sure." I pick up a towel and fold it into a neat square. "This is fun."

"For cripes' sake, Lydia, who wants to fold stuff? I'll be right back once I find Suze—you stay right here." She takes off into the crowd of women.

I watch the large group as I work. There are maybe twenty women and girls scattered around the room, and a few children are running back and forth. I'm surprised to see a couple of soldiers among the women. Most are in navy uniforms, blue with a white neckerchief knotted at their chests, while a few others wear army uniforms.

The women are in dresses or skirts. Their hair is short and curled, or long and softly waved, but no one is sporting an easy ponytail. No one is wearing sweatpants.

The castoff dress I'm wearing is nicer than most of the others in the room. Montauk, Amagansett, and even East Hampton are still poor fishing communities. No one has money to spare. The Hamptons that I grew up in, where the tourists pour in by the thousands, and where it takes hours to drive anywhere in the summer, clearly doesn't exist yet.

I set a folded towel down in front of me. My hand stills on the fabric, and goose bumps rise on my arm. I can feel someone's gaze. It's a heavy feeling, and it reminds me of the night of the bonfire when I *knew* someone was out there.

I look up. In the far corner, a dark-haired soldier is

staring right at me. I meet his eyes, and for a second I forget to breathe.

Wes.

I grip the table. I need to talk to him. I need to step forward. Only I can't seem to move my feet. I can't break his gaze. I'm anxious and a little scared, but there's something else happening too. Something dark. Something powerful.

His face is blank, impassive, like a mask has been pulled over his features. But I recognize the look in his eyes. Intensity, surprise, and anticipation, all at once—it's the same confusing mix of emotions he had written on his face when he forced himself to let go of my shoulders in the labs.

There's a loud noise behind me and I jump. I tear my eyes from Wes. A chair has fallen over; a laughing, embarrassed woman bends to pick it up. When I turn back around, Wes has disappeared. I scan the room, searching for him in the crowd, but it's useless—he's gone.

My heart is racing, and I press my hand against my chest to stop it. Wes is the only one who can give me some answers about the Montauk Project. I can't let him disappear again.

I start to walk around the table, but a small boy steps in front of me. I barely glance at him as I scan the crowd above his head.

"Hiya," he says.

"Hi." I keep searching. Women stand in tight groups, a soldier walks past carrying a large cardboard box, but there's no sign of Wes. "I'm sorry, but I'm trying to find someone."

"I could help you. What's your name? Who are you looking for?"

"Lydia," I say quickly. "Have you seen a soldier with dark hair around here?"

"There are lots of soldiers with dark hair here." He sticks a finger into the side of his mouth.

He's right. I look down at him.

He stares up at me through a fringe of dark brown hair that falls across his forehead. He's six or seven, wearing brown short pants, high socks, shiny black shoes, and a patterned short-sleeved shirt that matches his deep green eyes. "I'm Peter."

Peter . . . I crouch down so that I'm level with him. "What's your last name?"

"Bentley."

I stand up slowly and put one hand on the table to steady myself.

This little boy is my grandfather.

"My dad is a soldier," he tells me proudly, unaware of my distress. "When I grow up I'm gonna be in the war too. I'm gonna fly planes and shoot Nazis."

When you grow up there won't be a war anymore. "That's awesome," I say, distracted. This tiny person is my grandfather. My tall, gray-haired grandfather. Now he barely comes up to my waist.

"Huh?"

"Awesome? Cool. Great. Neato."

"Oh. I never heard that before. Awesome. Awwwesome. So is your daddy in the war too?"

I am saved from answering him by a slim blond lady who approaches, placing a hand on Peter's shoulder. I recognize her from one of the photos in the Bentleys' living room. This is Elizabeth Bentley, Dean's wife, and my great-grandmother.

"Is Peter bothering you?" She pulls him into her side. He curls against her tan, structured suit.

"Oh, no. Peter and I have been getting along great."

"It's been awwwwesome," Peter drawls. I have got to watch what I say around here. I've created a monster.

"You must be Lydia." She glances down at Peter, then back at me. "I'm Elizabeth Bentley. Dean Bentley is my husband."

"I know." I smile tentatively, not sure what she must think of me.

"Do you?" Her voice is suspicious.

"Mary pointed you out earlier," I say quickly.

She gives me an assessing look and clutches her pocketbook tightly under her arm. "Dean thinks the Bentleys are foolish to take you in."

I look Elizabeth directly in the eyes, refusing to be intimidated. "What do *you* think?"

She smiles slightly. "I guess I'll have to figure that out for myself."

I can work with that.

"Let's go, Peter." He waves as they disappear into the crowd.

My grandfather is a seven-year-old, my great-grandparents think I'm a threat, and I don't see Wes anywhere. I grab a towel and start folding again as neatly as I can. If I can't keep any order in my own life, I might as well try to create it elsewhere.

When most of the clothes are packed into boxes, ready to be picked up by the Red Cross, Mary comes back over to the table, pulling a short, dirty-blond-haired girl along with her.

"This is my best friend, Susie, but I call her Suze!"

I smile. "Hi, Susie."

"Hi." Her voice is soft and shy.

"My two best friends *finally* meeting!" Mary says, as if I've been here longer than two days. "Suze has been just dying to meet you. Haven't you, Suze?"

Susie makes a sound of agreement but doesn't say anything. Her hair is fine and lies in wisps around her face. Next to the vibrant Mary, she looks pale and thin.

"Let's all get ready for the USO dance together!" Mary chatters. "There's a picnic earlier in the day for the little kids and families, but we can go back to my house before the actual dance starts. What are you wearing, Suze? I've been mending that red dress I have. You should wear your black, with the tight bodice and the beads!"

"It's the only dress I have, Mary." Susie looks down at

the table. I notice that her shirt has a small hole in the sleeve.

"Well, then, aren't you lucky you look like such a bombshell in it?"

Susie gives Mary a look that is both amused and grateful.

"Is Mick coming to the dance?"

Susie's face falls. "He might have to work the boats."

"Suze is engaged to Mick Moriglioni," Mary tells me. "We went to grade school with him, but he left in eighth grade to go work in the family fishing business. His daddy's overseas now, and he has to run the business along with his younger brothers. He spends all his time down by the docks, and he *never* has time to see Susie."

Susie stares down at the table. "He's busy. I understand."

"Oh, phooey. He works too much, when he should be going out with you!" Mary flips her hair over her shoulder and huffs. "He's going off to war in just a few months. Suze is going to be all alone then. You'd think he'd want to spend time with her now!"

"Hello, girls," Lucas says from behind us. We all turn at the sound of his voice. He steps forward and catches my eye, smiling broadly. I can't help but smile back.

"Lucas!" Mary immediately starts to glow in his presence. "I was just telling Suze how Mick should take her to the USO dance this Saturday. You'll be there, won't you?"

He pretends to consider the question and Mary squeals, pushing at his shoulder. They both laugh.

"I'll be there if I can get leave. It shouldn't be a problem."

He looks at me. "Are you going, Lydia?"

"Do you think Mary would let me miss it?"

"Then I'll try to be there." He grins a little, his eyes bright. I blink at him, surprised by how flirtatious he sounds. I think of the way he laughs and jokes with Mary. He's probably just teasing me, too. Like an older brother or something.

Mrs. Bentley approaches the table. "You girls have done a wonderful job!"

"Thanks, Ma! We worked really hard," Mary says. I give her a look, but she just winks at me. "It was mostly all my work. Lydia barely helped at all."

I start to laugh. "You are such a liar!"

"Lydia!" She looks mock offended. "We're in a *church*."

Everyone laughs, including Mrs. Bentley. "Mary, I need to make sure the boxes are organized before they're sent out. Will you come help me?"

Mary sighs and glances at Lucas out of the corner of her eye. He's looking down at the table, drawing circles on the wood with his finger. He has a tiny smile on his face and I wonder what he's thinking about.

"Sure thing, Ma." Mary and Mrs. Bentley walk back into the crowd.

Susie, Lucas, and I stand around the table. Nobody says anything, and the silence quickly becomes awkward.

"I should go too." Susie glances between the two of us. She seems uncomfortable now that Mary is gone.

"It was nice to meet you," I tell her.

"You, too." She walks away.

"Bye, Susie." Lucas looks up, and his eyes find me instantly. "Alone again." He grins widely. There's something endearing about his crooked bottom teeth; I can't remember the last time I've seen teeth that aren't perfect. "It's nice of you to help out today."

"Of course. The Bentleys have been so wonderful, especially Mary. She's the best."

"She's a great girl." He says the words without any inflection and I can't read anything behind them. I want to ask him more about her, want to know if he feels the same way she does, but I don't.

"It's been like having a sister."

"Good luck to you then. I have three of 'em. They drive me up a creek."

"Three sisters?" I picture Lucas surrounded by a bunch of nagging, teasing little girls. "That's a lot of women."

"It's what makes me such a big hit with the gals." He laughs a little as he says it, but I don't doubt the truth of his words. I see the way other women in the room are watching him, aware of his tall, broad frame, blond hair, and pretty face. His features are too soft to be considered handsome, but he has an easygoing, boyish quality about him that's undeniably attractive.

I tilt my head as I study him. I only met Lucas two days ago, and I've been so distracted—by the Montauk Project,

Dean, Wes—that I never considered him as anything other than a nice guy who helped me when I needed it. But for that brief moment when I thought he was flirting with me, I became aware of him in a new way. Now I'm starting to see what Mary meant about him being "drooly."

My cheeks burn at the thought, and I glance down at the table. "You must miss them," I say quickly.

"We write." He shrugs, dismissing the topic. "So you're settling in okay?"

I nod and bite my lip. He mimics the motion and I laugh. Our eyes meet.

In my peripheral vision I see a navy uniform. I quickly turn my head to see Wes standing near the side door. His gaze cuts to me for a second, a flicker of black, before he slips out of the room.

I automatically jerk forward. "Lucas, I'm sorry, but I have to . . ." I rush from the table.

"What—?" I hear Lucas ask behind me, but I'm already gone.

The late afternoon sunlight is bright, with clouds moving in thin streaks across the sky. I stop outside the door of the church, scanning the yard in front of me. It's empty, with neatly cut grass stretching toward a few low, scrubby-looking trees. Beyond that the dunes rise up, covered in long, swaying grass. I can just glimpse the ocean through the gaps in the sand.

I walk across the yard, past the trees, until I reach a large dune. My shoes sink into the sand, some of it sliding into my short socks, rough against my ankle. I hop on each foot as I pull my shoes and socks off and hold them in one hand as I climb to the top of the bank.

Wes stands on the deserted beach. From a distance he looks like someone taking a casual moment to watch the waves break against the shore. But as I get closer, I see the contained way he carries himself: the subtle stiffness in his posture, the deliberate placement of his arms and legs.

As I walk up to him, he turns his head. The motion is so quick that I stop abruptly and drop my shoes onto the sand.

"The soldier you were talking to. Who is he?" Wes says it so quietly that I strain to hear him over the sound of the waves. His voice is different from how it was in the woods. It's no longer soothing and easy but stiff and slightly robotic. There is something in the way his jaw clenches that makes me think my answer is important to him.

He stares at me as he speaks. He doesn't fidget, he doesn't look around. For some reason it annoys me, and I cross my arms over my chest as I answer him. "That's none of your business."

He turns to face me without breaking eye contact. "Lydia. You being here isn't right. This isn't your time."

I step closer to him. I can smell the salt of the ocean, and something else—something spicy and clean, like pine needles and rain. "Why didn't you tell me I traveled through time? And why did you help me get out of the labs?" As soon as I ask one question, I think of another, and another, and I can't stop as they pour out of me. "Are you connected to the Montauk Project? Are you a guard there? Why didn't you kill me for knowing too much? *Who are you?*"

The corners of his lips tighten slightly.

"This isn't a joke," I say coldly. "I refuse to be in the dark, stumbling around trying to figure out what's happening."

"I know it's not a joke." He's serious again. "You're not supposed to be here."

I find myself growing defensive at his tone. "It's not like I meant to go back in time. I didn't know what would happen in that machine. Maybe I shouldn't have pressed a button, but I was trying to get away from *you!*"

He shifts closer to me. The movement is so small it's almost invisible but I notice it instinctively. "I wasn't going to hurt you."

"I didn't know that. I still don't know that."

Wes takes a full step closer and we're only a few feet apart. He's tall, just a little shorter than Grant. I'm not that short, but I have to crane my neck to look up into his face. The sun is behind him and it reflects off the metal buttons of his uniform. I wonder briefly where he found it—then where he's been sleeping and what he's been doing for these past two days. I look at his clean-shaven face, at his newly cut military-short hair and decide he can probably take care of himself.

"I won't *ever* hurt you, Lydia." He sounds so sincere that I feel most of my anger and fear dissolve. I'm not even surprised that he knows my name.

I take a deep breath. I won't let him distract me from the reason I'm here. I need answers. "Let's start from the beginning. Why was the bunker open?"

For a moment I think he won't answer. Then he says, "There was a security breach. That door opened automatically. It's not a commonly used entrance—it's usually sealed shut."

"A security breach? Who was it?"

"I . . ." he hesitates. "I left the Facility before the suspect was apprehended."

"Is that what you call the underground lab? The Facility?"

He nods.

The wind whips the curls around my face. I brush them away impatiently. Wes follows the movement with his eyes. We're close enough to touch, though he keeps his hands tight against his sides.

"I have questions about the Montauk Project," I say. "A lot of them."

His face goes hard at my words, and his mouth presses into a thin line. "There's not much I can tell you."

"What *can* you tell me?"

He doesn't answer.

"Do you work for them?"

No response. I lean forward, consciously invading his

space. The wet pine smell is stronger, and I realize that it's coming from him.

"Then tell me this. Why did you follow me?"

For the first time on the beach, Wes's eyes leave my face, dropping down to the sand below our feet. He seems . . . uncertain about something.

"I need to make sure you make it back to two thousand twelve," he says.

"Why is that important to you?"

He looks up at me again. "Have you ever heard of the butterfly effect?"

"You mean like when a butterfly flaps its wings in Texas and then there's a tsunami in China?"

One corner of Wes's mouth tilts up. "Sort of. It's a scientific theory about chaotic systems. Any small change can lead to unpredictable, potentially massive variations within a system."

"Isn't that what I just said?"

He smiles briefly, so quick I almost miss it. "It's not that a butterfly flapping its wings *will* cause a problem somewhere else, but that it *could*. We can't predict when or how those small changes happen, but they could cause untold amounts of damage to a system. Time is a system, Lydia."

"You're saying that my being here will change something."

"It could. The more interaction you have with this time, the more you might be altering future events that have unknown consequences." Any trace of humor leaves his face, and his voice is firm.

If I save Dean, I'll be changing the past. I'll be giving my grandfather the life with his father that he's always wanted. But no one can predict how that will affect the future.

I gaze down at the sand and picture my grandfather as he walked away from me in the woods, the rain falling on his shoulders. He seemed so old in that moment, so broken. I know that I would do anything to stop him from hurting. And now there's Mary, Dr. and Mrs. Bentley. If there's some small chance that I can save Dean, I'll only be making the future a better place for everyone.

But what will the consequences be if Dean never disappears? Will I even exist? Is that a risk I'm willing to take?

"You need to go home."

I look up at Wes, startled out of my thoughts. "What?"

"I'll take you. We can sneak into Camp Hero tonight."

I open my mouth, then close it. "I'm not going back yet," I say finally, surprising us both.

He stares at me for a minute. "Did you hear what I said? I'll take you home, Lydia."

Home. Safe. I think of Hannah, of my mother, my father, my grandfather. I miss them. But I'll find my way back there soon, I know I will.

I've never believed in fate or coincidence. I've always thought that we determine our own destinies. But there is something fated about me ending up in 1944. I stumbled into a secret government project by accident, and then

I pushed a button and it sent me to the exact time my great-grandfather is supposed to disappear. I *have* to believe this happened for a reason. Maybe I shouldn't have been so hard on Hannah and her signs.

Change isn't always a bad thing, and the butterfly effect is unpredictable. Wes doesn't even know what will happen if I stay and save Dean. Helping my family now might have *good* consequences. There are obviously risks, but the reward, if it works, would be great.

I take a step back, away from Wes. "I'm not going back yet."

His eyes narrow and I wonder if he's angry with me, or just confused. "If you stay here, you could change everything."

"I know."

I step away from him again. Wes sighs, turns his head, and looks out at the ocean. He looks like he's in a snapshot from World War II: the soldier standing in the sun as the waves break white and foamy near his feet.

I try to capture the image in my mind. Neither of us belongs in this time, but it doesn't mean we can't fake it for a little while.

"Lydia, I can't let you go." He turns back to me, and his expression is hard, set. "You don't understand how serious this is."

"I *do* understand."

"If you understood, then you wouldn't be staying in this

time period. You'd be coming back with me."

"Wes, I—"

"Lydia!"

We both freeze and turn toward the voice. Mary is standing on a high dune, one hand shading her eyes as she gazes at us from across the beach.

"I have to go," I say to Wes. I pick up my shoes and take another step backward.

"Lydia. Don't." His voice sounds ragged.

"I'm sorry." I move farther and farther away from him. "I have to."

Without another word, I turn and run back up the sand, where Mary is waiting for me.

CHAPTER 10

"*Would* you like more tea?" Elizabeth Bentley holds out a blue and white china teapot, steam drifting into the air.

"No, thank you." Mrs. Bentley places a delicate teacup onto the saucer in her lap.

We're sitting in Dean's living room, in *my* house, though it looks nothing like how I'm used to it. There's a hunter-green patterned couch in the middle of the room and a tall standing radio below the window. The walls are a soft, seafoam green, with gold leaf accents framing the ceiling.

Mary and I sit together on the couch clutching our teacups. It's the morning after the fundraiser, after I ran away from Wes on the beach. *You could change everything,* he said. I look out the window, into the familiar backyard where the branches of a dogwood tree hang heavy with thin white flowers. Wes doesn't know it, but his words have filled me with hope. I want to change everything. I want to fix my family.

But first I have to find out how—and if—Dean is connected to the Montauk Project.

Peter, my grandfather, sits on the floor in front of us playing war with small metal figurines. "Pow, pow, pow," he murmurs, knocking one of the army men onto the rug.

When his mother disappears into the hallway, I ask, "Who's winning?"

"The Allies." He doesn't look up from his toys. "We're bumping off those Jerrys one by one."

Mary fidgets in her seat. "I don't know why we had to come over for tea," she whispers to her mother. "Lydia and I were supposed to go to the beach with Suze and Jinx. You know I'm volunteering at Camp Hero later this afternoon. This was my only time to go."

"Shh," Mrs. Bentley scolds. "This is your brother's home. Be polite."

"My brother's not even here. . . ." She trails off as Elizabeth returns, carrying a tray of cookies.

"Help yourself." Elizabeth places it onto the low wooden coffee table.

Mary snatches up one of the cookies and takes a bite.

"Ohhh," she sighs, "real sugar." She finishes the cookie and reaches for another one. "How is it that you always have so many rations? First the tea, then the sugar cookies." She drops her voice. "It's the black market, isn't it?"

"Mary!" Mrs. Bentley exclaims. "The stories you come up with."

Elizabeth's pale skin stands out against the dark red of her high-necked dress. "Your brother brought tea, sugar, and white flour home the other day. He said the army gave him these supplies to pass on to his family."

"Lucas never has stuff like this." Mary eats the second cookie, closing her eyes as she chews.

Mrs. Bentley picks up a cookie from the tray. "I'm sure it's only for the senior officers."

"I thought we were all making do with less."

"That's for us civilians, not our soldiers. They're making the ultimate sacrifice. We do what we can on the home front." Mrs. Bentley touches Mary gently on the arm. "That means sacrificing in a different way."

"Well, it just seems like some of us are sacrificing more than others." Mary pouts.

"Oh Mary, have another cookie." Elizabeth hands her the plate. She sounds like she's trying not to laugh, even as Mary glares at her. "We can all benefit from your brother's important position."

Speaking of Dean. I glance toward the hallway. Mary might have been disappointed about this tea, but the minute Mrs. Bentley told us we were going, I started to plot. To find out what Dean really does at Camp Hero, I'll need to become the spy he originally accused me of being. What better place to start than in his own house?

I stand up, smoothing the fabric of my narrow blue skirt, another castoff from Mary. "Could you tell me where the bathroom is?"

"Of course." Elizabeth's tone is cool but polite. "It's down the hallway, to the right of Dean's study."

"Thank you." As they start to talk about the upcoming USO dance, I walk out of the room. Dean's study is across the hall from the kitchen and I find it easily. The door is slightly ajar. I check the hallway to make sure I'm alone, and then I slip into the room.

The blackout curtains are pulled tight across the small window, the only light coming from the open door behind me. There's a wide wooden table in the center of the room, with two straight-back chairs flanking it. Neat stacks of paper rest on its surface. A large black-and-white map of the world covers one wall, with careful lines drawn across it, marking where the Allies are advancing through Europe. Another large writing desk takes up half of the opposite wall, with open compartments built into the top and drawers along one leg.

I carefully rifle through the papers on the table. Most of the sheets are blank, and I put them aside, turning to the desk. The compartments are filled with letters, stamps, and envelopes. Moving quickly, I pull open the drawers. The top one is filled with pens and paper. The middle drawer has bills and receipts. I yank at the bottom one, but it's stuck. I pull harder. The wood creaks, then pops open.

I glance at the door. I've only been gone a minute or so, but I need to be careful. I don't know what Dean would do if he heard I was snooping through his stuff, but I know he wouldn't be happy. The top of the drawer is filled with papers, a deed to the house, a recent bank statement. I pull out a smaller stack of papers. They're covered in Dean's neat handwriting.

"The fuse box is in the basement near the furnace," the top one reads. "Flip the switch if one is blown." I rifle through the sheets. They're all like that—instructions on how to fix the furnace when it overheats, on how to refill the oil in the hot water tank.

Why is Dean leaving his family instructions on how to maintain the house? Is he *expecting* to disappear? Perhaps every soldier does this in order to prepare his family for the worst.

I put the papers back but notice a strange bundle in the very bottom, hidden underneath a file. I pull it out. It's a small stack of magazines, held together with twine. I cut the twine with a letter opener from Dean's desk. All six magazines are the *Electrical Experimenter* from 1919. One cover shows a red plane crashing into the sea. One is of a scientist holding a glowing lightbulb under the words THE TESLA WIRELESS LIGHT.

So this is Nikola Tesla. His face is thin, and he has a

neatly trimmed mustache. I open the issue. The article on Tesla is dog-eared. It's the beginning of a six-part series called *My Inventions* written by Tesla himself. I quickly rifle through the other issues. Each one has another part of the series, and each one has been bookmarked. Anywhere Tesla mentions magnetic theory, specifically his discovery of a rotating magnetic field, Dean has drawn a black line under the words.

According to conspiracy theorists, Tesla realized that if the rotating magnetic fields were charged enough, then time and space could be altered . . . which led to the development of the time machine.

Is this what I need to link Dean to the Montauk Project?

I hear a noise coming from the front of the house. A door opening. "Hello?" Dean's voice calls out.

I stuff the magazines back into the drawer and slide it shut. I tiptoe to the doorway and strain to hear what's happening in the hallway.

"We weren't expecting you till tomorrow," Elizabeth says.

"They let me go early. I report back on Sunday, twelve hundred hours."

"Two-day leave? You said it would be longer than that."

I peer around the door. They're standing in the entryway, facing this direction. I jump out of sight, frantically looking around the room. There's nowhere to hide if he comes back here.

"Something was changed. You know I can't talk about it."

"I know, I'm sorry. I shouldn't have asked."

"I'm going upstairs. I'll be down in a second." Dean's boots are heavy as he starts to climb the stairs.

"Let me make you something to eat," Elizabeth calls out to him, and I stare at the door in horror. If she walks to the kitchen, she could find me in here.

There's a pause, and I risk peeking out again. The hallway is empty. Elizabeth must have gone back into the living room, presumably to get the remains of the tea. I slip out of the study and make my way toward the living room.

"There you are!" Mary says as I rejoin them.

"Dean is home!" Mrs. Bentley claps her hands together. "Isn't it lucky that we caught him?"

I take a seat on the stuffed couch and reach for a cookie, hoping they don't notice my shaking hands. "Very lucky."

A while later I stand on the back porch, watching Peter run through the yard. He's holding a toy airplane, similar to the ones flying over Dean's childhood bed. "Vrooom," he calls out as he dips and twists the plane. It's humid and cloudy out. I slap at a mosquito on my arm.

The door opens behind me and Dean steps out onto the porch. We stand side by side, not speaking.

"That's a Warhawk," he says after a minute.

"What is?"

"The plane. A Curtiss P-40." He takes a cigarette out of a pack and offers it to me. I shake my head. He sticks it in his mouth and lights it, pulling in the smoke. I wrinkle my nose as the smell hits me, not used to the thick, bitter scent. Aside from my grandfather with his pipe, I hardly know anyone who smokes.

We're both silent as we watch Peter. I look at Dean out of the corner of my eye. He's changed out of his army uniform and is wearing a white undershirt tucked into dark pants.

"Lydia!" Peter yells. "Watch this!" He lifts the plane up, then down, takes a fast spin in the yard, and runs in the other direction.

"Awesome!" I clap my hands together.

Dean takes a drag of the cigarette, the end glowing red. "He likes you."

"I like him too."

Another drag, and the smoke swirls around us. "How do you like staying at my parents' house?"

I cross my arms over my chest and look at him directly. "They've been very welcoming."

"They're very trusting. It's my job to look out for them. Sometimes I get carried away." He throws the half-smoked cigarette onto the wooden floor of the porch and steps on it with his boot. "Do you understand what I'm saying?"

I shake my head.

He turns away from Peter to face me. "I shouldn't have been so harsh with you the other day. My father and mother trust you, and my boy likes you. That's enough for me for now. But I'll always do what it takes to protect my family."

I stare at him, not sure how to respond.

He smiles slightly. Before I can say anything, he disappears inside.

Peter runs through the grass, waving at me. I wave back, but my thoughts drift to what I found in Dean's drawer.

The *Electrical Experimenter* magazines are a clue, but it's not enough to prove that Dean is definitively involved with the Montauk Project. For all I know, he really will have a freak training accident in a few days.

I rub my bare arms. I have two tasks ahead of me: solve the mystery of Dean's involvement with the Montauk Project; then try to save Dean's life. I can't do the latter until I find out how he fits into Camp Hero.

For a moment, I consider telling Dean everything, blurting out the truth about who I am and what his fate is. But why should he believe me? I don't *know* anything yet. I don't know how he'll disappear. I don't know what's happening with the Montauk Project. I don't even know what to warn him about, other than a vague threat to his life.

I'll eventually need to tell Dean the truth about what happens to him, but first I have to get more answers. I have three days left to discover his connection to the Montauk Project and why he disappears. I've searched his home and didn't find much. But there's another place to explore. Dean's home away from home: the officers' barracks at Camp Hero.

As we leave Dean's house, I ask Mary if I can go with her to Hero later that afternoon. "Of course!" she cries, obviously pleased. But tea was early, and we have more time than we expected, so before Dr. Bentley drives us out to the field hospital, we go to the beach with Mary's friends.

It's still overcast but humid and sticky, and the heat is an oppressive weight. I lie on a towel near Susie, her fiancé, Mick, and their friend Jinx. Mary wades into the ocean with Billy, a classmate from school. She's wearing a white bikini with thick straps and a bottom that looks like a skirt. "Isn't it risqué?" she asked me earlier as she twirled in front of the mirror in her bedroom. "I can't believe Daddy let me buy it."

Compared to the bikinis I'm used to seeing in the Hamptons, this one could double as a nun's habit. I nodded and smiled anyway.

"Sorry, Lydia, you'll have to wear my old one."

Now I'm dressed in a dark blue one-piece halter top with bottoms that come down over my hips.

"Billy, don't!" Mary shrieks as the short, slim boy pulls her up against his chest. She pushes at him and he falls backward, splashing into the shallow water. It must be cold, frigid even, in early June.

"She's such a floozy," Jinx says affectionately. Jinx, short for Virginia, is tall and dark-haired, with large brown eyes. She lies facedown on a blanket to my right, staring out at the water.

The beach is practically deserted. There are a group of boys swimming not far from us and two young mothers letting their babies play in the sand up near the dunes, but other than that, it's empty. I've never seen a Montauk beach so bare in the summer.

"You're just jealous," Susie says from her other side.

"Mary's a doll, but she's khaki-wacky." Jinx grins. "Everyone knows it."

"Khaki-wacky?" I ask. I lean back with my elbows in the sand and look up into the hazy gray sky. I'm still jittery from sneaking around Dean's house, and I'm dreading what it will be like to break into the officers' barracks. But there's something comforting about hanging out on the beach with Mary's friends and doing normal stuff for a change.

"She's never met a soldier she doesn't like. Here, give me one of those." Jinx leans over to Susie and grabs a cigarette out of the pack next to her. Mick strikes a match and reaches over to light it. He's of average height, with curly brown hair and a long, narrow face.

"Mary's not fast." Susie sticks a cigarette into her own mouth. She offers one to me, but I shake my head.

"Of course not." Jinx's voice is rough and filled with smoke. "She'll settle down soon. I'm surprised she hasn't already run off with one of those soldiers."

I look at her, surprised. "But she's only seventeen!"

"Everything happens faster in wartime." Jinx points

her cigarette in the direction of Susie and Mick. "Am I right, kids?"

"Oh, you're right," Mick says. He smirks down at his fiancée. Susie blushes.

"What about you, Lydia?" Jinx asks. "Have you got a beau somewhere?"

An image of Wes standing on the beach flashes through my head. I push it far, far away. "Nope. Do you?"

She shakes her head, cigarette dangling precariously out of her mouth.

"How long have you two been together?" I turn to Susie and Mick, curious. Most of the couples at my school break up every other month, but these two are clearly in it for the long haul.

"Forever." Susie beams.

"It feels like forever," Mick mumbles under his breath.

"Hey!" Susie lightly taps him on his bare stomach and he laughs. She's like a different person when Mick is around—the shy girl I saw yesterday has disappeared. I watch the way they lean into each other and a sharp pang of jealousy shoots through my chest. Now is not the time to start thinking about boyfriends—I have enough going on to deal with—but I can't help wishing I had someone in my life who made me better just by being there.

"Mick enlisted a few weeks ago," Susie says. "But we're going to write each other letters every day when he leaves."

"When are you leaving?" I ask Mick.

"Shipping out in a little over a month. Don't know where I'll be stationed yet."

"What about Billy?" I glance toward the water, where Billy holds Mary around the waist and spins her into the air. In the distance I see the fishing boats, men throwing nets out into deep water. "Is he enlisting?"

"He got drafted. Army. We ship out at the same time." Mick grabs another cigarette, lighting the end. I stare at the slight boy in the water, wondering if he'll make it through the last remaining year of this war. He seems so young, splashing with Mary in the waves.

"What are your plans, then?" Jinx turns to me. Her pale skin is already starting to burn even though the sun isn't bright.

"What do you mean?" A light breeze stirs my hair and I smell the ocean, salty and fresh over the sharp, tingly scent of tobacco.

"Well, you don't have a beau, so you're not getting married anytime soon. Are you going to work in a factory? To enlist with the nurses like Mary?"

Now I need to have a life plan for the '40s? How will I ever be able to keep all of the lies straight? I decide to answer honestly for once. "I guess I haven't really thought about it."

Jinx puts her cigarette out in the sand. "Mary said you were a riveter. We're always looking for people up at the Watchcase factory in Sag Harbor. I could put in a word for you."

"You work there? What about school?"

"The war effort needed me more. I'm on the line, munitions. Lots of us girls are up there."

"My mother started working there after we lost my brother Davy." Susie stares out into the waves. "He was shot down in France two years ago." Mick puts his hand on her back.

"I'm sorry," I whisper.

She shrugs and smiles, though it doesn't quite reach her eyes.

Jinx gives her a sympathetic look, then turns to me. "Imagine, all us women working the line like the men used to!" She shakes her head and laughs a little.

"How crazy," I say drily, thinking of everything that hasn't happened yet in history. Feminist movements and social change. How bizarre it is to know so much more about the world than the people around me. But then I think of Billy getting drafted before high school is over, of Susie's brother dying in another country. It seems like everyone I've met here has lost someone because of the war. If they're not fighting, then they're at home, waiting to hear if their loved ones have died. I've never dealt with anything like that, and I wonder if maybe I'm the one who's naïve.

Mary and Billy walk toward us, their feet kicking up white sand. "You should go in!" Mary plops down next to me. She's soaking wet, and when she rings her hair out, cold drops of water splatter onto my bare shoulder.

"Are you coming to the movies tomorrow?" Billy asks. He's standing over us, but he never takes his eyes off Mary. Jinx catches my eye and makes a gagging motion.

"What's playing this week?" Mary asks.

"*Gaslight*?" Susie guesses.

Jinx groans. "Not *Gaslight* again."

"No, I think it's *Going My Way*," Mick cuts in.

Mary looks confused. "Is that Astaire?"

"Bing Crosby."

"Ah, Crosby," Billy sighs. *"I'm dreaming of a whiiiite Christmas,"* he sings in a comically low voice, waltzing around the beach with an invisible partner.

Mary smiles. "Billy, you're a dead hoofer."

"Then get up here with me."

"All right." She hops to her feet and puts her arms on his shoulders. He pulls her close, but she pushes him away, giggling. "Now Billy, you know I'm not that kind of girl." They start to step in a wide square pattern as Mick taps a beat on his leg.

"Oh, quit grandstanding." Susie laughs.

"We'll show you how it's done." Mick stands up and yanks her to her feet, pulling her into his arms. They start to waltz close together, their heads almost touching.

"Everyone has flipped their wigs," Jinx says to me.

I laugh. I've always pictured the past as this frozen thing, as moments captured in old-fashioned photographs. I never imagined how real life was in 1944. The war makes choices more urgent, more important, as everything could so easily disappear. It makes my old problems—deciding which college to go to, worrying over an internship—feel less real.

I'm glad I'm here. I'm glad I went back in time. The thought whispers through my head, a fragment, a lost feeling. I let it float away as I watch the couples dance in the sand.

CHAPTER 11

Mary hands me a piece of cloth and I take it cautiously. "Put that in the bin." She points to a metal bucket near the door. I carry it across the room and drop it into the pail. As I turn back around, I wipe my hands on the white apron that's protecting my dress. A rust-colored stain streaks across the side of my hip.

The field hospital at Hero is not how I remember it from a few days ago. Instead of a lovely peach-colored, sun-filled room, I'm standing in a large open space separated into cubbies by white sheets that hang from the ceiling. At least ten soldiers lie on beds that are pushed up against the walls. Most are sitting up and talking, though a few are sleeping, covered by thin sheets. The room smells like rubbing alcohol, body odor, and blood.

I realize now that my room on that first day was a private one—the nurse didn't want me sleeping around all the injured men. The real hospital is downstairs, and Mary and one other Red Cross nurse flit and buzz around the room like hummingbirds. They serve food, change bandages, and help the soldiers bathe. Thankfully, most of the injuries are minor: small cuts or wounds sustained during training.

"Lydia, I need you!" Mary's voice cuts through the loud murmurs in the room and I scurry back over to her side. This is a Mary I haven't seen yet—focused and serious. I join her next to a bed where she's tending to a boy around our age with a large cut on his shoulder.

"Hold this down on his chest." She hands me a long, thin cotton bandage. I hesitate, my hand hovering over the soldier's bare skin. He sees it and laughs.

"I won't bite, darlin'." His deep Southern accent reminds me of Lucas, but his dark eyes remind me a little of Wes.

What is wrong with me? Why am I even thinking about either of them? I put my hand roughly on the boy's chest. He grunts, and Mary shoots me a look.

I hold down one corner of the bandage while Mary wraps the other end around and around his shoulder before securing it. She sits back, wiping the sweat from her forehead.

"You're all set, Private Marshall. I bet it'll heal up real quick." She smiles flirtatiously at the young, dark-haired soldier. Now that the job is done, Mary's back to being Mary.

Private Marshall leans in closer to her. "It will with such a pretty nurse to take care of me."

I roll my eyes. "Mary," I interrupt, "I need to get some air."

She winks at the injured boy and then stands up. "Go ahead, Lyd, I still need to feed Private Jenkins, and Nurse Linny wants me to sort some supplies. It might be a little while before we can leave. Is that okay?"

"Yeah, don't worry about me." I pretend to grimace. "I just can't handle all this blood." It's not exactly true, but I *do* need an excuse to get outside so I can sneak into the officers' barracks.

Mary looks concerned. "If you want, I can go get Daddy and we can leave. . . ."

I wave my hand at her. "No, no, it's fine. Just give me a minute. I guess the hospital isn't really my scene."

She laughs. "You say the strangest things sometimes."

As soon as I'm outside, I scan the clearing. There are four buildings in a wide semicircle. Three of them look almost like houses, with windows and decorative roofs. The fourth is the fake white "chapel."

The clearing is empty in the late afternoon. In the distance I can hear trucks driving throughout the camp, and every once in a while the sound of gunfire. I put my head down and quickly walk toward the officers' barracks. Mary pointed it out to me earlier, saying that Dean lives there when he can't leave Camp Hero.

No one is outside the building, but when I peek through the windows, I see a guard standing just inside the entrance. I duck down when he looks in my direction. Trying to find another way in, I walk around the building. There's one large window in the back that faces a hallway. I push at the glass. It's unlocked and it slides up with a low creak. I freeze. My back is to the dense woods, but the guard might have heard the noise. I wait, holding my breath. One minute, two. Nothing happens. My hands slowly unclench.

Using the ledge, I pull myself up and through the open window. I crawl into a long and narrow hallway. It's empty; all of the officers must be out training. Before I start to explore, I carefully shut the window behind me, worried that if someone sees it open they'll sound the alarm.

There are several doors in the hallway. I slowly open one of them. Inside is a medium-sized room with two beds and two small desks pushed up against each other. Dean probably doesn't have to share a room, and so I shut the door again. I notice there's a small plaque next to it that says SECOND LIEUTENANT QUARTERS.

I search until I find the door that says FIRST LIEUTENANT QUARTERS and carefully step into the room. This space is smaller but there's only one bed and one desk. A high window in the corner gives the room a little bit of light. Everything is covered in a thin layer of dust, as though it's been a while since anyone was last here.

I open one of the desk drawers. On the top is a letter addressed to Dean Bentley. At least I know I have the right room. I set it aside and pull out a large, folded piece of paper. I spread it out on the desk. It's a map, showing an aerial view of Camp Hero. All of the concrete bunkers have been highlighted.

Dean supposedly stays here all the time. So why does this room seem unused? And why does he need a map of the concrete bunkers?

I put the map back and try to open one of the smaller drawers. It won't budge. Kneeling down, I notice a keyhole. I reach up to the bun at my neck and pull out two bobby pins. I bend the metal into a straight line. Using a technique my dad taught me after I'd been locked out of the storeroom in his shop one too many times, I push one pin into the keyhole and hold it there, then put the other pin into the top of the lock and jiggle it. There's a small clicking noise and the drawer springs open.

I peer inside. The drawer is empty. Defeated, I move to shut it again. But as it closes, I notice something glint from far in the back. I reach in, and my hand closes over a long piece of metal. I take it out. It's a thin, rectangular shape with several holes and squares cut out of it. My heart starts to race as I realize where I've seen it before.

"Lydia."

I whip around, holding the piece of metal out like a weapon.

Wes is standing in the doorway wearing an army uniform. I was so caught up in what I just found, I didn't even hear him open the door. Some spy I make.

"Where did you get that?" His voice is low and a little dangerous. I tense automatically.

I'm too rattled to come up with a good lie. "I found it in the drawer."

He stares at me and doesn't move an inch. "Put it back."

"This is the same key you used to open the bunker that leads to the underground labs. What is it doing in my great-grandfather's desk drawer?" My voice is high and breathless, the words falling out of my mouth before I really have a chance to process them. As soon as I see Wes's face, I know I've said too much.

His jaw tightens, like he's clenching his teeth hard. But then he sees me flinch and he sighs. He walks forward slowly. "Your *great-grandfather*?"

I squeeze the metal key tightly in my hand, but I don't say anything.

"I suspected that you could be related to the Bentleys . . . but I didn't know how."

"Why?"

"Because you look like them. You share mannerisms. The way you run your hands through your hair, just like Mary Bentley. And you bite your lower lip when you're uncertain about something." His gaze drops down to my mouth, and all of a sudden the room feels like it's too small, too tight. "Which is something Mrs. Bentley does as well."

I hadn't noticed that, and I'm surprised that Wes has. But that also means— "You've been spying on me!" I look at the door quickly, horrified that someone might have heard me.

"Don't worry." Wes's mouth tilts up in a sort-of-but-not-really smile. "I took care of the guard."

I glare at him. "But you *have* been spying on me."

"Yes." He says it without any regret or explanation.

I raise my eyebrows. "That's it? Yes?"

"Lydia." He meets my eyes. Even in the dim light coming from the small window, I feel myself get pulled into his stare. "I'm trying to keep you safe."

It's not easy, but I turn my head away. "Right. So that I don't step on an ant and cause an earthquake in fifty years."

"It's not a joke," he says, but there's something in his voice that makes me think he's a little amused.

"I know." I slump back onto the desk and hold up the strange key. "I just found proof that my great-grandfather is a part of the Montauk Project."

"You should put it back and come with me."

"I can't." I straighten and walk over to the high window. I'm not tall enough to see out of it, even when I stand on tiptoe. "Dean disappears in three days, and all I know is that he's somehow involved in the Project. I need more answers."

I turn back to Wes, not really sure why I'm telling him

all this. It's not that he puts me at ease. If anything, it's the complete opposite. But he's the only one who knows the truth about me. And I feel like I can trust him. He seems serious about wanting to help me—or at least to get me out of here so that I don't screw up the future.

Wes runs his hand along his jaw as he watches me. "Dean Bentley disappears?"

"Yes. I don't know why or how, though now I know it has to do with the Montauk Project. But the possibilities are endless." I start to pace the small room. "He could go on a time travel mission and get lost. God, he could even fall down a flight of stairs in those labs. Maybe it's time I told him the truth."

Wes goes stiff. "No, Lydia." He steps forward and takes hold of my arms. "You cannot tell him. You don't know what the consequences would be."

I'm frozen. This is the first time he's really touched me since he grabbed me in the woods. Only this time my arms are bare and I can feel his skin against mine.

I pull away from his grasp. "Do *you* know what the consequences would be?"

"No. No one does, that's the whole point. But if you tell Dean you're a time traveler, that's a . . . huge interference."

"How do you know? Maybe this is fate. What if I'm *supposed* to come back here to warn Dean? Maybe we can't change the future, even if we try."

His eyes darken, until they look black in the thin light.

"Trust me, you can."

I feel my patience start to wane as I remember that I know nothing about Wes and who he really is. "How do you know that?"

"I . . . work for the Montauk Project. I know that we can change history because I've seen it happen before, and I've seen the ramifications, too. You being here is a rift in time, and what you do here will affect everything that happens along our time line."

I try to work out the logic in my head. "But if history changes, then how can anyone be aware of it? Wouldn't we all just conform to the new version?"

He turns away and stares at the blank wall above Dean's bed. "It doesn't work like that." When he looks back at me, another mask has fallen over his face. "The minute you got into the TM you stepped outside of time."

"TM?"

"Tesla's Machine."

"Seriously?" I give him a look.

He ignores it. "You don't exist in the time line right now, and therefore anything that changes within it can't affect you."

I push my bangs up off my forehead, thinking hard. "So if I alter history and then go back home, the world could be completely different."

He takes a step closer to me. "You'd be the *only* one who knew that something had changed. Your friends and families could have different memories of you. You might be an entirely different person to the world around you, and you'd be playing catch-up with your own life."

"What if . . ." I pause, taking a breath. "What if I erase my own existence? What if my parents never meet?"

He tilts his head slightly, watching me carefully. "You wouldn't stop existing because you're outside the time line. But if you went back to your time, then no one would know who you were. There would be no record of you ever existing."

I close my eyes. It's comforting to know that I can't erase myself by accident. But is a life without friends or family who remember me, who know me, even worth living?

If I screw this up, if I guess wrong, then everything I know might disappear. Should I just go back with Wes right now?

As hard as I try, I can't shake the image of my grandfather walking away from me in the rain. I know what he would do in my place. He would try to save his father, regardless of the risks. And I think of Mary. Of Dr. and Mrs. Bentley. They seem so happy now, like such a loving family. Losing Dean won't rob them of that, but it will change them forever. If I save Dean, then I'd be saving them from that pain.

"Lydia, you can't tell Dean." Wes's voice is firm.

I put my hands up. "I get it. You don't want me to mess with time. I understand, Wes."

Even as I say the words, I realize that I've made up my mind. I'm going to try to save Dean, regardless of the consequences. I have to believe that changing his history can only improve my family's future.

"Promise me you won't talk to him."

"I promise," I agree, and I mean it. I can't see how talking to Dean will help yet anyway. He won't tell me anything, and I still don't know what I'm warning him about. I need more information. And there's only one place left to look.

Unfortunately, it's also the last place I want to go.

Wes stares at me for a long minute, so long I start to worry that he can tell what I'm thinking. But he just says, "Good," and then turns to the door. As soon as his back is to me I slip the metal key into the pocket of my skirt. "We need to get you out before the guard wakes up."

I follow him into the hall. "Won't he be suspicious that he was knocked out in the first place?"

Wes raises his hand, signaling me to be quiet. He moves silently down the hallway, with the purposeful, quick movements I've come to associate with him.

The guard is sprawled on a chair, head lolled to the side. He looks like he's sleeping. We slip out the front door. The sun is setting and the clouds are pink and purple above the tree line.

As soon as we're in the middle of the clearing, Wes turns to face me. In his borrowed uniform and in my stained apron, we look like just another soldier and volunteer nurse talking in the late afternoon.

His face is set in hard lines. "I've explained the consequences of staying in the past. How else can I convince you that you need to go back to your own time, for all of our sakes?" He keeps his voice low and private.

"I'm not ready, Wes." I whisper the words. "There are things I *have* to do here."

"Lydia." He looks down at me through half-closed eyes. "I'm worried about what I suspect you're planning. I should stop you. I know it's what the Project would want me to do." There's something dark in his expression that makes me want to step farther away from him. I don't even ask him what he means, though I'm dying to know. "But I've never . . . I don't . . . I want to . . ." His brows draw together. He looks confused, like he doesn't know how to find the words he wants to say.

His expression is the same one from that first day in the bunker, and then again at the fundraiser when he saw me from across the room. Wes seems so confident, but I keep seeing these flashes of vulnerability in him. It makes me wonder what he's hiding from me. It also makes me want to touch his arm and tell him that everything will be okay.

Before I can respond, Mary walks up to us. She has taken off her apron, but I notice blood on her sleeve. "Lydia. There you are."

She comes to a stop when she sees that I'm talking to

Wes. "Who's this?" Mary scans Wes's long, lean body.

"This is Wes—" It occurs to me that I don't know his last name.

"Private Wesley Smith," Wes cuts in smoothly. Any trace of vulnerability has disappeared now that Mary is here. His voice is steady and sure again.

Mary beams up at him. She looks like she's about to melt all over the lawn.

"I'm Mary. I haven't seen you around here before. How do you know Lydia?"

He looks at me. I see his chest rise and fall as he takes a deep breath. "We met in the hospital on Wednesday."

I nod and glance down at my feet, suddenly embarrassed but not sure why.

Mary gives me a knowing look. "Well, I'm sorry to steal Lydia away, but we have to be going. Daddy is ready to drive us home, and we have to get back for dinner." She puts her finger on her chin, like she's just had a brilliant idea. I'm afraid to hear what it is. "Why don't you come to our house for dinner, Private Smith? Ma always makes extra food and I'm sure Lydia would love to have you join us. Wouldn't you, Lyd?"

I grit my teeth. "I'm sure Wes has other things to do."

He half smiles. "I'm sorry, but I have to decline. I always eat in the mess with the other privates."

"Phooey." Mary sticks out her bottom lip, then brushes her hand through her curls. I notice the gesture and automatically look at Wes. He raises one eyebrow and I bite back a smile.

"Well, let's go Lydia. Daddy's waiting." Mary takes my arm and we start to walk away. We cross the clearing and head toward where Dr. Bentley parked his car.

Wes's gaze never leaves my back. I can feel it on my skin, as intimate as a touch.

CHAPTER 12

$\mathcal{O}n$ the drive back to the Bentleys' house, I can't stop thinking about Camp Hero. If I'm going to find out more about Dean's involvement with the Montauk Project, I have to sneak back into the Facility. And I need to do it tonight.

Dean disappears in three days. I'm running out of time to find answers. I pat the pocket of my skirt, feeling the outline of the strange metal key. It must open one of the bunkers, and I wonder if it's the same one Wes and I snuck out of. If only I had found a way to test it this afternoon. But first I was with Wes, then I was with Mary, and there was never any time to sneak away.

It's probably for the best. I don't want to draw any more suspicion to myself, and I need the cover of night. Now I just have to figure out how to get back there.

As we pull into the Bentleys' driveway, the first thing I notice is that Lucas's truck is here. A truck he's driving back to Camp Hero later tonight. And it has a large, canvas-covered truck bed. Perfect for someone to hide in undetected.

"I didn't know Lucas was coming to dinner," I say to Mary and Dr. Bentley as we get out of the car.

"He's always welcome." Dr. Bentley pulls his medical bag out of the backseat. "And he usually takes us up on it. Hates the mess food."

Mary grins at me, and I know she's thrilled Lucas is here. I grin back, thrilled for a different reason.

That night at dinner I pick at my food, half listening to the conversation around me. We're eating something called liver loaf, mashed potatoes, and tomato salad with chunks of cheese on top. Mrs. Bentley cuts a thick slice of the loaf and puts it on my plate.

I glance at the black curtains pulled tight over the windows. Out in the fading twilight, Lucas's army truck sits in the dirt driveway. I think about what's ahead of me tonight: sneaking into Lucas's truck, around Camp Hero, into the underground labs. Trying not to get killed.

Wes was so appalled when he thought I was going to talk to Dean, and this is—potentially—an even bigger step. But now that I know Dean really is somehow connected to the Montauk Project, I need to find out how. Both for my own desire to know the truth, and because knowing that truth is the only way I can hope to save Dean.

I promised Wes I wouldn't talk to Dean, and I won't . . . at least not yet. Three days. It's not a lot of time, but it could be enough to stop a man from disappearing.

I push at the liver with my fork, staring down at the plate.

"Lydia, are you all right?" I look up to see Mrs. Bentley standing over me. She has a glass in her hand, and she's obviously trying to clear the table. "You've been so quiet all night."

I hand her my plate. "I guess I'm feeling a little tired. I'm all right. Thank you, Mrs. Bentley."

Dr. Bentley leans forward. "I meant to tell you, Lydia, I've been asking around town about your aunt."

I sit up straight. "Really?"

"No one has heard a thing about her. Are you sure you have the name right? Julia Roberts?"

I press my lips together and nod.

"I asked my church group, too," Mrs. Bentley says. "No one has heard of a Julia Roberts."

"That's strange." My voice comes out sounding a little strangled. "I know I had the address and name right."

Mrs. Bentley waves her hand at me. "Don't worry about it, dear. You can stay with us for as long as you need to. You've been such a help, volunteering with Mary and going to tea this morning at Elizabeth's."

I suppress a wave of guilt. I only did those things to get more information about Dean. "Thank you, I really appreciate it," I answer quietly.

"You're not getting sick, are you?" Mary looks concerned. "The dance is tomorrow. Can you imagine if you missed it?"

"Mary," Dr. Bentley scolds, "there are more important things than dances."

"Well, I know that! I was just saying."

Lucas smiles, though he looks worried as he watches me. "*Are* you getting sick?" he asks quietly.

"I don't know." I'm not, but it's a good excuse to leave the table before I have to sneak out into Lucas's truck without them knowing. I lean forward and press my hand against my forehead. I can hear them all murmuring as I close my eyes.

"Maybe you should go lie down," Dr. Bentley suggests.

"Yes, that would probably be a good idea." I get up from the table slowly.

Lucas stands up from the table as I do. "Let me walk you upstairs."

"Um . . ." My eyes dart from him to Mary.

"Let him," Mrs. Bentley says. "You shouldn't go up the stairs alone if you feel faint."

"Okay." I awkwardly wait as Lucas comes around the table. He grasps my arm gently and leads me out of the dining room.

The trip upstairs seems to take a thousand years. I'm pressed up tight against Lucas's side and his arm is around my waist. Finally we get to Dean's old room, where I'm currently sleeping. Lucas seems reluctant to let me go. I pull away and hold the door with one hand as I turn to look at him.

"Okay, well, thanks for walking me up." I smile, hoping to dismiss him quickly.

He leans down, looking like he has every intention of sticking around. "Are you sure you're okay, Lydia?"

"I'm sure I'll be fine. I just need to sleep. Why don't you go back downstairs?"

His eyes go soft. "I hate the thought of leaving you like this."

"Lucas, I'm just feeling a little tired. I'm not dying."

He smiles, then straightens a little. "Lydia, there's something I wanted to talk to you about."

"Lucas!" Mary's voice calls from the bottom of the stairs. "Ma cut you a piece of cake!"

He glances over his shoulder, then back at me. He hesitates.

"Lucas!" Mary yells again.

He shrugs. "Well, good night, Lydia."

"Good night." I watch Lucas walk down the stairs, a little confused by his attentiveness. *Could he like me?* The thought starts to twist and turn in my head again.

Lucas is cute and sweet, and I enjoy being around him. He's also a soldier in World War II, and I'm pretty sure my great-great-aunt has a crush on him. Maybe if I met him in my own time, then things would be different. But they're not.

I think of Wes and those flashes of vulnerability I keep seeing in him. He's an even less realistic option than Lucas. So why can't I stop thinking about how his hands felt on my bare arms? How black and impenetrable his eyes are when he looks at me?

I shake my head and step into Dean's room, shutting the door firmly behind me. I don't have time for boys; I need to prepare for tonight.

I rummage through Dean's closet, looking for something to wear that won't draw attention to myself. There are no army uniforms. I pull on a thick blue work shirt that's so big I have to roll up the sleeves three times before I find my hands. There's no way his pants will fit me, so I yank on my own jeans, washed and folded on a chair near the bed. I tuck in the shirt, then pull on the saddle shoes Mary loaned me—the only pair of shoes I have that fit. I twist my hair up into a high ponytail.

Then I sit and wait.

I cross my legs and jiggle my foot impatiently and think about my plan once I'm in Camp Hero. I have no idea where they might be keeping information about Dean, but if it's there, I'll find it. This is 1944, and there are no security cameras or thermal alarm systems yet, so I have some hope of being able to sneak inside the bunker. And I have Dean's key. I try not to think about those endless white corridors, and the fear that a guard is hiding behind every corner. If I think too much about it then I won't go. And I *have* to go if I'm going to solve this mystery.

Restless, I get up and wander around the room. I pick up a trophy and put it back down. I run my fingers along the belly of a model airplane. Then I notice Mary's sketchbook is sitting on the bureau. She must have left it here after she showed it to me last night.

I was amazed by her charcoal portraits, her ability to capture not just the likeness but the essence of her subjects. It's the perfect thing to distract me while I wait. I pick it up and carry it to the bed, where I start to leaf through the pages.

The first sketch is of Dean, the lines of his face serious, a touch of laughter in the shape of his mouth. There's one of Mrs. Bentley and Dr. Bentley sitting in the parlor, listening to the radio, theirs heads close together. A self-portrait of Mary. I am again startled by how similar we look. I have slightly darker hair, and larger, wider eyes, but we have the same pointed chin, the same full shape to our lips. We could definitely be sisters.

I keep flipping through the pages, watching Mary's life emerge in the well-drawn pictures. There's one of Lucas, laughing, and I stare at it for a long time. Mary captured every detail, from the crinkling around the corner of his eyes to the way he smiles with his whole face. She really knows him.

I stop, staring down at a picture of myself toward the back of the book. In it, I'm wearing Mary's green dress. I look strong, fierce almost. My shoulders are back and my mouth is pulled into a serious frown. But there's also a certain sadness, and a lost expression around my eyes. Is this how Mary sees me? As some sort of tragic heroine?

I'm about to put the sketchbook aside when a piece of paper falls out and drifts to the floor. I pick it up. It's the charcoal rendering of Lucas. There's some writing on the back that I didn't notice before. I scan it as I place the picture back inside the notebook. *Lucas Clarke, February 1944, "Georgia Boy."* I smile. Didn't Lucas tell me he grew up on a farm in South Carolina? I try to think back to our conversation at the fundraiser. No, he'd said Georgia. White Plains, Georgia, "a tiny town in the middle of nowhere." Where did I get South Carolina from?

As I close the sketchbook, a memory tugs at the back of my mind. My grandfather's room in the morning, light falling through the lace curtains. A mourning dove calling outside. Grandfather's voice: "She eloped with a soldier from the base not long after my father left, and they moved back to his family farm as soon as the war was over. I think it was in South Carolina? Maybe Georgia."

How could I not have put the pieces together before now? Lucas is Mary's future husband.

I carefully close the sketchbook and place it neatly on the bed. It was confusing and exciting to think about Lucas harboring feelings for me, but he's *meant* for Mary. I don't want to get in the way of her happiness—their happiness. If Lucas *does* like me, then I need to discourage him as much as I can. It's not like I don't have enough going on to be convincing about it.

I abruptly stand up from the bed, determined to carry out my mission tonight. Opening the bedroom door a crack, I listen to the voices downstairs. They've finished dessert. They're walking into the living room, laughing and talking. The radio clicks on and the tinny, high voice of an announcer talks about the night's programs. Then a news announcement, and everyone falls silent. The troops are moving through the European theater, the front lines in the Pacific are expanding. A detective program comes on and conversation starts again, a low murmur.

I sneak out the door and into Mary's room. Her window is open a little, and the light breeze is cool on my flushed skin. I push the blackout curtains farther aside and lean out into the night, looking for the rose trellis that crawls up this side of the house. Moving slowly, I work my way down the wooden slats. When I reach the bottom, I crouch near the windows, inching my way around the dark house. The crickets are louder at night, a constant clicking sound. I pause near the blacked-out window that I know leads to the den. The window is open beyond the heavy curtains and I hear the hum of the radio, Mary's laugh, Lucas's deep voice.

I make my way over to the truck. It's darker near the front of the house, and I creep through the shadows. The military truck has a large truck bed, with olive-colored canvas stretched over the back. It reminds me of those old covered wagons people used to take out west.

As I tiptoe closer, I hear the front door of the house open.

"It was a pleasure, Sergeant Clarke," Dr. Bentley says. His voice is muffled, and I can tell he's standing inside the entryway.

"Thank you for having me." Lucas sounds clearer, and I picture him standing on the front steps, his cap clutched between his hands. "Tell Lydia I hope she feels better."

"I will."

"Bye, Lucas!" Mary calls out from somewhere far away. I can hear the happiness in her voice.

There's a moment of silence followed by the sound of footsteps in the dirt. I have to move quickly. I climb onto the back bumper, trying to keep my movements steady. Slowly, I crawl forward until I'm all the way inside the truck. It smells like an old basement, dusty and earthy and wet. There's a black tarp on the floor, covering a pile of empty crates. I lie down on the floor next to the crates and pull the tarp over my body. As soon as I'm settled, I hear the driver-side door open. The truck shifts under Lucas's weight as he gets in. A moment later the engine roars to life, and we start moving slowly away from the Bentleys' house.

———

The ride to Camp Hero is bumpy and uncomfortable. One of the crates is digging into my side but I don't dare move. I stay tucked under the tarp, not sure where we are or what's happening outside of this dark space. It's disorienting in the near blackness, and I find myself losing track of time, as if I'm drifting in and out of my body.

The truck finally comes to a stop. I hear laughter, Lucas's slow drawl. It must be a checkpoint. We start moving again, and the road is even bumpier, rocking my body hard against the rough sides of the crates. We drive for a short time before Lucas turns off the engine. I hear his door open, then slam shut. His footsteps disappear. I pull the tarp off me. It's dim inside the truck bed, but light trickles in through the open back. Somewhere in the distance I hear a man shouting. I crawl forward and peer around the edge of the canvas. We're parked near the officers' barracks. Beyond them I see the steeple of the fake chapel rising into the night.

There are a few outdoor lights illuminating the open space, and soldiers mill around, some leaning against the steps of the buildings, some smoking cigarettes in small groups. Lucas's truck is parked in the shadows, in a long line of similar army vehicles. To the right is a large stretch of forest. As quickly as I can, I jump out of the back and run into the woods. I stop behind a large tree trunk, listening for shouting behind me, waiting for a soldier to burst through the trees, gun in hand. But everything is quiet.

I walk carefully through the woods, keeping to the edge of the trees, my eyes on the clearing and the soldiers scattered near the white buildings. The men are all wearing olive uniforms, some with hats, some carrying guns. I don't want to think about what will happen if I'm caught here again.

I circle the wide space until I find the main road. I follow it for a quarter of a mile, then veer to the right, heading into the trees. The bunker is to the southwest, and I walk in that general direction, grateful, for once, that my grandpa used to drag me here so often—at least I know where I'm going. But the forest is harder to navigate at night, and it's less familiar in this time period. I trip over low roots and large rocks, and branches knot in my hair, swiping at my shoulders and cheeks. It reminds me of the night of the bonfire, where I felt like someone was following me. Now I wonder if someone *was* following me, if even then I was getting too close to the mysteries underground.

The moon is bright; it's a cloudless, star-filled night. But instead of lighting my way, the moon just seems to make the shadows deeper, the trees taller. I hear a noise up ahead and I duck on instinct, curling my body around a rock. A group of soldiers walks through the woods in front of me, crackling the leaves underfoot and rustling tree branches. Someone laughs, a quick, abrasive sound that makes me flinch. I smell the smoke of their cigarettes as they pass.

I stay there for a moment and close my eyes, wondering if I'm making a mistake. Then I see that image of my grandfather again, shuffling through the trees, and I stand up. I can't back out now.

I move deeper and deeper into the woods. I am aware of every sound I make: branches snapping under my feet, the rustling of leaves on the forest floor. I move more slowly, more quietly. Soon I am almost at the clearing. I hold my breath as I walk the last few feet and then quickly let it out in a rush of air. I can just make out the black outline of the concrete bunker in front of me.

The space around the bunker is empty and quiet. I pull the metal key out of my pocket and take a step forward.

Something grabs my shirt and yanks me back. I open my mouth to scream, but a warm hand covers it. An arm snakes around my middle and holds me tight. I'm dragged back into the woods.

I struggle against the hands that hold me, blood rushing through my veins. Suddenly I'm released, and I swing around, ready to face my attacker head on. I freeze when I see Wes staring down at me with his eyes narrowed and his mouth tight. He's pissed. I'm used to having to try to read what he's thinking, so it's a shock to see his emotions so clearly written on his face.

"What do you think you're doing?" I spit the words at him. I rub at my stomach, still able to feel his arm there.

"What are *you* doing here?" he snaps. "No, let me guess.

You're sneaking into the Facility." His voice is annoyed, even sarcastic. I'm a little taken aback. I've seen uncertainty and confusion in him before, but this is like he's on the edge of a cliff and any little move will push him over.

I don't answer.

He clenches his jaw. "That's what I thought."

"I need to get inside."

He steps closer to me. We're almost touching. "Have you been listening to anything I've said?"

"I heard what you said."

"Obviously not. Or you don't care?"

The outline of his body is dark against the trees. He's completely tense. I can practically feel the anger vibrating off of him.

I'm surprised by how mad he is. But then, I don't really know him. He doesn't really know me.

Both of us are keeping secrets, only giving out tiny pieces of information.

I raise my hands, ready to be diplomatic. "Look, I'm not trying to make you angry. I know you want me to go back to my own time, and I promise I will eventually. But there's something I need to do first."

He stares at me hard, then rubs his jaw with one hand. "Tell me why."

So I do. I tell him about my grandfather, about Dean, about June 5. "If I can just get into the Facility, then I can find out information about what Dean is up to. Then I can know why he disappears, and the mystery will be solved. My grandfather and I will know the truth."

"You're *only* looking for answers? You're not trying to change anything?" His voice is softer, more thoughtful.

"I'm not trying to change anything," I lie. I wish I could tell him the truth. I want him to know how conflicted I am, that this isn't an easy decision for me, and that I'm terrified of what might happen. But it's the only one I can make if I want to save my family from the pain of Dean's disappearance.

Wes sighs and looks at me for a minute. I can barely see his eyes in the dark forest, and I can't read his expression. "Okay. Let's go."

My mouth falls open. "What?"

"I'll help you get into the Facility. Let's go," he repeats.

I give him a suspicious look. "Why do you want to help me now? You don't agree with what I'm doing."

"You're right, I don't. But I know you're going to do it anyway, unless I physically restrain you." At my alarmed expression, he keeps talking. "Which I'm not willing to do. If you go into the Facility alone, you'll get caught and the guards will kill you. Or worse. If I go with you, at least I can keep you alive. And if you're only after information, then you probably aren't a threat to the time line."

I wonder again why Wes cares so much if I live. Is he trying to prevent me from changing the past—or is it something else, something about me that keeps him here?

"Okay." I grin at him in the dark. Sneaking into a heavily armed government lab doesn't seem half as scary with Wes coming with me. "Let's go."

Instead of going directly to where I know the bunker is, Wes circles us through the woods.

"Why aren't we using the entrance?" I whisper as I follow behind him, my eyes glued to his dark form.

"Too conspicuous. And loud."

We walk for a few minutes before he stops at a random point in the trees. I can't see anything special about where we are, but then Wes points to a metal disk set into the ground.

"We're going in through the vents." He crouches down next to the round metal and pushes it. It makes a loud grinding noise as it slides open, and I look into the woods. Distorted shadows hide in the forest and the moon is heavy in the sky. Something moves in the grass near my feet and I jump.

Wes looks unconcerned as he stands and holds out his hands. Our eyes meet as I slip mine into his. He pulls me forward. The metal disk has been pushed to the side to reveal a large hole that seems to drop into blackness.

I look up at Wes. "Once we're inside, we need to be quiet, and we need to be fast," he says, his voice urgent and low. "I'll be right behind you. I'll direct you through the vents. If there's trouble, you need to do what I say, even if that means running for your life. Can you do that?"

I nod, my eyes wide. My heart is pounding, so loudly I imagine Wes can hear it. I start to panic. Maybe this is a mistake. But then Wes squeezes my hands and I feel a little bit better.

I sit down on the edge of the hole, still holding on to Wes. He slowly lowers me into the depths of the Facility.

CHAPTER 13

I drop down into a dark, narrow vent. It only curves in one direction, and I crawl forward on my hands and knees. I hear Wes enter behind me.

"Follow it," Wes whispers, so soft I barely hear him. As quietly as I can, I crawl through the tight space. It comes to a fork.

"Left."

Sweat drips into my eyes as I move. It stings, but there's no room to sit up and wipe it away. The air is stale and filled with dust and it smells like old batteries again, mixed with the burning scent of bleach. I have to cough but I fight the feeling, a tickling sensation growing and growing in my throat.

Wes guides me left again, then right.

Up ahead is a patch of light and I crawl toward it on my hands and knees. It's a metal grate, an air vent, looking down into a fluorescent-lit room. There's an empty desk, a hard-backed chair. Nothing else. "Keep moving," Wes whispers.

There's another grate up ahead, a glow of light. I crawl toward it, then suck in a breath as I realize there are people inside, sitting on the white floor of a large, empty room. No one speaks or moves. They're all dressed in matching gray nightgowns, and their bodies are small and delicate—too small to be adults.

I crawl closer, then freeze. I feel Wes tense behind me. The room is filled with *children*, maybe ten of them, anywhere from five to twelve years old. Some are pale, some have darker skin, but they're all skinny to the point of starvation, and their hair has been cut razor short. They are covered in bruises. One of them, a gaunt, yellow-haired girl in the corner, lifts her head and looks right at me. I flinch, though I'm unable to pull away from her vacant stare. She's like a zombie, there's so little life in her face.

"Lydia." Wes's voice is hard, completely devoid of emotion. "Don't stop moving."

"What is this place?" I breathe.

I remember Grant telling me that the Montauk Project kidnapped children to use for experiments. I never could have believed that he was *right*. But here's the proof, right in front of me. Acid rises in my throat as I unconsciously press one hand into the sharp metal of the grate. As if I can reach out and touch them. Pull them to safety.

"Lydia." Wes says it firmly, but I feel his fingers gently graze my ankle.

It takes all my will to move away from the grate. I crawl forward into a new, twisting section of the air duct. My hands and feet feel numb, but I force myself to keep moving away from that room.

Wes turns us in two more directions.

I stop again when I hear a noise coming from somewhere below me. A muffled sound. Words, someone talking. I press my ear against the vent, then jerk away when the sound changes from low tones to high-pitched screaming. Screaming, screaming. Pain, madness, I can't tell. It doesn't matter. The sound goes on and on. I curl my fingers into the tin surface below me. I'd cover my ears if I had room to sit up. But instead I just listen to it, praying that the noise doesn't belong to one of those broken children.

It stops eventually, but I hover in place, shaking and sweating. This time Wes is silent as he waits for me to recover. I can sense him behind me, and just having him nearby makes me feel less afraid.

Finally he whispers, "We're close to Dr. Faust's office." I've heard that name before—when the two guards were talking while I was hiding in the time machine room. He must be one of the scientists with the Project. I wonder if

Nikola Tesla is down there somewhere too. Nothing seems too far-fetched now.

When I move again, my muscles feel even more locked up, tighter and aching. Wes leads us to the right. After a few minutes, we come across another grate. Even before I reach it, I hear noises, the scratching of a pen, a man coughing. I move forward slowly, peering down into another room. There's a desk directly below us. A man with slightly balding brown hair and hunched shoulders sits at it. He's wearing a white lab coat. Wes grabs my foot, holding me in place.

There's a muffled knock. "Come in," the man at the table says. The door opens, and a soldier stands in the entryway. I can't see his face, just the lower part of his body. He's slim, wearing a black uniform similar to the army ones. He raises his arm, holding a rigid pose.

"At ease," the man below me says. He has an accent that I can't place. "Have they concluded the experiment?"

"Yes, Doctor," the soldier says. His voice is softer, younger.

The man sits back in his chair, dropping the pen onto the table. "Give me the report."

"Subject twenty-one did not return from the field, sir."

He sighs, rubbing his eyes with his fingers. "Was it like last time?" I watch the slope of his nose, the angles of his elbows as he lowers them back to the desk. Wes is completely still behind me.

"Yes, sir." The soldier hesitates, his formal tone wavering slightly. "He just disappeared, sir."

"So we've lost another one."

"Yes, sir. General Lewis is asking for you, sir."

"Fine." He sighs again, pushing his chair away from the table. He disappears from view, then reenters, moving toward the soldier. He's a short man, heavyset, with wide shoulders. The younger soldier steps back to let him walk through the door first. It shuts behind them with an echoing bang.

I pull air into my lungs, the first real breath I've taken since they started talking. Wes nudges me. I crawl forward until I'm past the grate. As soon as my feet have cleared it, he yanks it up and out of its frame. He leans it against the side of the vent, then slides down into the office. I peer into the room.

Wes is standing on the doctor's desk. He raises his arms to me. Using the side of the grate for leverage, I lower my feet down, and then let myself drop. Wes catches me easily. He holds me for a fraction of a second before letting go. Moving silently, he jumps off the desk and glides over to the door. He gives me a look and gestures at the desk. He'll keep watch; I need to do the snooping.

I hop off the desk, then rifle through the papers on top. The doctor was writing in a leather journal filled with mathematic equations. I flip through it, catching the name "Tesla" printed at the top of a page. I can't make sense of the math, so I close it carefully. There's a filing cabinet near the wall and I head for it. All of the drawers are locked—complicated combination locks—except for one near the bottom, which is slightly ajar. The doctor must have forgotten to shut it before he left.

Wes watches me, but I can tell his concentration is on the hallway. I pull the drawer fully open. Inside are numerous files, all marked with the words "Confidential," "Subject," and numbers rising in sequential order: "Subject 1," "Subject 2," and so on. I pull out "Subject 1."

The plain folder contains several pieces of paper. A black-and-white photo of a soldier rests on the top of the pile. He's blond and smiling, wearing an army cap. The page below is covered in facts: name, age, occupation before the war, family, medical history. I flip past it.

The second page has a detailed account of how he volunteered for something called Operation Victory. I flip again. There's a page of handwritten text; it looks like it was ripped out of a notebook. I skim it, catching words here and there: *Subject did not respond as we anticipated . . . little contact after initial launch . . . subject appeared in machine two days past delivery point, his cognitive abilities severely altered.*

I put the paper aside, then recoil in horror. I'm looking at another photograph, an "after" shot of the soldier. His eyes are glazed and unfocused, his mouth is permanently twisted.

I remember a story my grandfather likes to tell about

something called the Philadelphia Experiment: In 1943, the government supposedly made a ship travel through time and space. The ship vanished and then showed up in another location before reappearing in the original spot. There were rumors that when the ship disappeared, the men aboard went mad, driven insane by traveling through magnetic waves. I think of my own trip through time, the ripping feeling, as if my body was a puzzle being slowly taken apart and put back together again.

I hold up the photo. "What is this?" I hiss.

Wes looks down at it. "The TM was still being perfected in nineteen forty-four," he whispers. "There were complications with the traveling."

My eyes widen. "Is this going to happen to us if we try to leave this time period?"

He shakes his head, then holds up a finger so I'll be quiet.

I'm not very reassured, but I gather up the file and stuff it back into the drawer. I pick out another folder, and another. Either there's a large red LOST stamped over the face or the "subject" looks like the man in the first photograph. A few have lost body parts. An ear here, a finger there.

I shove the second-to-last folder back into the drawer. There's only one left and I pull it out slowly. This one is different. There's a stamp on the front that says THE RECRUITMENT INITIATIVE. Inside is only one sheet of paper—a mission statement for something called "Project Hero." I scan the paper. On the top, right under the title of the mission, is the name Dean Bentley.

I swallow hard as I stare at the words. Dean must be going on this mission. He must be one of these subjects, which means he's in even more serious trouble than I thought.

Suddenly Wes is at my shoulder. "We need to go now," he whispers. I jump to my feet and stuff the confidential file into my shirt when his back is turned. He grabs my hand and pulls me to the door. We fly out into the hallway.

Wes takes a left and sprints down the brightly lit hall. He moves so fluidly, so fast. I trail behind him, desperately trying to keep up.

I hear a sound coming from a connecting hallway. It sounds like someone running. Wes and I hurry in the other direction, turning right when we hit the end of the hall. The new corridor is empty, blindingly white—the floors, the walls, the ceilings. There are stairs at the end and we glide down them.

I'm breathing hard by the time Wes stops. He presses me against the wall and angles his body in front of mine. "Did you find what you needed?" he asks quietly.

I nod, panting too hard to answer. He smiles slightly. He grabs my hand again, pulling me behind him. We turn into a new hallway and Wes slows. I glance around. All of the hallways look the same, but there's something familiar about this one. I see a door on one side, and my stomach starts to sink.

Sure enough, Wes slides it open. We're not in the time

machine room like I feared, but we are in the observation room next to it. This must be the other side of the two-way mirror. It's a dark, narrow space, with a few chairs, a desk, and a large monitor.

I can see the TM through the tinted window. It looks innocent enough sitting there; the metal is dulled and the room is barely lit. But I know better.

Wes grabs my hand to pull me through a connecting door, which will lead down to that room. I yank away from him.

"What do you think you're doing?" My voice is low and rough.

He turns to me. His eyes are narrowed. "You said you have what you needed. We can both go back now."

"Wes." I press my hand to my forehead. Anger is rising inside of me. "I have things I need to do here. I thought you understood that."

He takes a step closer. "You said you wanted to find the truth. You found it. Time to go."

I back away from him until my body hits the door we just came through. "It's not that easy," I snap.

"Why not?" He has a stubborn set to his jaw that puts me on edge. "Are you hiding something else from me?"

My mouth falls open. "You're one to talk. You haven't told me *anything*. I don't know who you are. I don't know why you're here. I don't know what you want from me. I don't know anything about the Montauk Project."

My voice gets louder and louder but I'm past the point of

caring. "What about how dangerous that machine is? I saw the pictures of those men who went insane. Were you even going to tell me?"

His voice rises too, and I don't think he's even aware of it. "I'm trying to protect you! I'm trying to get you back home where you'll be safe. Why do you keep fighting me?"

"Because I need to save Dean! I need to save my family!" I shout it at him without thinking, and as soon as the words leave my mouth, something that's been holding Wes together cracks. His eyes go glittery and he comes for me, lightning quick. I don't know what he's going to do, but I don't wait around to find out. I yank at the door handle behind me and fall into the hallway.

I take off the way we came. I can hear Wes following me. I turn a corner, and another one, barely aware of what I'm doing. Finally I slow down. My anger is cooling, and common sense returns. I can't run from Wes *and* the guards. I won't let Wes take me back to the time machine, but running away from him down here is stupid. I can't tell where I am and I don't know how to get out of here without Wes.

I stop in a hallway, waiting for Wes to catch up with me. But I don't hear anything. Puzzled, I turn around to look for him. There's no one coming.

I press my body against the wall, wondering where Wes is. He should be here by now. What if something happened to him? What if he's given up on me? I have to find him again. I pull myself up, and I hear a footstep behind me.

"Wes." I start to turn but freeze when I hear a clicking noise near my ear.

"Don't move," an unrecognizable male voice says.

The stranger pushes something into the back of my head. Something cold and metal.

"Or I'll shoot."

The barrel of a gun.

CHAPTER 14

"*Turn* around."

I automatically raise my hands and slowly pivot. Blood pounding, breath short. The man holding the gun is probably in his late twenties, and he's dressed in the black guard's uniform. He's a little taller than me, and has light brown hair that's cropped close to his head.

He barely looks at me as he reaches out and clamps onto my arm with one hand. He tugs me forward. I dig in my heels.

"Where are you taking me?" My voice sounds faint.

He doesn't answer, just squeezes my arm tighter and jerks. I stumble. Before I can find my footing, he starts to drag me.

He pulls me down the hallway. My ears are ringing, and all I can hear is the sound of the screaming from earlier, the noise ringing through the metal vent.

"Faster." The man's voice is harsh, like he smokes too many cigarettes. He yanks on my arm and I barely catch myself before I ram into the wall.

Will Wes come for me? Maybe he's finally decided that I'm not worth the trouble. Maybe I'm on my own here, waiting to be killed by the men behind this project. Or worse, waiting for them to use me in their experiments. That thought makes me straighten up. I'd rather die quickly from a bullet than become one of those subjects.

Using all of my strength, I quickly twist away from the guard. I catch him by surprise and his hand stays outstretched for a moment before he fully realizes what just happened. I see my opening and bring my knee up hard between his legs. He makes a strangled noise and I lunge, ready to run. But he's faster, and he grabs me around the middle before I can get away. He pushes me up again the wall, my face scraping against the uneven cement.

Suddenly his body jerks and my head hits the wall. The guard starts to fall. I move to the side to get away from his weight. He drops like a stone, hitting the tile floor with a dull thud.

I turn around slowly. Wes is standing there, watching me. He holds out his hand. I take it without a word.

We run through the white hallways of the Facility. There's no point in saying what we're both thinking: the fallen guard will be found quickly. Someone will be aware of the breach, and this place is about to go on high alert.

I'm a little dazed from my head hitting the concrete and have a hard time keeping up. Wes notices and slows his pace, but we don't have much time left. Just when I think I can't go any farther, he stops and opens a random door on the left. We enter a large room, filled with what look like oil tanks. Wes weaves through the huge containers, and I follow, the scent of grease heavy in the air.

Back in the hallway, he took the gun from the fallen guard. Now he holds it close to his chest as we enter a different room. There's only one other door on the far wall. He approaches it, glancing back at me.

"I need you to do what I say," he whispers. "Promise me."

"Okay."

He raises an eyebrow.

"I promise, all right?"

"Stay here." He steps through the door. I hesitate for a moment before I peer around it. The room is filled with blinking machines. There are two guards in uniforms. One stands near the door; the other is over by the machines.

I watch as Wes sneaks up behind the first guard. He brings his hand down in a sharp motion and the guard crumples. Before the second guard can even turn around, Wes kicks him in the chest. The guard slumps onto the machine in front of him. It all takes less than a minute.

I walk into the room. Wes turns at the sound of my footsteps. "I told you to stay back." I shrug, staring down at the fallen guards. He sighs, placing his hand on my shoulder. "Go," he says, steering me toward another door.

We enter a new room. This one is filled with cars and trucks of all sizes, gleaming in the bright light overhead.

"Are we taking one of them?" I whisper.

"No." His breath tickles my ear, and his hand lightly grips my shirt. "Too dangerous."

He leads me to a door that's obscured by a big army truck. There's a combination lock near the handle. He fiddles with it and it slides open.

"Go," he says again.

I step out into the dark, quiet woods of Camp Hero.

Wes winds through the forest like he's part of it. I struggle to follow. My arm aches from where the guard yanked on it, and my cheek feels like it's on fire. I'm not sure where Wes is headed, though I know we're near the south side of the camp, not far from the vent we crawled through only hours earlier.

"Where are we going?" I ask after a minute. He halts abruptly, and I barely stop myself from colliding into him. He turns around. Only a little moonlight filters through the trees above our heads, but I can see the shape of his features in the darkness.

"Can you keep walking?" His voice is soft.

"Yeah, but can we rest for a minute?" There's a pounding on the side of my head. I reach up to feel a large bump forming under the skin. "Just a minute, then I'll be fine."

He watches me silently. The air around us smells of fresh dirt, cut grass, and gasoline; we're close to the central part of the camp. "Come here," he says.

I give him a suspicious look, not moving any closer. Now that we're out of the Facility, I think about our argument, about running away from him. I'm not sure how to act around him.

He takes a step forward, bends down, and hooks his hand under my legs, pulling me up into his arms.

"I can walk by myself!" I struggle and push my hands against him. I don't want to rely on his support. He ignores me and continues through the woods.

"You're about to fall over. We're still not clear of the lab. We need to get you back to the Bentleys' house." His voice is still soft, hushed.

His arms are solid against my knees, my back. He carries me as though I weigh nothing. I stop fighting, one hand rising up to his neck almost involuntarily.

"Are you still mad at me?" I blurt out the question.

Wes gazes down at me through long, dark lashes. He looks different from this angle; his bottom lip is even fuller, his chin more pronounced. He looks innocent, as if his armor is falling away. I wonder if that's true or if it's just a trick of the moonlight and shadows.

"No. Seeing him hurt you . . ." He trails off and his arms tighten around me. "I'm not mad."

I'm silent as I digest this. He might not be mad, but he doesn't want me to try to stop Dean either.

"Are you still mad?" His voice is curiously blank, and he stares straight ahead as he asks the question.

"Not anymore." I wait a beat. "I wish you didn't try to trick me though."

Wes walks us around a tree trunk, then through a thicker part of the woods. He ducks so I can push branches out of the way as we pass.

"I wasn't trying to trick you," he says quietly. "I honestly thought you would want to leave once you had the information."

"I still have things do to."

"I gathered that." His voice lowers. "You want to save Dean."

He doesn't sound very happy about it, and I don't say anything. After a few minutes, he stops at the edge of an open clearing. There's one large building in the middle of it, with several army-green jeeps parked nearby. I slide down out of his arms, holding on to his shoulder as my head spins a little.

As soon as I let go, Wes motions me forward. We move through the trees in a wide arc, stopping when we're close to a wooden structure. It looks like a utility shed; there are no windows and only one wide metal door.

"Where are we?" I whisper.

"Old supply area. There aren't any guards, but a patrol

comes by every half hour. I'm not sure when they were last here. We should wait." But then he looks at my tired, bruised face and seems to reassess. "We'll go now."

He crouches down and runs toward one of the small all-terrain jeeps. I run after him, gritting my teeth against the pounding in my head. He holds the passenger-side door open for me and I dive in. The jeep is low to the ground, with a thin canvas top and no windows.

Wes slides into the driver's seat. I duck down as he yanks at something under the steering wheel.

"What are you doing?" I whisper.

"Hot-wiring it." He does something with his hands, there's a spark, and the jeep roars to life. "It's easy with these old cars." He throws it into gear and we back up quickly.

I stare at the wires hanging near his legs. "Will you teach me how to do that?"

He glances at me, surprised. "You want to learn how to hot-wire a car?"

"It seems like a useful skill."

His lips tilt into a smile, but he doesn't respond.

The headlights are off as we drive quickly out of the clearing. Soon we're on the main road that curves through the camp. It's empty this late at night, though I can see lights glowing in other parts of the base.

"What about the guards at the gate?"

"We're not going through the gate." Wes veers the jeep onto a tiny dirt road that leads through a maze of trees. We turn onto another run-down path. This one curves west through the southern part of the camp, not far from the cliffs near the beach. After a while the road ends and turns into forest. I expect Wes to stop, but he keeps going. We drive around trees, over a tiny stream. I hold tight to the dashboard as we bounce through the woods.

The trees open into a wide field, and Wes drives along the edge of a grassy pasture. It's too windy inside the jeep to try to talk to each other, but I keep glancing at him out of the corner of my eye. Everything unsaid seems to stir and boil between us, and the air grows thicker and thicker with tension.

When the field ends and turns into the beach, Wes cuts the engine. We're parked on top of a dune, and the ocean is in front of us, dark and unending. It is almost impossible to see where the black water turns into the night sky.

Wes opens his door. "Wait there." He gets out of the jeep and disappears. I hear him rummaging around in the truck bed.

I breathe in the scent of salt water and listen to the sound of the waves running onto the shore. Being on the beach feels like coming home again, especially after the night I've had.

My door opens and I look up. Wes is leaning over me. His face is stark in the moonlight, all angles and dark hollows. I feel something tighten inside my chest.

He slowly takes my chin in his hand. I flinch, but I don't pull away. Using his other hand, he touches my cheek with a piece of cloth that he must have found in the back. His movements are jerky, like he's not used to doing this. I wince as the fabric rubs against my torn skin.

"Does it hurt?" His voice is tight with emotion, but I can't tell what he's thinking.

I shake my head—a difficult task with Wes holding on to me—and our skin rubs together. "I feel a little dizzy."

He lifts my chin and looks into my eyes, and I feel my pulse pick up. "I don't think you have a concussion. But you'll probably have a headache tomorrow."

I scrunch my nose. "Just what I need."

His lips curve slightly. It makes him look younger. "How old are you?" I ask, curious.

"Seventeen." He lets go of my face and steps back. The moon is so much brighter out here than it was in the forest, and I watch as he folds up the dirty cloth and tucks it into the pocket of his black pants.

"That's how old I am. When's your birthday?"

He raises his eyebrows. "Why do you want to know?"

I open my mouth, surprised when the truth tumbles out. "My best friend has this thing about people's signs."

This time his lips curve up even more. I can see the hint of a dimple in his right cheek.

"The beginning of August," he answers.

"That means you're a . . . Leo. Right?"

The softness vanishes from his face, and I wonder what kind of nerve I just struck. "I wouldn't know."

"Leos are strong and independent." My voice is quiet. He stares down at me as he leans against the open door of the jeep. "And loyal and protective."

"Do you believe in that stuff?"

I shrug and laugh a little. "I make fun of Hannah mercilessly, but sometimes I think there's a little bit of truth in it."

"Hannah. She's your best friend?"

I nod and bite my lip. He follows the movement. "You miss her."

It's more of a statement than a question, but I answer him anyway. "Yes, a lot." Tears start to form behind my eyes and I blink rapidly, feeling like an idiot.

Wes, of course, misses none of this. "If you're sad, and have people you love at home to go back to, then why do you insist on staying here?" The question isn't hostile—he genuinely sounds like he doesn't understand.

But for me it brings back all the unanswered questions and all the secrets. I swing my legs around to face him. "You can't ask me questions like that. Not when you've been keeping so many secrets from me. You say it's to protect me, so I haven't pushed you very hard for answers. But I can't keep being in the dark. You *need* to tell me what's going on. Starting with who you are."

His face goes blank. "You need to tell me why you want to save Dean."

I lift my hands. "Isn't it obvious?"

He doesn't answer.

"He's my *family*, Wes. If I can save Dean then I can give my grandfather his life back. I can make sure Mary doesn't lose her brother, or that the Bentleys don't lose a son. Can't you see that?"

The mask covering his features cracks a little, and I see the naked vulnerability in his eyes again. I realize then that he *doesn't* see, but that he wants to.

"Wes." I lean forward. "Please tell me who you are and what your role in the Montauk Project is."

"I don't want to put you at risk. If you know too much . . ."

I reach out, placing my hand on the bare skin of his wrist. He looks down at the soft pressure, then back at me, his jaw clenched. I realize it's the first time *I've* touched *him*, at least when we weren't running for our lives. I'm surprised by how much it seems to affect him.

"Don't you think I already know too much anyway?" I say it lightly, but he obviously doesn't take it that way. His hand is rigid under mine.

"Lydia, you don't understand what they're capable of. You don't understand what they would do to you if you got caught in the Facility."

I think of the screaming noises and of the room full of children.

The room of children. Wes. I sit up straighter and my hand falls away from his. The pieces come together in my head, and I gaze at Wes with a mixture of sympathy and horror.

"Are you . . . ?" I can't even finish the sentence. "Were you . . . ?"

He turns away from me fully, looking out at the water. "Wes . . ."

"I was born in nineteen seventy-three in New York City." His voice is lower than I've ever heard it. "It was nineteen eighty-four when I was . . . taken. I was eleven or so, running with this gang of kids, living in an abandoned subway station uptown. I was walking down the street one day when someone grabbed me, threw me into a van, and knocked me out. I didn't see his face. I woke up in Hero. And then the training started. If you can call it that."

"What happened to you?" I force myself to ask the question, afraid of what he'll tell me.

"I was *reconditioned*, or that's what they called it. Beaten. Brainwashed. They use children because they can travel more easily. After adolescence, usually older than eighteen or nineteen, someone is more prone to going crazy, to getting hurt. Especially if it's his first trip through time. Children seem mostly unaffected. And children are more easily controlled."

I close my eyes, picturing everything he's not telling me. What it was really like for him, the hell of living through the Montauk Project. "God, Wes."

Then I remember those "after" photos, with the men either lost in time or lost in their own minds. "Is that why the subjects in this time period can't travel?"

Wes nods. "The TM is still unpredictable in nineteen forty-four, and they can screw with dates and times. But yes, the reason those soldiers are going crazy is because they're not young enough for their bodies and minds to handle the pressure."

Something occurs to me and I grip my knees with both hands. "You said you were born in nineteen seventy-three. Shouldn't you be"—I do the math in my head—"thirty-nine?"

"I'm seventeen." He sounds amused. "For you, it's the year twenty twelve. For me, it's earlier. I would need to go back to nineteen ninety to be a part of the normal time line again."

"So because we're younger, we can travel without a problem." I press my hand to my forehead. "But if Dean goes in . . ."

He watches me silently.

". . . he won't make it. Don't you see why I have to help him then?" My voice sounds unnaturally high.

Wes's shoulders tense.

"He's going to get sucked up by the Montauk Project just like you are."

"Then he's already dead, Lydia." The words sound as if they're ripped from his throat. "Anyone who knows about the Project dies the moment they're not useful anymore. Sometimes before."

I look at him in shock. "How are you useful for the Project?" I breathe.

He tears his gaze away from me, staring down at the sand under his feet. "I'm a recruit. We travel to different periods to find information or to subtly change a moment in history."

"But you were so angry with me because of the butterfly effect!"

"*Subtle* changes in history, Lydia. The scientists calculate the odds of unintended changes and the recruits perform the missions."

I try not to think of what it was like in the TM. "You're constantly traveling in that machine. How have you been doing that for six years?"

He runs his hand over his jaw, a gesture I'm starting to recognize. "You get used to it."

He rests his hand on the door of the jeep. It's almost as bright as day out here with the moon reflecting on the water.

"How many times have you seen the world change?" I ask quietly. "How many different versions of time have you lived through?"

His eyes go black. "Too many." He turns away from me until he's facing the ocean. His profile looks cut from stone.

"Why do you stay, Wes? If it were me, I would run."

"No, you wouldn't. They'd find you. They always find you." He refuses to raise his eyes; his fists are tight against his sides. I reach out to him, then drop my hand, not sure how he'll respond to my touch.

"It doesn't matter anyway." His voice is blank, emotionless. "Pretty soon I'll be too old to travel, and then I'll be useless."

I breathe in sharply. "Are you saying they'll kill you?"

He doesn't answer.

"You can't just give up. You *can't*." I lean forward. "Giving up is the same as dying, isn't it?"

He finally lifts his gaze to mine. "There's not a lot of hope in my world, Lydia. That's why I need to keep you away from it."

"Wes," I whisper.

He slowly bends down until our faces are only inches apart. I feel my cheeks burn as I stare at the full curve of his bottom lip. "I don't want you to give up," I whisper, realizing, as I say them, that the words are true.

His eyes flicker to my mouth. I press my hands onto my knees. His lips are almost on mine—

We're interrupted by a shout: "Who's there?"

We pull apart. There's a shadowy figure standing on a dune not far from the truck.

"Move back," Wes says softly. I swing my legs into the cab and he shuts the passenger door. A man is coming down the sand toward us. As he gets closer, I see that he's wearing rough fisherman clothing, with a blue Coast Guard cap on his head—he's a civilian volunteer, a member of the home guard.

"It's all right, I'm a soldier at the base," Wes says.

"What's your division?" The man approaches the truck.

He shines the flashlight into my face, and I shrink away from the light.

"Hmm." He gives Wes a different kind of look.

"We would appreciate if you didn't say anything," Wes replies. "Her parents . . ."

The man cocks his head at us. I hold my breath. Finally he laughs. "I remember what it was like to be young. You kids better get on out of here now."

Wes nods. "Appreciate it." He gets into the truck and starts the engine. We drive through the sand until we reach the old highway.

We don't speak again until Wes parks on the Bentleys' road, a few feet from their driveway. He sits back against his seat and looks at me. I stare straight ahead, trying to organize my thoughts.

I almost kissed Wes. I *wanted* to kiss Wes. But there's no future for us. His life is chaos and torture and time travel. Once I leave here, I'll probably never see him again.

"You're a recruit." I break the silence, trying to sound businesslike and brisk. "Which means you should have tried to kill me when I stumbled into the time machine. Why didn't you?"

"I—" His fingers tighten on the steering wheel. "You went back in time by mistake. Once I knew you were in nineteen forty-four, I had to get you out. Like I said, you being here could change things."

I bite my lip. There must be something he's not telling me.

"So I'm just a job to you. Another mission?" He doesn't answer. "Is the Montauk Project expecting you to bring me back to twenty twelve?" A dark thought flashes through my mind and I say it out loud. "Are you going to kill me the minute I get back to the future?"

"No." Wes sounds offended, and his gaze cuts into mine.

"But if I'm a mission, then they must want you to kill me at some point." I shrink away from him slightly.

He sees the movement and his eyes narrow. "I'm not going to kill you, Lydia. I snuck you into Camp Hero. If they had found either of us, we'd both be dead."

I look at him, surprised. "Why would they kill you? I thought I was the only one in danger."

"I'm not . . . supposed to be here either." His voice is flat, and he rubs his jaw again.

"I thought this was a mission. I thought they knew you were here."

He faces the front of the jeep, and I wonder if he's avoiding my gaze. "The scientists in nineteen forty-four don't know about the recruits. We never travel back to this time period. I've been sneaking around, just like you have."

"But—" I wave my hand up and down, indicating his clothes and his short hair. "You have uniforms. You cut your hair. Where have you been sleeping?"

He smiles slightly. "I've been posing as a soldier at Camp Hero. Blending in as much as possible."

"I don't understand." I tilt my head back against the seat. Outside I can hear the crickets chirping, and the long, high call of a bird. It must be getting close to morning. "Y~~ ~~id

His ~~voice changes, and he is saying~~ something he's heard a thousand times: "Certain points in time are more precarious than others. The Facility was built in nineteen forty-three. Only one year ago. If one tiny thing goes wrong with the time line, then the entire Montauk Project could cease to exist. The people in charge don't want that to happen, so they keep us away from this time period."

He still hasn't let go of the steering wheel, and he's completely still as he speaks. "The recruits start getting involved again in the nineteen fifties. You're lucky you were sent here."

Outside, the sky on the horizon is shot through with streaks of light. "It was purely an accident," I say.

"I know. For some reason the TM was set to this time period, which is strange. When you didn't input a new date, it brought you here automatically."

"How does it work anyway, the machine? I know about the alternating magnetic waves, but hearing about it is different from living through it. . . ." I shudder.

"It acts as a vessel by tapping into time tunnels that already exist. The TM essentially transports you to a connecting TM."

My hair is starting to come out of my ponytail, and pieces fall down around my face and shoulders. I tuck them behind my ears. "But wasn't the TM only invented last year? What if you go to a time that doesn't have a TM?"

"Then you'd be stuck there," he says matter-of-factly. "You can't travel without a TM."

I sigh. "I guess it *was* lucky that I came to nineteen forty-four."

He lifts his chin, his eyes on the sky in front of us. "You should go now. It's starting to get light out."

I open the door but don't step out.

"Wes."

He looks at me, and I forget what I wanted to say. We stare at each other in the early, early dawn.

In a quick movement, he finally lets go of the steering wheel and leans toward me. I freeze as he gently pushes a strand of hair away from my face. His fingertips trail along my cheek and I automatically close my eyes.

When I open them, he's sitting back in his seat, gripping the steering wheel again. "You should go," he repeats.

I slide out of the truck but pause before I shut the door behind me. "Where does this leave us? You know I want to help my family."

His mouth tightens and he won't look at me. "I can't support that. It's too dangerous."

"I don't expect you to keep helping me," I say. "I just don't want you to stop me from doing what I know is right."

He doesn't answer. I slowly shut the door. A moment later the engine turns over and he drives away. I watch him go, standing by the side of the road long after the truck has disappeared.

The Bentleys keep their back door unlocked, and I open it slowly. I slip into the dark kitchen, then down the hallway and up the creaking stairs. My bedroom door is open a crack and I tiptoe into the shadowy room. Closing it with a soft click, I lean forward to press my forehead into the smooth wood, aware of every bump and bruise on my body. I want to crawl into bed and stay there for a hundred years.

A light suddenly flickers on behind me and I spin around.

"Where have you been?" It's Mary. Her hands are on her hips and she's glaring at me.

"You scared me!" I gasp, pressing my hand to my chest.

She walks over to stand in front of me. She's wearing a white nightgown that pools around her ankles.

"What happened, Lydia?" she asks. "I came in here to see how you were feeling and you were gone. I thought you were abducted until I saw that some of your clothes were missing. Where did you go in the middle of the night? And what happened to your cheek?"

"I, uh . . ."

"Well?" Mary folds her arms across her chest. "If you don't tell me where you were, I'm gonna have to wake up my parents."

"I met a boy," I say quickly. "I snuck out to see a boy."
It isn't technically a lie.

The anger fades from Mary's face.

"A boy?" She starts to smile. "Where did you meet a boy? What's his name?"

"It's . . . Wes. The soldier from Camp Hero."

"Wes?" She tilts her head. The soft glow of the room shines through her hair like a halo. "Oh, Private Smith." Her voice gets breathy. "The dark hair and the eyes and the . . ." She holds her hand up high, indicating Wes's height.

I nod. "We met at the hospital, and one thing led to another." I pause. "I might be falling in love with him." I say the words automatically, and a heavy feeling settles into the pit of my stomach. Is this *true*? Could I be falling in love with Wes?

Mary studies me carefully. Whatever she sees in my face meets with approval, because she suddenly squeals and grabs my arm.

I'm almost panting, my breath becoming short at the thought of falling in love with Wes. I've never even had a real boyfriend, but in the past few days I've *almost* fallen for Lucas, and I've maybe, sort-of-already fallen for Wes. One is destined to marry my great-great-aunt and the other is a slave to a top-secret government organization.

What am I supposed to do with that?

Mary pulls me over to the bed and squeezes my arm. "Tell me everything."

I shake my head, trying to clear my thoughts. "Wes is . . . good looking." Mary gives me a *duh* look. "He wants to protect me," I say, relaxing slightly as I think about how he makes me feel when I'm with him. "He keeps showing up when I need him. I don't know how he does it, it's like he has this radar or something. And I feel like I can be myself around him. Even when that self isn't very pretty. Does that make sense?"

She nods, a small smile tugging on the corners of her lips.

"There's something dark and dangerous about him, but there are these moments where I see something deeper inside of him. He's capable of so much more than he thinks he is. And sometimes I look at him and our eyes lock and it's like I'm physically incapable of pulling away."

"All that in just a few days?" Mary teases.

I smile. "It's been a long week."

"It's like something out of a fairy tale." She studies my face more closely. "But how did you get all hurt?" She straightens and her smile fades. "Did he do that?"

"No! No," I protest. "I, uh, fell off the rose trellis. I climbed out your bedroom window but fell halfway down and hit my head. Wes was really sweet. He took care of me." I feel the ghost of his fingers skimming across my cheek.

"You're blushing!" Mary exclaims. "You must really like him."

I stare down at my hands, remembering the way his

skin felt under mine, and wondering when I'm going to see him again.

"So, Lydia." Now Mary's the one blushing. "Did you . . ."

"Did we what?"

"You *know*. Did you do anything with him?"

"Like, did we kiss?"

"Or other things."

"Mary!"

She grips my hands excitedly. "There's this girl Theresa from school who everyone knows is *fast*, and last year she had to be sent away for a little while. Suze told me she had a *baby*. Can you believe it? Suze knows all about it. She told me her and Mick have gotten *really* close to doing it."

"We didn't even kiss!"

Mary sighs, clearly disappointed.

"But I wanted to," I say honestly.

Mary's face lights right back up. She leans forward and her voice drops to a whisper. "Have you ever been kissed?"

"A few times. Have you?"

"Oh, lots of times. I had a beau a few years ago. Tommy Sullivan, I told you. And then there are all those soldiers, missing home. Someone has to provide a little comfort." She winks, and I laugh.

"Anyway, those kisses didn't mean much." She looks up toward the ceiling. "It's easy to get caught up in the excitement. I still write to some of them. But if I kissed someone like Lucas, I think it would be different. I think it would *matter.*"

I picture Lucas, his earnest face, those crooked bottom teeth. "You're probably right." I smile, and realize that any small feelings I may have had for Lucas are starting to dissolve completely. He and Mary are clearly meant to be together, and I can't get Wes out of my head.

"I'm glad that you care about someone. Now you don't have to get bored listening to me blather on about Lucas." She stands, pulling her long nightgown down around her legs. "Anyway, you should get some rest. And put on a nightgown. Why are you wearing those factory clothes again? I can't imagine what Wes thought of you." She moves to the door. "Good night, Lydia."

"'Night."

As soon as she leaves, I unbutton my shirt, ready to pull on a nightgown. But my fingers brush against course paper instead of skin. I completely forgot about the file tucked into my shirt. I pull it out, sitting down on the bed as I place it in front of me. CONFIDENTIAL is stamped across the back in bold red ink. I open it and pull out the Project Hero mission statement again. I read the brief report:

Subject has volunteered for the highly selective mission . . . On the 5th of June, 1944, in a coordinated attack against Axis forces, Subject will travel in Tesla's Machine to 1920. Subject will go to Germany to find and eradicate Adolf Hitler, then a rising public figure . . . Subject will use any means necessary to dispose of this threat to the United States of America.

Dean's name is the only one on the paper. He *must* be the Subject.

I drop the paper. It floats onto the bed, resting gently against Dean's old blue quilt. In two days, Dean is going to be sent to 1920 to carry out a mission that's destined to fail. Even if by some miracle he makes it through the machine unscathed, there are no Tesla Machines in 1920. Dean will be trapped there forever, unable to return.

CHAPTER 15

Montauk Manor gleams in the bright sun. Red brick and brown woodwork accent white stone walls that rise into massive gables. The flagpole stands tall on the front lawn, an American flag twisting in the wind.

It looks like it does in my time. But instead of tourists in beach gear, uniformed soldiers roam the dirt paths surrounding the main road. Gray navy jeeps are parked near the entrance. Gear is thrown across the white porches, replacing beach chairs and outdoor dining tables.

"Lydia! Over here!" I turn to see Mary waving at me from the sloping lawn on the south side of the mansion. She sits with her parents on the edge of the hill, surrounded by children and soldiers and families spread out on blankets.

Montauk's annual spring picnic is hosted by members

of the neighboring towns in support of the navy and army bases stationed in Montauk. Tonight is the USO-sponsored dance, and they're holding it on the lawn of the old tennis auditorium. Mary can't stop talking about our dresses and which soldiers we'll dance with, and her enthusiasm is infectious. But I keep thinking about Dean and his doomed mission. How can I prevent him from going?

I know it's time to tell Dean the truth and I'm dreading it. I don't know how to make him believe me, short of pulling out the file I found. But then he'll know I snuck into the Facility, and he might even accuse me of being a spy. I also can't get Wes's words out of my head. The minute I tell Dean the truth, I've changed the future forever. I want to believe it will be a good change, but I'm still afraid of the unknown possibilities. What if I erase myself and return to a life where no one knows me? I'm not ready to face that fear yet.

My grandfather remembers saying good-bye to Dean on the morning of June 5. It's also the date of Project Hero. That gives me two days—including today—to work up the nerve to talk to Dean.

I wave back at Mary and make my way toward the buffet table, covered in an array of jellies, tiny sandwiches, and dark, thick cookies. I take a little bit of everything. I walk through the groups of people, clutching my plate. Mary and Mrs. Bentley are sitting on a checkered blanket, looking out over the crowd, while Dr. Bentley lounges on the grass nearby, smoking a pipe and contemplating a deviled egg. I sit down next to Mary, who tosses an apple in my direction. Mrs. Bentley hands me a cloth napkin from a basket by her feet.

"Are you ready for the dance later, girls?" Mrs. Bentley asks.

"Of course!" Mary exclaims. "We're going back to the house to get ready. Suze is coming too. I'm wearing my red dress, and I've been mending the blue for Lydia."

Mrs. Bentley smiles at me. "I'm sure it will be just lovely on you, Lydia."

"Thanks." I smile back.

"Oh, look, there's Dean." Mrs. Bentley stands up and smoothes the wrinkles from her wide, flowered skirt. "Dean!" she calls out. He turns toward the sound of his mother's voice and starts walking in our direction. He's wearing his uniform and holding hands with his wife, Elizabeth. Her hair is so blond that it glows almost white in the sun.

Dean's face is tanned and healthy, his body lean and slightly lanky. He's a young man, about to go on a mission that he thinks is going to save his country. But he has no idea what really awaits him.

"Hello," Elizabeth says as they approach our blanket. She's wearing a plain brown dress.

"Elizabeth, dear." Mrs. Bentley smiles and the two women hug. Elizabeth won't let go of Dean's hand, and they end up forming an awkward triangle.

"How are you?" Mrs. Bentley asks.

Elizabeth shakes her head a little. "Dean has to report to the base again. He says they need him for a few days and he doesn't know when he'll be back home."

Dean looks grim as he watches his wife. There's a restrained quality about him, as though he wants to break down into tears or anger and he's barely keeping himself together.

Dr. Bentley stands up too, and puts an arm around his son. "Let's take a walk," he says. Dean nods, though he glances back at his wife. He too seems reluctant to let go of her hand. Dr. and Mrs. Bentley gently pull them apart and lead them away, softly speaking to each half of the married couple.

"Dean is *always* leaving," Mary says in a whisper. "He's usually home in a day or two."

"They're just worried about him." I jiggle my foot against the blanket, frustrated and confused. It's a terrible burden knowing someone else's fate.

"You're right." Mary sighs and gestures to where her mother is hugging Dean's wife. "I guess I wouldn't want to watch my husband go off every few days either. Especially when he can't tell me why."

I don't know what to say.

"Oh, look!" Mary brightens. "Suze is coming. And Jinx!"

The two girls plop down on the blanket. They're both wearing plain sundresses.

"Hi, girls." Jinx smiles. She sees my expression and

pauses. "What's the matter?"

"Dean has to leave for a few days and everyone's upset." Mary's voice is soft and concerned. I bite my lip.

"He's always back in a few days," Susie says gently.

Mary smiles slightly. "You're right. I'm sure everything will be fine."

"Yeah, but what if it isn't this time," I snap. The three girls look at me, then exchange glances.

"Sorry. I just need something to drink." I wave limply at the refreshment table, where large glass pitchers of lemonade and ice water sweat in the afternoon sun. I stand.

"Are you okay?" Mary shades her eyes as she looks up at me.

"Yeah, I'm fine. I'll be back in a minute."

"Get me a lemonade," Jinx demands.

"Sure." I quickly walk away from them, turning toward the Manor. I walk around the large building until the picnic is out of sight.

There's a small field past the hill and I step into the middle of it, running my fingers through the tall, pale grass. I break some off and twist the stalks in my hands. They smell sweet and fresh, like dry hay.

I'm turning it all over in my head—Dean, Mary, Wes— when I hear a noise. The grass rustling and swaying. I back up slowly, my eyes darting around the field. A head suddenly pops up not far from me, and I scream out loud.

"Lydia?"

It's Peter. My seven-year-old grandfather.

"Peter? What are you doing out here?"

"Shh," he whispers, his small body half-hidden in the reeds. "You'll wake them up."

"Wake who up?"

He beckons me closer. The grass parts around my heavy skirt. I'm wearing the green dress again, with a wide-brimmed straw hat that keeps the sun out of my eyes. I lean over to see what Peter's pointing at. There is a bird's nest tucked into the grass, three tiny brown chicks pressed tightly together inside.

"They're so small," I whisper.

"I know. The mama will be back soon. But she'll attack us if she finds us here." He reaches up, slipping his fingers into mine. "Let's go." He tugs me forward and we walk toward the picnic.

"My daddy's going on a mission soon," Peter says.

"I know." I squeeze his fingers in mine. They're sticky and warm.

"He's a big war hero."

My throat feels tight. "He is. A big war hero."

The lawn is covered with people. "Look." I point into the crowd. "There's your mother. I think she's lost her baby bird."

"I'm not a bird, Lydia." He sounds highly offended.

"Really? These aren't feathers?" I rumple the dark spikes of his hair.

He giggles, pulling away. "No!"

"Here comes your dad," I say as Dean breaks away from his walk with Dr. Bentley and starts walking in our direction.

Peter lets go of me, running forward until he reaches his father.

"Where have you been?" Dean places his hand on Peter's head.

"I found a bird's nest."

He smiles, though his tone is gruff. "You can't go wandering off like that. Your mother was worried."

"Sorry." Peter grinds the toe of one leather shoe into the grass.

Dean looks at me. "Thank you for bringing him back."

"No problem."

"Can I go now, Dad?"

"Find your mother." Dean lightly nudges Peter forward. "She's looking for you."

Peter scampers down the hill. Dean and I stand there awkwardly. He crosses his arms over his chest and stands with one leg out to the side. It's a pose I've seen my father take a thousand times.

"How are you, Lydia?" he asks, his tone overly polite.

"I'm well. I really like staying with the Bentleys." It's difficult to get the words out.

"I'm sure you heard I'm leaving soon?"

"Yeah, I heard." I open my mouth, then shut it again. Is this the right moment to tell him? Will there ever be a right moment?

"I don't know when I'll be back, so I won't be around to keep an eye on you anymore. Let's hope you are who you say you are."

I look at him and am shocked to find that he's smiling at me, that he's joking around. He's always so serious that it's hard to think of him in any other light. "You can trust me," I say. "I've started to think of them as my own family."

He stares at me for a moment, taking in the red hair curling out from under my hat, my green eyes, so similar to his own. "You look like Mary."

"I do?"

He nods, reaching into his pocket for his cigarettes. "You could be sisters."

"That would make you and me related too, you know."

He smirks a little, lights the cigarette, and inhales deeply. "Now, let's not get carried away."

I smile.

"Take care," he says. He starts to walk away.

"Wait!" I reach out, my hand hovering in the empty space between us. He pauses and turns slightly. "Where you're going, it's dangerous, right?"

He doesn't say anything, squinting at me in the sun.

"Be careful. Please. It would hurt your family if something happened to you. And if you have the option of not doing it, then don't. Do it, I mean." I mentally cringe, not knowing what to say, not knowing how to tell him the truth.

He takes a drag of the cigarette. "Good–bye, Lydia."

I watch him walk down the hill to where Elizabeth and Peter wait for him near the Bentleys' blanket. Mary talks rapidly to Dr. Bentley as Mrs. Bentley stands to hand Peter an apple. Dean joins them, his arm curling around Elizabeth. Mary says something and they all laugh. They're a family, connected by love, by affection. They're *my* family.

I had a chance to tell Dean the truth, but I didn't take it. I only have one more day to make things right. Tomorrow I can't fail. I won't be a coward.

That evening, Susie and I sit in Mary's bedroom, watching as she does her hair. She's still in her slip, and the lines of her girdle press into her skin. Susie is dressed already, in a slim black dress with a high neckline and short sleeves. Beads dangle from the hem, making a clinking noise as she moves. She looks pretty, her light hair pulled back in a soft swirl around her face.

Mary helped me get ready a little while ago. My hair is twisted up on one side with pins. The rest falls in heavy curls around my shoulders. Mary insisted on doing my makeup, and now my eyes are heavily lined, my cheeks tinted pink, my mouth a deep burgundy. It makes me look less like a high school girl and more like a young woman. She even covered my scraped cheek with a thick foundation, and you can barely see the cut. I'm in a slip, waiting until the last minute to put the blue dress on.

"Here, let me do that." Susie takes the bobby pins from Mary's hand. Mary expertly applies bright red lipstick, then makes a kissing face at her reflection. Susie giggles.

"Are my legs dry yet?" Mary turns to examine them in the mirror. They've been painted with something called "Stocking Stick"—a cakelike makeup that's supposed to look like stockings.

"I think so," I say. She tried to put it on me, too, but I resisted the heavy texture of the stuff.

Susie hands Mary her red dress and helps her zip up the back. The fabric hugs Mary's curvy frame, with a narrow waist and full skirt. She slips into the matching jacket. Her hair is a dark enough red that it doesn't clash with her dress, and her lipstick perfectly matches the bright fabric. She looks like a pinup girl.

"You look amazing!" I tell her.

"Oh, hush." She waves her hand, dismissing my comment. "So will you once you put your dress on."

I smile, overwhelmed by my affection for her. Mary has made this past week so much easier.

"So." Mary blots her lipstick with a tissue. "Is your beau going to be there tonight?"

"Wes? Maybe. I don't know." I have no idea. At the fundraiser he told me he's been spying on me, and considering how he surprised me at Camp Hero last night that's probably still true. I can't picture him showing up to a dance, but the thought of seeing him again makes my heart start to race.

"He's so drooly, Lyd," Mary gushes.

"Lydia has a fella?" Susie bends to apply her own lipstick in the mirror.

"She does, and he is . . ." Mary is uncharacteristically at a loss for words, and I don't blame her—Wes is certainly hard to describe.

"He's . . . nice," I say, for lack of a better word. *Nice* really isn't how I picture Wes, but somehow *intense* doesn't seem very romantic.

"And the way he looks at Lydia." Mary sighs, and mock fans herself. "I've never seen anything like it."

"Not even from my Mick looking at me?" Susie pouts into the mirror.

Mary scoffs. "Oh, you know Mick thinks you hung the moon, and it shows all over his face. But Wes . . . I thought he'd set Lydia on fire with just his eyes."

"That's not true." I look down, embarrassed.

"It is too true. That boy would swallow you whole, if he could."

"So he's nice, good-looking, and he loves you." Susie looks at me in the mirror, still holding the lipstick in her hand. "Sounds like a good thing to me. Maybe you'll be engaged soon too."

"I want to be a bridesmaid," Mary cuts in. "And I want to wear pink. Maybe we can have a double wedding, you and Wes, me and Lucas."

I shake my head at her and she laughs. But her words

make me pause. I have feelings for Wes, but it still feels so hopeless. We're from such different worlds. We're even from different time periods.

Wes chased me into the past against every order he's ever had. I think he's starting to feel something for me now, but I can't be sure. He was raised in a cold place, with no love and no warmth. Does he even know what loving someone means? Could we ever care about each other in the same way?

Mary nudges me and I turn to her. "Here." She holds out a tube of lipstick.

I point to my lips. "I already have some."

"I know, silly! But this is for later, when you go to the powder room. You don't want a pale mouth."

"Where am I supposed to put that? I don't have a purse."

"You can put it in mine." Susie holds up a tiny beaded clutch. "Though I might not have room."

"Just stick it in your bra," Mary says.

"What?"

She rolls her eyes, holding out the tube. "Your bra! Put it in."

"You're kidding."

"Everyone does it." I gawk at her. "Fine, I'll do it for you. Come here." She lunges at me, lipstick in hand.

"Get away from me!" We both fall back onto the bed, a tangle of red taffeta. I roll over, shrieking with laughter.

"Okay, okay!" I push her away. "Give me the tube."

Still laughing, she shoves the curls out of her face and hands it over. I stick it down my cleavage, tucking it into my bra.

"Happy?"

"Very." Mary gets up from the bed, smoothing down her dress.

"Oh no," Susie gasps. "Don't look."

"What, what it is?" Mary asks. She lifts the hem of her dress. "Drat!" Some of the leg makeup must have rubbed off on the skirt, which now has a slight tannish smear near the bottom. "What am I going to do?"

"We'll put cold water on it." Susie steers Mary toward the bedroom door. "Let's get a washcloth from the bathroom."

The two girls disappear. I reach for the blue dress that's hanging near Mary's closet. I step into it, struggling to zip up the back by myself, then turn to examine myself in the mirror.

My dress is a shiny, sapphire blue that falls around my body like liquid. The dress has princess shoulders with long sleeves, a scooped neck, and a slinky skirt. The color is bright against my pale skin and makes my eyes look even greener. I slip on the short white beaded gloves that Mary left out for me, and step into low black heels. I twirl around, watching the skirt flare out around me.

Since I've been in the past, I've been consumed by thoughts of Dean and the Montauk Project. Tomorrow I *have* to tell Dean what's going to happen to him. I have to confront the new future I'm trying to create.

But tonight I want to put those thoughts aside. Tonight I want to drink punch and dance and laugh with Mary and her friends, knowing that tomorrow everything could change forever.

I hope that Wes *is* spying on me, because right now I don't care if we've been doomed from the start. I want, for just one night, to close the distance that always seems to separate us.

CHAPTER 16

Mary, Susie, and I sit in the backseat of Dr. Bentley's car, our skirts a waterfall of red, black, and blue. It's a short drive to the Tennis Auditorium, a large Tudor clubhouse not far from Montauk Manor. In my time it's a playhouse and a community center, but in 1944 it's another building occupied by the navy.

The road around us is dotted with parked cars, army trucks, and navy jeeps. We pass a group of girls, their heels sinking into the dirt. Dr. Bentley drives slowly, stopping when we're near the entrance. Toward the side of the building, I can see glowing lights and bodies moving through the shadows in between them.

"Thanks for driving us." Mary climbs out of the car. Susie and I follow her. We walk through the dark, weaving around parked cars as we make our way toward the bright spot on the lawn. I hear music, the blare of a trumpet, the low moan of a saxophone.

"Jimmy, no. We can't!" A girl's voice giggles from behind one of the cars, and I see the shape of a couple embracing, his head in her neck, his hand high on her thigh. He whispers something to her and she giggles again, leaning into his arms. I look away, my face hot, and I can't help but think of Wes leaning over me on the beach last night.

The dance has been set up on the side lawn, a large open space surrounded by trees. A wide dance floor has been created in the middle of it, and a band is raised on a small stage made of plywood. Two trumpeters stand toward the back of the stage. A saxophone player and a clarinetist sit in front of them on wooden folding chairs. There's a man holding a stand-up bass, while a blond woman in a tight dress sings into a microphone. She's belting out a fast song, about bugle boys in Company B, and she twists her hips and hands as she sings.

"What is this song?" I ask.

Mary gives me a strange look. "'Boogie Woogie Bugle Boy.' Everyone knows that, Lyd."

Wooden poles with hanging glass lanterns surround the dance floor. As we get closer, I realize that they're actually large mason jars with candles inside. The makeshift lanterns swing from side to side in the breeze. More jars are scattered around the lawn, dangling from nearby trees or tucked into the grass.

We walk across the lawn. The dance floor is already packed with couples, some pressed close, oblivious to the music, most twisting and turning to the fast beat of the song, their legs kicking to the sides, their arms tight around each other. The men lead, twirling the women in circles, whipping them to the sides and then back, sometimes lifting them up in the air, so high their skirts fly in different directions. I pause, taking it all in. I've never seen anything like this, never been to a dance that didn't have a DJ playing overproduced techno. This is different, strange . . . magical.

Mary sees me standing still, a little dazed, and she grabs my arm and yanks me to the edge of the dance floor, where wooden folding chairs have been set up on one side. She pulls off her jacket, throwing it onto a nearby chair. "Let's get a drink first!" she shouts over the music. Susie nods and we follow Mary toward a refreshment table. Mary picks up a glass of pink punch, sipping it as she sways from side to side.

"Hi," a boy shouts into her ear, smiling. He's on the short side, with brownish hair and kind of a square head. He's wearing a white navy uniform. "You're a real blackout girl." Mary giggles. "Let's dance." He grabs her hand and pulls her into the crowd. She has just enough time to shove her drink in my direction and give us a playful shrug before she's swallowed up in the sea of dancers.

"Are you going to dance too?" I ask Susie as the song

changes. It's slower, but still swingy and loose.

"Of course she is," a male voice says, his arm swooping in and pulling Susie forward. It's Mick, her fiancé. Apparently he didn't have to work tonight. He sweeps her out onto the floor.

"Hey, sugar, are you rationed?" A nearby sailor asks me.

"I don't know." I take a sip of the sugary punch. I'm pretty sure there's rum in it. "What does it mean?"

I feel someone beside me, and I look up to see Lucas standing near my shoulder. He's glaring at the soldier. "Scram," he says.

"Looks like you are, honey." The sailor winks at me and turns to join his buddies.

I face Lucas. He gives me an appraising look, taking in my slinky dress, my curls. His eyes linger on my dark red lips.

I fidget under his gaze. So much has happened since I last saw him: I discovered that Mary is his future bride. I started to realize my feelings for Wes. I'm not sure how to act around Lucas now.

"Do you want to dance?" he asks.

I look out at the couples, at the swingy steps they all seem to know by heart.

"I don't really know how to dance like that."

"The jitterbug?" He points to a couple moving their arms and legs in quick, bouncing steps.

"Or any of it."

"Hmm." He leans forward. "Some of that Lindy hopping might be a bit hard, but we can certainly teach you how to swing. You *do* know the triple step, right?"

I shake my head.

"It's real easy." He holds out a hand. I hesitate for a second, but then I take it. Lucas and I are friends, and he's never given me any real indication that he wants more. We can certainly share a harmless dance. "Just follow my lead."

He pulls me onto the dance floor. We're surrounded by sweating, bouncing couples. Someone bumps into me and we're pushed closer together. The music is loud, the woman's voice high and staccato.

"Put your arm on my shoulder," Lucas says. "And give me your other hand." I close my fingers around his. "Step forward as I step back. Then back as I step forward." We complete the short movements.

"Now to the side, and then in a circle." He guides me with a hand on my back, and my body moves with his. We turn in a circle, not quite as fast as the other couples, but I'm not tripping over myself either. He steps me backward, then spins me around, catching me as I twirl into him.

"See? Easy." He smiles, holding me against his chest.

"Easy," I repeat, grinning back.

There's a tap on my shoulder. It's Mary, standing with her partner.

"Time to switch!"

Lucas opens his mouth to say something, then pauses,

glancing from me to Mary. "Of course. Let's dance, Mary."

I step away from Lucas and take the square-headed soldier's outstretched hand. He's not much taller than I am, and his palms are slick. I almost trip as he twirls me, pulling me forward roughly. When the song comes to an end, I quickly escape back to the refreshment table.

I pick up my glass and take another sip. There's definitely rum in this punch. I consider leaving it on the table. But tonight I want to step outside myself, and that includes trying something new. I toss back the punch, grimacing as the sugary liquid slides down my throat.

Mary and Lucas join me at the end of the next song, laughing and fanning themselves. Mick and Susie come to grab a drink, and Lucas entertains us with stories about growing up on the farm. I drink another glass of punch.

Mick puts down his cup and grabs Mary, pulling her onto the dance floor. They start to jitterbug, their legs kicking up in unison, their arms bouncing and swaying.

"They're so good!" I say to no one in particular.

"Yeah, and they know it." Susie laughs. "I need to go get my man." She cuts in on the couple, pulling Mick close. Mary is snatched up by another boy, and they start dancing, her skirt flying up around her makeup-covered legs.

I see Jinx in the crowd, dark hair bouncing as she flies across the floor. The music changes again, and the song is slow. I'm starting to feel the effects of the rum punch; the lights are hazy inside their glass jars, the couples spin and spin, blending together. I don't even flinch when I feel Lucas close his hand over mine. I think he's leading me to join our friends on the dance floor, but instead he pulls me away toward the other side of the lawn.

He stops near the edge of the trees, where a single lantern hangs on a branch above our heads.

I look up at him. "What is it?"

"I think we should talk." He taps his finger against his pant leg in a nervous gesture.

"Okay." My voice is slow. "About what?"

"I know we haven't known each other for very long." He pauses. It's dark, but I think he might be blushing. "I've been thinking about you lately. A lot."

My mouth falls open. "What?"

"I wanted to ask you tonight." He still won't look me full in the face. "To go with me to the dance."

"Lucas—" I try to cut him off, but he plows ahead.

"But then you were sick and I . . . lost my nerve." He shrugs, one corner of his mouth lifting into a lopsided smile. "I feel like I know you, Lydia. Like we have this connection I can't explain. Maybe it's because we both lost someone we love. I don't know. I just feel different about you, and I have since we first met on the base."

Guilt blossoms inside of me. Guilt from my lie. Guilt about Mary. Even guilt over Wes, though I still don't know how he feels about me. "Lucas, there's a lot you don't know. . . ."

"I'm willing to learn. I want to *know* you, Lydia." His face is so open and trusting. I turn my head away quickly and then close my eyes as the world realigns.

"So I guess that's all I wanted to say." He glances down, shy again. "That I want to know you. If you'll let me."

I look over at the dance floor, where Mary rests against her new partner, and I feel my heart sink. "Lucas, I can't . . ."

He shakes his head. "Don't say anything right now. Just dance with me. Please."

"I—"

"Please, Lydia."

He looks so fragile in that moment that I nod reluctantly and let him pull me onto the dance floor. Another slow song is starting, and the singer's smooth voice pours thickly over the trumpets, low and mournful. Lucas draws me into his arms.

My body is rigid against his, but he doesn't notice. I can't stop thinking about what he just said. He and Mary are meant to be together. If I never came to the past, they'd probably be falling in love right now. Am I screwing up their destinies just by being here?

"Can I cut in?"

Lucas suddenly pulls away and my head jerks up.

It's Wes.

"What are you doing here?" I breathe the words as I smile at him. His black hair gleams in the soft candlelight; an army-issued shirt is snug over his shoulders. He meets my eyes. He has that uncertain look about him again, and I find myself stepping toward him automatically.

"Do you know him?" Lucas asks. His voice is strange, stripped of its usual warmth.

"This is Wes. I mean, Private Wesley Smith." I glance between the two of them. Wes is taller than Lucas, and leaner. His face is sharper too, his features more defined. Lucas, though older than us, suddenly seems younger.

Lucas drops my arms. "What division are you with, GI?"

Wes doesn't look away from me as he answers. "I'm with the Seventy-seventh Infantry Division, sir."

Lucas crosses his arms. "The Seventy-seventh is in the Pacific right now, Private. They shipped out from Hero in March."

Wes finally turns to Lucas. "I was injured while training in Hawaii and sent back to Hero not long after. Lydia and I met in the hospital the other night. Sir."

"Wes, this is Lucas Clarke," I cut in.

"*Sergeant* Clarke," Lucas interjects, one eyebrow raised.

Wes stands straighter, saluting Lucas with his right hand tight to his forehead.

"At ease," Lucas drawls. He seems to savor the words.

"Lydia." Wes holds out his hand, and I immediately take it. He pulls me close, and I sink into him. Lucas stares at us for a moment, then turns and walks off the dance floor.

Wes draws my entire body to him and I forget all about Lucas. We're closer than we ever have been, so close that

I can feel him take a long breath. I place one hand near his neck, almost touching his bare skin. He pulls my other hand between our bodies and holds it pressed to both our chests. We spin in a lazy circle. The candles above me seem to move closer together, tiny flickering bursts that blend into one long stream of light.

"What are you doing here?" I ask again.

"I—" He pauses, and for a second I think he won't answer me. "I wanted to see you." His voice sounds raw, unused.

I pull back so that I can see his face. "Really?"

He doesn't answer, but his hand tightens against my back.

"I thought . . ." I stop and clear my throat. "I thought you just wanted me to go home."

He shakes his head. It's an abrupt movement, without his usual deliberate care, and I smile. A rush of warmth spreads through me. Wes came here for *me*, not because he wants to force me to leave things alone.

The last thing I said to him was that he didn't have to help me, but that I needed him to accept my decision. If he's here tonight, then he's willing to stand aside while I try to fix my family's future. He's going to support me.

My hesitant smile grows.

He peers down into my face and then his mouth draws into a thin line. "Have you been drinking?"

I blink.

"You have." His tone is accusing. "You're drunk."

"Wes, I had two cups of rum punch." I roll my eyes.

"I'm hardly drunk."

"Your eyes are unfocused. I don't like it."

I shrug. "This is my night of fun. Get over it."

"Your night of fun?" He raises an eyebrow.

"Everything could change tomorrow. I want one night where I can be free from all this conspiracy stuff. I want to do something fun."

"Like what?" Wes smiles, and I see the dimple flash in his cheek.

"Like dance."

He immediately spins me faster and I start to laugh.

"What else?" He sounds amused.

"Drink punch."

"I think you've succeeded there. Anything else?"

I look up at him, and my smile fades. I bite my lower lip, and then I press my body closer to his. I feel him tense and watch the laughter vanish from his eyes. In its place is something dark and consuming.

We freeze in the middle of the dance floor, our eyes locked. The music changes to a fast song, but neither of us moves.

Suddenly Wes releases me, grabs my hand, and guides me out of the crush of people. Lights and faces blur around me. I briefly see Mary waving as Wes and I half walk, half run together across the lawn and into the shadow of trees.

We don't stop until we're out of sight of the party. Then Wes drops my hand and turns to me.

He steps close. His expression hasn't changed. Still intense. Still overpowering. A little unnerved, I retreat until my back hits a tree trunk. He follows me.

"Lydia." His hands come up to my face and linger just above my skin. My eyelids flicker.

"I'm not . . . I don't know how . . ." He sounds lost. I look up at him. His mouth parts, his eyes are searching.

I reach up and press his hands until they cup the sides of my face. His palms are cool against my skin.

"It's okay," I whisper.

He leans down until our faces are only a breath apart. His eyes are open and watchful. We breathe the same air for a minute, and then he closes the distance and gently presses his lips against mine.

My eyes shut. He tilts his head and opens his mouth and then I can't think of anything anymore, not how soft his lips are, not how this feels like the only real kiss I've ever had, nothing but Wes.

What started as soft and sweet suddenly becomes demanding and urgent, lips meeting quickly over and over. Wes pulls me closer to him, one hand cupping the side of my face, the other pressing hard on my back. I slide into him, letting his body support my weight, overwhelmed by his mouth on mine. My fingers catch in his hair.

He pulls back. My breath is short and I look up at him, hands still locked behind his head. He gently pushes my bangs back.

"Wes." I sigh his name and he smiles. I fight the urge to trace the dimple at the corner of his mouth.

He leans down again and I close my eyes, tilting my face toward his.

His voice is a whisper against my lips. "Now will you come back with me?"

My eyes snap open. "What did you just say?"

He pulls back slightly, still watching me. I can't read his expression. "Will you come with me to Camp Hero?"

My body tenses. All of my fears about Wes twist together in my head. He didn't come here for me. He doesn't feel the same way I do. He's just trying to get me to go back to 2012.

I push at his chest. He drops his arms and I wrench away, stumbling across the forest floor.

I turn to glare at him. "Did you kiss me so that I would agree to leave with you?"

His face goes blank. "No."

But I shake my head, almost choking on the bile that rises in my chest.

"Did you dance with me and tell me you came here to see me and *manipulate* me just to get me into the TM?" I press my fingers to my mouth, still feeling him against my lips. The kiss felt so perfect. I thought it meant something.

"No." There's a little more force behind the word this time, though his face is still expressionless. He's so different from the Wes of only a few moments ago.

"How could you do this? I thought you felt . . ." My voice breaks on the words.

He steps forward, the movement slow and careful. "I would never hurt you."

I put my hand out to stop him from getting any closer. "What do you think you're doing right now, Wes?"

He turns his head away and when he looks back, the mask over his features is gone. His eyes are soft and uncertain. He looks almost—confused, like he doesn't understand what's happening, or why.

"I didn't mean to hurt you, Lydia," he says, low and soothing. "I didn't . . . I just want to keep you safe."

I cross my arms over my chest and look away from him, back toward the bright lights of the dance. I see the couples moving slowly, the tiny lights flickering through the trees.

"Last night in the Facility I discovered that Dean is going on a mission to kill Hitler." I keep my tone deliberately even, though I feel like I'm breaking apart inside. "If Dean survives the TM then he'll be stuck in the twenties forever. I'm going to stop that from happening because I want to help the people I care about. Because I have to."

My voice gets louder. "I thought you were starting to understand." I press both hands to my forehead. "I'm such an idiot."

I feel his gaze on me, but I refuse to look up.

"Lydia . . ." He trails off.

I lower my hands and finally turn to him. He's standing perfectly still, his arms loose at his sides. "What?" I prompt. "What do you want to say?"

He reaches up and rubs at his chin, then takes a step away from me. He doesn't say a word.

"Right. Good night, Wes," I say coldly.

I leave him and walk back toward the dance. I so badly wanted to believe that he felt the same way about me. Now I just feel used, and a little embarrassed that I kissed him like that.

I'm almost out of the tree line when I pause. I can't help it. I look back at him. He hasn't moved at all—a black silhouette against the forest.

I turn away.

CHAPTER 17

I get dressed in the late morning as the sun starts to pour through my window. I walk downstairs and into the kitchen, picking up an apple from a bowl on the counter. The Bentleys' kitchen is modern for 1944, with a red, diner-style table, a refrigerator with round sides, and white and red tiled counters.

Feeling restless, I walk through the ground floor of the house until I come to the only place I haven't been in yet. Dr. Bentley's study. I knock on the door, and it swings open into an empty room. I notice floor to ceiling bookshelves and a heavy wooden desk with piles of paper spilling over it. The dark green wallpaper, framed medical degrees, and blackout curtains make it feel serious and grown-up.

I take a bite of the apple and move toward the shelves

to study the rows of books lining the walls. When I'm home I like to read for hours. I touch the stiff spines with my fingers, wishing I had time to do that now. But I stop. Thinking of relaxing with a book makes me think of my ruined night of fun, which makes me think of Wes. And I really don't want to think about Wes right now.

"There you are," Dr. Bentley says from behind me.

I jump, turning toward him.

"Were you looking for a particular book?" He walks into the room and places some papers on the desk.

"Not really. I was just curious."

"You're welcome to read anything on these shelves. The fiction is to the right. You'll want to stay away from that one." He gestures to the bookshelf closest to the window. "All medical journals."

"Thanks." I take a step closer to the shelves of fiction, still clutching the half-eaten apple. "I love to read."

"That's nice to hear." He leans against the desk and smiles at me above his salt-and-pepper beard. My dad hasn't gone gray yet, but I imagine he'll look like Dr. Bentley when he does: distinguished but approachable. "You'd be one of the only readers in this house. Mrs. Bentley and Mary don't seem to have the patience for novels. They'd rather be out having their own adventures than reading about someone else's."

"When I was in school I wrote for the paper," I say absently as I examine the bookshelf. "I want to be a journalist."

"Have you thought about college? There's Barnard, in

New York. Right next door to Columbia, my alma mater. Mary thought about applying, but now she's set on joining the army to become a nurse."

I look up, surprised by his tone. "Do you not want her to enlist?"

"It's her decision. I want her to be happy. And she's happiest when she's helping people." He shrugs and picks up a pipe from the cluttered desk. "And when she's drawing. That's how she relaxes. Mary has an artistic soul. She's very sensitive."

I bite the apple again, chewing thoughtfully. "I know. I've seen her sketchbook."

"Really?" Dr. Bentley raises his bushy eyebrows, and he brings the pipe to his mouth. He lights it with a match, puffing on the end as the flame disappears into the wide rim. "She must trust you. She doesn't show her work to many people."

"But she's so talented!"

"She is." He puffs twice and smoke curls toward the ceiling. It smells warm and spicy and safe somehow. I think of my grandfather and wonder what he's doing right now. Is he smoking his pipe? Is he looking for me? Has time stopped while I've been gone?

"I hope I can admit now that I had my doubts about you staying here, Lydia. But I know that Mary feels so close to you. And now that Dean has left . . ."

I freeze, one hand resting on an old leather-bound book. "What did you say?"

"Mary's really come to care about you."

"No, about Dean. What do you mean, he left?" My hands clench automatically, and apple juice squeezes over my fingers. It drips onto the wood floor.

He sees my stricken expression and cocks his head at me. "It's only for a few days, most likely."

"But I thought he wasn't leaving until tomorrow. That's what he said at the picnic. Not until tomorrow, the fifth." I can't seem to stop talking as I try to digest this news.

"Are you feeling all right?" Dr. Bentley looks at me with concern. "You're pale. Come sit down." I let him lead me over to the large leather chair behind the desk.

"You're sure he's gone already?"

Dr. Bentley nods.

"Why did he leave early?" My chest feels heavy. Dean isn't supposed to disappear until *tomorrow*. What does it mean that he left a day early? Has my grandfather had the date wrong all these years, or has something changed? Was Wes right? Has my presence altered the time line somehow?

"These things happen, especially where Dean is concerned." Dr. Bentley smiles a little sadly. He turns toward the window, looking out on the backyard. Sunlight is streaming through the trees.

"Dean was always the adventurer. I suspect that's why he's risen in the military so quickly. There's nothing he won't volunteer for, nothing he won't try. It's a miracle he wasn't injured overseas. I spent most of his childhood patching him up after his big stunts." He takes a drag from the pipe, his eyes shadowed. "He wants to make the world safe for the people he loves. It's a trait that Peter will inherit, I suspect."

I picture my brave, stubborn grandfather, who has never given up on trying to discover the truth of what happened to his father. "I know he has."

Dr. Bentley straightens. "What do you say you and I have some breakfast? I've been eyeing the leftover pie Mrs. Bentley made last night. But fair warning—I make no promises if she catches us. In fact, I'll most likely blame it all on you."

"That would be great." I smile weakly. Why, *why* did I chicken out yesterday? Why didn't I tell Dean the truth when I had the chance? Now he's gone before I had a chance to stop him. He's probably inside the Facility already, preparing for a doomed mission. How am I going to save him now?

"It's every man for himself in the trenches." Dr. Bentley walks out of the study. We're almost to the kitchen when a honking noise has us both turning toward the window.

"Looks like Lucas is here," Dr. Bentley says.

I open the front door. Lucas is standing on the bottom step. His eyes are hard and his mouth is pulled tight at the corners. "Lydia. I was hoping I could talk with you."

"Of course." I smile tentatively and open the door wider.

He shakes his head. "I don't want to come inside."

"All right." I close the door behind me and follow him onto the lawn. It's sunny out and starting to get warm.

Lucas stops next to his truck. "Is anyone here?" he asks.

"Mary and Mrs. Bentley went to church. Dr. Bentley is still inside."

He nods, then leans against the door of the truck.

"Lucas, is everything okay?"

"Are you stuck on Smith?" he blurts out.

I gape at him. "Stuck on . . . ? Do you mean am I *with* Wes?"

He looks at me, waiting for an answer. His cheeks are even pinker than normal.

I laugh nervously and run my fingers through my messy curls. "Why are you asking me this?"

He crosses his arms over his chest. "I saw you with him last night. Dancing. Running off into the woods. I saw the way he looked at you." His voice is filled with hostility. It dawns on me that although Lucas is easygoing, he wears *all* of his emotions on his sleeve, including anger.

I look down at my bare feet. I didn't have time to put on shoes, and the gravel from the driveway is digging into my toes. I'm still angry with Wes, still hurt, but I can't deny my feelings—even if he doesn't feel the same way.

"Yes," I say softly. "I think I am."

Lucas's mouth falls open. "What? What about . . . I thought . . ." He trails off, looking shocked.

My voice is small. "I'm sorry, Lucas. Wes and I . . . it's really complicated."

He sighs. "I told you I wanted to get to know you better.

I thought you wanted that too."

"I know. I'm sorry. I should have told you last night."

He takes a step toward me. "I know I didn't invent this." He waves his hand back and forth in the air between our bodies.

"I didn't know how you felt until last night. I should have said something then, but I didn't want to hurt you. . . ."

"You only met him a few days ago!" Lucas exclaims, apparently forgetting that I only met *him* a few days ago too.

"It doesn't matter."

He makes a noise in his throat. His blue eyes are burning as he asks, "What about me?"

I bite my lip. If I had met Lucas in my own time, I might have fallen for him. And I can't deny that a small part of me is attracted to his easy charm. He made life simpler when I desperately needed it to be. But there was always Mary—and Wes—between us. It could never work.

I don't want to upset Lucas, but I can't give him hope that I might change my mind either. The whole situation reminds me of my relationship with Grant. I realize now that Hannah was right—I *should* have been honest with him from the beginning. I'm always saying that the truth is worth knowing, even if it hurts. Maybe it's time for me to start practicing what I preach.

I push my shoulders back and face Lucas. "I'm sorry." My tone is firm. "I'm falling in love with Wes, and I . . . don't feel the same about you."

His eyes shut.

"Lucas." I say his name like a plea. "Trust me when I tell you there's a great girl out there for you. I know that for a fact."

"But she's not you," he says softly.

I shake my head slowly. Then I make a choice, one I know Wes wouldn't approve of. "You should think about . . . Mary."

He opens his eyes. "Mary?"

I nod. "Mary."

He raises one hand to scratch the back of his neck. "Mary?" he asks again.

I laugh a little, trying to break the tension. "You can't tell me you haven't thought about it."

"I mean, I guess . . . I just never really . . ." He looks up and I see that some of the disappointment has left his face, replaced by a thoughtful expression. "Mary?"

We're interrupted by the sound of an approaching car. Lucas and I both step back as Mrs. Bentley pulls into the driveway. As soon as the car rolls to a stop, Mary hops out of the passenger side. Mrs. Bentley gets out too and waves to us on her way into the house.

"Lucas!" Mary sounds breathless. "What are you doing here?"

Lucas looks at her, and I see his gaze start with her feet and work his way up. She is pretty and flushed in a bright yellow sundress, her auburn curls tumbling around her shoulders. "I was . . ." He can't seem to take his eyes from her. "I was just . . ."

"Church was so boring," Mary chatters. "Mrs. Potter was wearing this huge hat and you couldn't see anything over it. And the sermon was an hour, I swear it."

Lucas opens his mouth and closes it again. "I was just leaving," he says abruptly.

"Oh." Mary's smile fades. "When will we see you again?"

He glances at me, then turns back to Mary and smiles so wide you can see his crooked bottom teeth. "Soon. Real soon."

She beams at him and I step back. I try to contain my own smile and fail miserably. The more I meddle in the past, the more I'm tempting the butterfly effect, and I know I need to be careful. But I may have been the reason Lucas wasn't focused on Mary in the first place, and that seems like an even larger interference. Fixing it was obviously the right thing to do. Lucas and Mary are meant to be.

Lucas walks to his truck. "See ya, Mary." He turns to face me and his expression drops a bit. "Good-bye, Lydia."

He doesn't wait for a response, just gets in and starts the engine. A loud rumbling sound fills the yard. "Good-bye, Lucas," I say, even though I know he can't hear me anymore.

CHAPTER 18

Not long after Lucas leaves, Elizabeth appears with Peter and the whole family has lunch. Everyone is quiet after Dean's sudden departure, and we all pick at our food, not saying much. When the meal is over, Peter plays with his soldiers in the backyard. Mrs. Bentley asks me and Mary to weed her victory garden while she has tea in the parlor with Elizabeth.

We wear old baggy jeans with rolled-up hems. "Dungarees," Mary calls them as she ties a scarf around her head. It takes forever to pull all the dandelions and grass peeking out among the early summer vegetables. Mary complains about the heat and her aching muscles until I find a long, wiggly earthworm in the dirt and dangle it in her face. She squeals and shrieks and I smile, happy to distract her—and myself—from thoughts of Dean.

"Don't look now, Lydia," she says, pointing at something over my shoulder, "but I think you've got a visitor."

I look up from the dirt to see Wes standing near the edge of the backyard. At the sight of him, my heart starts to beat faster, even as the anger and disappointment from last night washes over me.

I walk over to him, stopping a few feet away. Caked dirt falls from my fingers and sprinkles onto the grass beneath our feet. "What do you want, Wes?"

He stares at me, his eyes darker than usual. He's acting as though nothing is different, as though he didn't try to manipulate me just a few hours ago. "I need to show you something."

"What is it?" I ask.

He looks behind me, where Mary is avidly eavesdropping. She doesn't even pretend to look away.

His voice drops, low and deep. "I need to show you something," he repeats, and he sounds so forceful, so intense, that for a minute I forget to be mad at him.

"Come with me." He turns and walks away. I follow him around the side of the house and into a small section of forest, far away from the eyes and ears of the Bentleys.

"Wes, what's going on?"

He turns to face me and reaches into the pocket of his olive army jacket. He pulls out a folder and holds it between us, his face grim.

I take it from him. My dirty fingers leave brown smudge marks on the surface. On the back of the folder is a red CONFIDENTIAL seal. On the front are the words THE RECRUITMENT INITIATIVE stamped in black. I turn it over in my hands and look up at Wes. "This is the same type of file I took from Dr. Faust's office."

Wes nods, then gestures for me to open it.

Inside are only two documents. One is a picture of Dean. He looks stern, an army cap pulled low over his head. The other is a document with "The Recruitment Initiative" typed across the top.

I skim the words as Wes watches silently. *The recruitment program has been established to locate and train soldiers and selected civilians to participate in missions related to the Montauk Project, specifically Tesla's Machine. All recruits are taken on a volunteer basis with the understanding that these missions may result in failure.*

And then, at the bottom of the page: *The program was initiated by Sergeant Dean Bentley on special assignment. Volunteers are approved and selected at this time by Dr. Josef Faust and Lieutenant Dean Bentley.*

I grip the folder with both hands. "Dean . . . recruits?"

Wes doesn't say anything, letting me put the pieces together myself.

"Dean isn't going on the mission," I realize. "Dean is *finding* the soldiers for the mission. That's why his name was on the Project Hero mission statement. He was the one who found the subject for it."

"There's something else you should know." Wes steps closer to me. "The Recruitment Initiative has two branches. One branch is called Retrieval and the other is Training. Retrieval is the process of bringing recruits in. All recruits, Lydia, not just the volunteer soldiers."

"Kidnapping," I whisper.

Wes's jaw is clenched tight. "Training has four different modes: survival, tutoring, combat, and brainwashing."

"The torture."

"Yes." His voice is blank as he speaks, as if he's removed himself from the experience. As if it happened to someone else entirely. "Brainwashing is the first mode of training." He leans down. "Do you understand what this means? The Recruitment Initiative is the program that snatched me off the street. They kidnap children. And Dean is responsible for it."

I frantically shake my head, trying to block out his words. "But I saw the men whose photographs were in the folders in Dr. Faust's office. They weren't children; they were grown men. Dean might be recruiting volunteer soldiers, but he wouldn't hurt innocent kids."

"Lydia. You saw the room of children. It's only a matter of time before Faust starts approving use of them—if he hasn't already. The Montauk Project becomes more and more ruthless as time goes on. If Dean's working for them, then he's ruthless too."

"Oh my god." Wes puts out a hand, trying to warn me about something, but I don't notice. "I never thought Dean Bentley would turn out to be the bad guy," I say roughly.

There's a small sound behind me, a tiny squeaking noise. I turn to see Peter pop up from behind a rock, one of his toy soldiers clutched in his hand. He stares at me in horror.

"Peter—" I reach for him, the folder in my hands falling to the ground. Peter whirls around and runs back into the woods.

"Did he hear me say that his father is a bad guy?" I whisper. Wes nods and I press both palms against my forehead.

I feel Wes's touch on the back of my neck. It's only a slight sweep of his fingers, but it's enough to make me feel calmer. I lift my head, unable to erase the image of my grandfather's face. He worships his father, he always has. What must he be thinking of me right now?

"Do you want to go after him?" Wes's voice is soft.

"No." I bend down and pick up the folder. "I'll find him later and apologize. You and I need to sort this out."

I think of all I know about Dean, what my grandfather has told me about his father. He was supposed to be a good man. I *thought* he was a good man. But now I'm not so sure.

Wes watches me struggle with my thoughts and says, "People get caught up in stuff like this for a lot of different reasons. He probably thinks he's doing the right thing."

I scoff. "Nobody could think kidnapping and torturing children is the right thing."

His mouth twists a little. "I've met a lot of scientists at the Facility as I travel across time, and all of them think what they do is for the greater good. And sometimes it is."

At my horrified look, his voice gets firmer. "Sometimes the past *does* need to be changed, Lydia. If you could stop a huge disaster from happening, and save thousands of people, wouldn't you do it?"

I nod reluctantly.

"Do you know how many events like that I've stopped over the years, just by changing one tiny moment in the time line?"

"But, Wes, you can't be advocating for what they do. They use children. They *torture* them."

He turns away so that I'm staring at the hard angles of his profile. "I'm not saying I agree with their methods. But sometimes the world isn't always so black and white. People can do bad to do good."

"No." I shake my head. "I don't believe that." I picture Dean at the picnic, his hand cupped around Peter's head. "And I don't believe that Dean could be kidnapping children off the street and then brainwashing them. Maybe he doesn't know everything."

Wes looks back at me. "Lydia . . ."

"He *doesn't*, Wes. He might be sending soldiers on these missions, but he doesn't know about the room of children. I know it in my gut."

"How can you be sure?"

"I just am." I look at the sky, where the tree branches weave together in the wind. The sound of the leaves rustling is oddly soothing. "I don't know how to explain it. Dean is family. And if he could raise someone as kind and as loving as my grandfather, then he can't be a part of something like this."

Wes gives me an assessing look. There's a war going on behind his eyes, and I can tell he's wrestling with some kind of big decision.

Finally I watch as a strange peace settles over his features. "So what do we do next?" he asks, and his voice sounds lighter than it ever has.

I tilt my head at him. "We?"

"We." He smiles slightly.

"You want to help me?"

He nods.

I step closer to him and lift the tan folder. "How did you get this?" I ask slowly.

His eyes drop down at the movement. "I broke into Dean's office in the Facility."

"Why?"

"Because I knew you needed more information," he says quietly.

"You did this for me?" I can't keep the surprise out of my voice. "I thought, after last night . . ."

"Lydia." He steps closer. "Last night was a mistake."

"You didn't mean to kiss me," I say flatly.

"That's not it." He looks at the ground. "I didn't kiss you because I was trying to get you to do something. I kissed you because . . . I wanted to."

My breath catches.

"I'm not good at this," he says, his voice hoarse. "I don't know how to deal with . . . feelings."

I step closer. We're almost touching.

"I don't think that's true, Wes." I'm finally starting to understand the magnitude of his actions. "You went into the Facility for me. You took out this file."

I lift the folder again. "What about the butterfly effect? What about all your beliefs?"

"I don't believe in what you're doing, Lydia." His voice has lost that uncertain quality. "I've seen what can happen when people mess with the past. But I thought about everything you said last night. You keep fighting so hard for the people you love. You'll do anything, even if it means risking your own future. I've never seen anyone act like that before. That's why I want to help you."

His words flow through me, warm and comforting. I let go of my anger, of my fear, of all the unanswered questions I have about Wes. He is going against all his beliefs to help me.

I still don't know why he helped me the first time I stumbled into him. I don't know why he followed me into the past. But, surprisingly, I don't care anymore. I usually insist on knowing the truth about everything. It's what led me here in the first place. But for Wes, I'm willing to put that instinct aside to be with him.

He catches my eye and I start to lean in to him. We're only inches apart when the folder I'm holding scrapes against his arm. I pull back, flustered.

"Dean. We need to concentrate on Dean." I clear my throat. Wes smiles slightly.

"He's in the Facility right now," I say. "He wasn't supposed to disappear until tomorrow, but something changed. I think I might have already altered the time line."

Wes's eyes narrow, and his rubs his jaw again. "That's not good, Lydia."

I frown. "I don't know how much time Dean has left. I need to find him tonight, before it's too late."

"What are you going to do once you find him?"

I sigh. "Warn him about his disappearance. Hope he believes me."

"He might not," Wes says. He looks skeptical.

"I don't know what else to do."

"Do you have any proof?"

I shake my head, feeling defeated. "And now I also need to warn him about the Recruitment Initiative. He needs to know what's happening—or what's going to happen—with those children."

"If Dean doesn't already know about the kids—"

"He doesn't," I cut in.

Wes gives me a look. "*If* he doesn't already know, he still might not want to hear about how his project is corrupt. He might not believe you about any of it."

"Wait." I reach out and grab Wes's arm. "If I can show him the room of kidnapped children, then he *has* to believe me. He won't be able to deny it after he sees it with his own eyes."

"Lydia." Wes looks alarmed. "You can't forget all about the butterfly effect. Showing him that room could produce a huge change in the time line. If the Recruitment Initiative is gone, then my role in the Montauk Project disappears completely."

"But if the recruits are dismantled, then won't you have a better life?"

He grits his teeth and the movement makes his cheekbones look even sharper. "That's a big if, Lydia. My life may not be perfect, but I don't want to chance an unknown future."

I meet his eyes. "You said that if anything in the time line changed, then it wouldn't affect us because we're outside of it. That means you'd still exist, even if the Recruitment Initiative was destroyed. You'd be free, Wes."

He looks at me and there's something hopeful and raw in his expression. "If I can give you that life, then I will," I say. "I *have* to do this, for you and for my grandfather. It's a risk, of course, but isn't it a risk worth taking? Especially if you could leave the Montauk Project behind forever?"

He frowns, but I can see that he's thinking about my words.

"Fine. We'll sneak into the Facility tonight at midnight. You can warn Dean, and then . . . , Lydia, once you save Dean, there won't be any reason for you to stay in the past." His voice goes soft, hesitant. "Will you let me bring you back to your own time, after this is over?"

My gaze swings involuntarily toward the Bentleys' house. He's right: I said I would leave this time period once the business with Dean was over, and it will be tonight. But am I ready to leave yet?

I think of my family on both sides of time. This has been an adventure, but I can't stay here forever, and I know that Wes won't rest until I'm back in 2012. Leaving won't be easy, but this isn't my life. It's time to go back home.

"Okay," I whisper.

He smiles. "You should go talk to Peter."

Of course, Peter. I had forgotten about him overhearing me. I need to make it right.

"I'll be here at midnight," Wes says, stepping away. He half smiles, then disappears into the trees.

Finding Peter isn't as easy I thought it would be. I check inside the house, around the yard, and then I start to search the woods.

I eventually spot his small, dark head behind a boulder. I walk through the underbrush until I'm facing him. He won't look at me, just looks straight ahead into the forest. I can see faint tear marks running down his face. My stomach clenches tight.

I crouch next to him. I'm still holding the folder, and I set it down next to me on the damp ground so I can rest both hands on my knees.

"I shouldn't have said what I did. Your father isn't a bad man."

He tucks his face into the side of his shirt. "Then why did you say he was?" It's hard to make out the muffled words.

"I was angry. But I'm not anymore."

He peeks out at me with his green eyes. "Why not?"

"Because I remembered that your dad is a big war hero. And that he's kind and a good husband and a good dad."

Peter nods and turns his face a little more toward me. "He plays airplanes with me and he always lets me win."

I smile. "That sounds like a good dad to me."

Peter lifts his head. "Are you sorry for saying that about him?"

"I'm very sorry."

"And you didn't mean it?"

"No way."

He sighs and the movement makes his whole body lift and then fall. I hold back a smile. "Then I guess I can forgive you," he says. He scampers to his feet and grabs my hand. "I want to show you the other bird's nest I found."

He tugs at me and I laugh, rising to my feet. I almost forget to snatch up Dean's file before Peter pulls me farther into the woods.

Later that night, I sit on the edge of Dean's old bed, studying his quilt and waiting for midnight. Mary is in the next room, probably asleep by now. The thought of leaving her and everyone else is a physical ache inside of me. I had no idea that I could become so attached to someone in such a short period of time. But I promised Wes I'd go tonight, and I can't stay in the past forever. I miss my parents. I miss Hannah. And of course, I miss my grandfather.

Leaving the Bentleys, especially Mary, will hurt. If only there was a way to bridge these two time periods so that I could have all of the people I love in one place.

I pull on the clothes I arrived in: tattered Levi's jeans and a thin button-down shirt. I grab the file I stole from Faust's office and the file Wes gave me and tuck them both inside my shirt.

I glance at the clock next to Dean's bed. It's almost time for me to go, but I find that I can't just run away. I have to at least say good-bye to Mary. I slip into the dark hallway and knock quietly on her bedroom door. "Who is it?" I hear her whisper through the thick wood panel.

"It's me. I need to talk to you."

"Come in!" Her voice is hushed and excited. I press

my lips together, hating how much I know I'm going to disappoint her.

I ease the door open and shut it softly behind me. Mary is sitting on the twin bed closest to the window. The lights are out but the blackout curtains have been pulled back, and the full moon illuminates the room.

"I couldn't sleep either." Mary giggles, but when she sees my face, her smile fades. "Lydia, what's wrong?"

I cross the room, to sit next to her on the bed. "There's something I have to tell you," I start.

"Okay," she says slowly.

"You're not going to like it."

"Lydia, you're starting to scare me. Why are you dressed like that? What's going on?"

"I have to leave." I say the words quickly, afraid I won't be able to get them out.

"What are you talking about?" She laughs softly.

"I'm leaving here. Tonight."

She shakes her head. "You're not."

"I am. I'm so sorry."

"But I don't understand; this is your home. Why would you leave?"

"I have to go. I wish things could be different, but this isn't my home. Not really."

"What are you saying?" Her voice rises, and she reaches forward to grasp my arm. I gently pry her fingers off me and take her hand in mine.

"Mary, I don't think we'll see each other again."

"Why? Tell me why, Lydia."

"I'm . . ." I turn away from her, looking out the window at the shadowy lawn. In the far corner I can see the dark mounds of Mrs. Bentley's garden. I think of the dirt slipping loose and dry between my fingers. "I'm eloping. With Wes."

"Really?" She squeezes my hand in hers, her voice dropping to a whisper.

I nod. "Really."

"You can have the wedding here, though. We'll have a big party and everything." She smiles tentatively.

I look away. "No, we need to go now. Wes is getting shipped out. There's no time."

"So get married quick and then stay with us when he goes." She's so insistent, so eager. I knew she would be, but somehow it makes it worse. I wish that I didn't have to lie to her again.

"We want it to be private, just us. Neither of us has any real family. We want to make one together. And I'm going to . . . train as a nurse and follow him overseas. Like you. You inspired me." And it's true. I've never met anyone like Mary before. She's so open and bright and vibrant, and I hope I take a little bit of that with me when I leave.

"But we'll write. Come back after the wedding," she pleads.

I blink away the tears that threaten to fall. "I'll try."

"Lydia, I don't want you to go."

"I know, but I have to."

She sits back, tears gathering in her eyes. "Wes is really the one?"

I think of how it felt to kiss him in the woods and it's easy to say, "He is."

"So you fell in love with a soldier and now you're running off with him. You really are like the Lydia Bennet in *Pride & Prejudice*." Mary smiles, though I see the tears streaming down her cheeks in silver tracks. I smile back, tasting salt on my tongue. And we sit there in the moonlight, crying and smiling at each other.

"If you have to go, then you have to go." She struggles with the words. "Though I wish you wouldn't."

"I know." I squeeze her hand again. "Will you tell your parents that I left, and why? That I said thank you—for taking me in, and trusting me when they didn't have to. And that I'm sorry I'm leaving like this."

"I will."

"Thank you for believing me from the beginning. You fought for me, and I know that's why your family helped me."

"I knew you were trustworthy." She smiles. A familiar guilt settles in my stomach, as heavy as stone.

"Mary." I hesitate, searching for the words. "You're going to be happy. In the future. You'll get what you want . . . I know it."

"Are you a fortune-teller now?" She laughs a little.

"Something like that." I look over at the clock near her bed. Only a few minutes till midnight. Time to go.

"Will you let me climb out your window?" I ask.

"Of course."

"I'll miss you." My voice cracks on the words.

"I'll miss you too." She leans forward and I rise to meet her, and the two of us hug tightly and don't let go for a long time.

"You're wrong, Lydia," she finally says. We stay locked, our cheeks pressed tightly together. "You *do* have family. You have me."

CHAPTER 19

Wes is waiting for me a few yards down from the Bentleys' driveway. He sees my face and doesn't say a word as he opens the passenger door of the army jeep. I slide into the vehicle and clench my hands in my lap. I hardly pay attention as Wes gets in and starts the engine. Instead I gaze back at the Bentley house, the windows black and hidden. "I can't believe I'll never see them again," I say softly. Wes brushes his fingers against mine before he shifts into gear and pulls onto the road.

We drive through the streets in silence. I don't want to talk and am consumed by thoughts of what I'm leaving behind and what awaits us in the Facility. Wes keeps glancing at me, sensing my dark mood. Finally he pulls over, parking on the side of the road just out of town.

"Why are we stopping?"

He turns to me. "Are you okay?"

I press my lips together and shake my head.

"I'm sorry that you have to leave them." His voice is low. "But this isn't your time. You're not supposed to be here."

"I know." I take a deep, shaky breath. "But knowing that doesn't make it any easier."

He watches me try and collect myself. "I don't know what it's like to have a family." His voice is so quiet I barely hear him.

"You don't remember your mother at all? Or your father?" I turn to face him.

"Sometimes I think I do. The sound of a woman's voice. Arms around me. But who knows if it's even real." His face changes, hardens. "They're gone now, and I'm alone. I do what I have to in order to survive."

"You're not alone anymore." I reach out and touch his hand. He flips it over, so that he's cradling my fingers in his.

"I can't remember the last time another person was kind to me."

My heart is in my throat as I listen to his words.

"I live in the Facility. I have no friends. I don't even have my own bed . . ."

"Don't you have anything that belongs to you?" I ask.

He hesitates, then pulls away from me. He reaches into the collar of his shirt and tugs out something gold. It's a pendent on a chain, and he slips it over his head. "Just this."

I pick it up from his outstretched hand. I'm holding a small gold pocket watch. The decoration is plain, a leaf border and thinly etched lines. I notice that the time is frozen at a few minutes after four o'clock.

I turn it over in my hands. The moon is bright through the window of the jeep, and I can just make out the inscription on the back: *With Love, WLE.*

"What does this mean?" I ask, rubbing my thumb over the tiny letters.

He shakes his head. "I don't know. I've had it for as long as I can remember."

I look at him in surprise. "They let you keep it? When you were taken?"

"No." He pauses, and I know the memory isn't one he's comfortable with. "I wasn't wearing it when they took me. One of the first round of sessions I had was on forgetting my past. Anytime I remembered my old life they would . . ." He doesn't finish.

"What?"

He looks away from me, his eyes shadowed. "You don't want to know, Lydia. And I don't want you to."

My stomach turns over as I picture the room full of lost children, knowing what will happen to them, if it hasn't already.

"I'm sorry." I squeeze the watch in my hand, more determined than ever to get to Dean and stop the Recruitment Initiative. I can't save Wes from his memories, but I might be able to save others from the same fate.

"Training lasted two years," he says. "Once that phase was over, they started to send us on missions. I started time traveling. I would report back to a scientist or general in one time period and then I'd need to do something else. The head scientists stay connected to each other by using the recruits as their go-betweens."

"Throughout all of time?"

"Certain periods are more active than others. I've never traveled past twenty fifty, or before nineteen fifty." He looks at me. "At least, I hadn't before you."

I smile.

"After I was doing missions for a year, they sent me to New York to find out what would happen if some small event was changed. I don't even remember what it was anymore. But I was out doing reconnaissance when I realized I was near my old home in the subway station. And I just thought, if I go down there, no one will know."

His eyes are sort of glazed, and I know he's reliving it: the fear, the thrill rushing through him. I touch his arm in an effort to bring him back to the present. He jerks a little and his eyes clear. "I went in and got the necklace and I've kept it ever since," he finishes quickly.

"A moment of defiance."

His gaze locks on me. "One of them," he says slowly.

I feel my cheeks heat up, but before I can ask him what he means, he takes the watch from my hand and lifts the chain back over his head, tucking it beneath his shirt again.

"We need to go." He glances at me one more time before he starts the engine and pulls out onto the road.

When we're close to Camp Hero, I crawl into the back of the jeep, pulling an oil-stained blanket over me. I listen as Wes speaks quietly with the guards, and then we rattle and bump through the uneven roads of the base. In what feels like no time at all, we've reached the south side of the park.

I stay still and silent as Wes pulls the truck over. His door opens and closes, and in a few moments he's yanking the tarp back. I blink and take his hand when he offers it to me.

We jog through the trees until we reach the vent again. "It's the quickest, safest way in," he tells me as he pushes the heavy metal covering aside.

This time Wes drops down first, and catches me as I lower myself after him. It's dark and musty inside. I take shallow breaths. The smell of bleach and acid hangs in the air.

Wes leads and I follow. Somehow he's graceful even when he's crawling through an air duct. The thought makes me smile.

We're only inside for a few minutes before he stops over a metal grate. He yanks it up and shoves it to the side, then lowers himself into the hole. I follow, trusting him to catch me as I fall.

The room isn't lit, and it's hard to see where we are. I sense Wes standing in front of me and I step closer to him. From the smell of cleaning supplies, I would guess we're in a supply closet, and I wonder briefly if it's the one I ran into by mistake a few days ago.

"Why are we here?" I whisper.

I feel, rather than see, Wes walk to the door. "The vents don't access Dean's office. I discovered that when I snuck in to get you that folder."

Wes opens the door a crack and light spills into the small room. He motions me forward.

The hallway is empty, and we inch along the side, keeping close to the wall. I hear the sound of a door opening, and Wes puts his hand out, stopping me. I hold my breath. We stand there, frozen and listening, but no one comes.

We continue through another door and down a short flight of stairs. I think I might recognize some of the hallways we pass through, but it's hard to tell—everything looks the same. White concrete, gleaming metal doors, wide tiles covering the floor. We pass through another door. Pause to wait for a sound of footsteps to pass. Go. Stop again. Go. Another door.

Sweat glides down the center of my back, and my hands shake against my sides. We enter a silver corridor that I know I've never seen before. The floor, the ceiling, everything is metal. Dozens of doors line each side.

I jump when I hear the sound of someone moaning. I think it's coming from one of the doors near me and instinctively turn toward it. Wes shakes his head and grabs my arm. He leads me down the hallway and out into another white hall. "What was that?" I whisper.

"Cells," he replies under his breath.

I shudder. We turn a corner and then Wes points to a narrow door on the right. I step forward, but Wes pushes me gently behind him. He opens the door to Dean's office quickly and slips inside.

Dean is hunched over a large desk with his fingers pressed against his temples. The room around him is gray and bare. I notice that he's wearing a black uniform that matches those of the other guards in the Facility.

Dean bolts upright when he sees Wes. "What—"

He notices me and goes still.

"Lydia. What the hell are you doing here?"

"Dean." I step forward. Wes stays by the door, keeping watch. "We don't have much time. I need to talk to you."

"What's going on?" he demands. "Who are you?"

There's a gun lying on the surface of his desk. Dean's fingers twitch. Wes has his eyes glued to the weapon.

I take a step forward. "I'm here to warn you. I know about the Montauk Project. And about the Recruitment Initiative. It's not what you think."

"You *are* a spy." Dean's face twists; his voice is grim.

"No. I'm a time traveler. And I'm your great-granddaughter."

His mouth falls open as I tell him about stumbling into the time machine and ending up in 1944.

"Peter is my grandfather. I'm a Bentley, and I have

something really important to tell you."

His face is white, ashen. "Prove it."

"What?"

"If you are who you say you are, then prove it."

My mind races. "How? I can tell you something that happens in the future, but you won't know if it's true or not yet."

"Tell me something about Peter. Something only he and I would know."

I desperately try to think of a memory involving both of them. "He hates peas," I blurt. "He's always hated them, because he said that once you made him canned peas when his mother wasn't home and that he put cold butter on them to try to make them taste better, but they turned into cold gray-green mush. You wouldn't let him get up from the table until he finished. After that he couldn't eat them without throwing up."

Dean's eyes widen slightly. "How do I know he didn't tell you that story in the past few days?" Though I might have shaken him, he isn't convinced.

"He has a scar," I say frantically. "On his stomach. His appendix ruptured when he was only three. It's in a straight line, next to his belly button."

"You could have seen that anytime."

I look helplessly at Wes. He meets my eyes briefly. There's a steadiness in his eyes that makes me start to think more clearly.

I turn to Dean. "There's a cubbyhole in Peter's room. Under his bed. He doesn't think anyone knows about it. It's where he hides his treasures. There's a red tin box with a picture of a bear on the top. He's only ever shown it to you after you gave him a picture of yourself."

Dean is silent, his green eyes wide.

"Look, you can argue with everything I say, but here's the truth: you disappear forever. Tomorrow or today, I don't know anymore."

I shake my head, frustrated. "Peter grows up without a father. At first I thought you were going on the Project Hero mission to kill Hitler."

He looks at me with surprise, but I ignore him. "But then I found out you're the one who runs the Recruitment Initiative. So now I don't know *how* you disappear, I just know it happens. You need to be careful, Dean."

He drops back down into his desk chair and buries his face in his hands. "You came to tell me I'm going to die."

I take another step forward. "I came to warn you."

He looks up. His face seems to have aged in an instant; the grooves near his mouth look deeper; his eyes are drooping at the corners. "Is that all?"

I exchange a glance with Wes. "No. It's about the Recruitment Initiative."

Dean stares at me. "How do you know about this?"

"I . . . broke into the Facility. I had to do it, Dean—I had to know if you were connected to the Montauk Project like my grandfather always suspected."

He presses his fingers to his temple. "I knew you were trouble," he mumbles.

Wes makes a small sound under his breath and I turn to glare at him. He raises an eyebrow.

I turn back to Dean. "I'm not trouble," I insist. "I'm here because of Peter."

"My son," Dean breathes. For the first time since I entered the room, he doesn't look like he's about to lose it. "Tell me about him. What kind of man is he?"

I close my eyes, picturing my grandfather. "He's kind and he's funny. He married young, but he always says it's because he found the love of his life, and why would he wait around to be with her forever? And he had a son, my dad. They have a hardware store in Montauk. Grandpa always helps me with my homework, even when I can tell he doesn't want to. He makes the best lasagna. And he always has a million things in his pockets."

Dean chuckles. "That sounds like him."

"He's the most important person in my life." My voice cracks and I blink as tears gather behind my eyes.

Wes steps forward and rests his hand on my shoulder. I reach up and touch his wrist gently. His hand tightens on mine before he lets go. I straighten and look back at Dean. He's lighting a cigarette, though his eyes are wet.

"Grandpa spent his whole life searching for you," I say. "He's *always* looked for you. When I came to nineteen forty-four I knew I had to give him a chance at a life with his father again. So please take my warning seriously."

He watches me for a moment and then nods gravely. "I will."

Relief is like a warm blanket. I haven't failed my grandfather. I haven't failed the Bentleys.

Dean stands and takes a drag of his cigarette. Smoke fans out through the small space. His eyes are thoughtful as he watches how Wes stands protectively behind me.

"Who is he?" he asks, pointing his cigarette at Wes. "Did he come with you?"

"No, but—" I step forward. "There's something else I need to tell you."

"I don't think I like the sound of this." He goes to sit on the edge of the desk, then motions at me to continue. "All right, out with it."

"The Recruitment Initiative isn't what you think it is."

"I created the Recruitment Initiative. I know what it is. We find volunteer soldiers and civilians to travel in Tesla's Machine. We're perfecting the science, and we're sending people on missions to try to change certain historical events."

"That's not all." I tell him about the kidnapped children, about the torture and the brainwashing. I watch his face get darker and darker and I breathe a little easier—he didn't know.

He stands straight, his cigarette abandoned. "You're saying that the RI eventually starts . . . using children?"

I nod. "They learn that children travel more easily,

and so they start kidnapping them for training. It's already happening, Dean."

"No." He shakes his head. "I won't believe that's true. I can't believe that the program would be used like that. We're trying to build something good here. We're trying to learn more about the TMs so we can protect—maybe even save—our world. Dr. Faust and General Lewis wouldn't condone that. Faust was Tesla's protégée. They created the TM together. Faust has devoted himself completely to the Project since Tesla died last year. And General Lewis is a good man, a good soldier. We're doing good work here."

His voice gets firmer as he speaks, and I know he's convinced himself that he's right, that I must be wrong about what the Project becomes.

"I saw the children," I say desperately. "I've seen what they're doing to those lost kids already."

Dean's eyes narrow. "Show me."

Walking through the halls of the Facility with Dean is an entirely different experience. He has an air of authority that I know means he's important down here, and the guards stand aside for us as we pass. Even if our presence arouses suspicions, Dean doesn't seem to care. He wants us to show him the children. Now.

Luckily Wes knows his way around the Facility enough to remember where the room is. I'm already lost as we move through white hallway after white hallway. We walk for a minute when Dean says, "This is the scientists' wing. I don't come here often." The way he says it makes me think he's starting to believe that something isn't right.

Wes stops in front of an unmarked door. Dean glances at me once before pushing it open. It leads to a small room. The three of us step inside.

We walk into a high, narrow observation area. It has one long glass wall that's angled toward the ceiling; the only light comes in through the window. The rest of the space is empty and dark.

The window looks down onto an open room. Dean approaches it slowly, almost fearfully. I follow him, but Wes stays near the back wall. Just like the other day, the space is filled with tiny bodies. Dean is silent as he stares down at the gaunt, broken faces.

Suddenly he runs to the door and rips it open. "Guards!" he shouts. A man in a black uniform appears in the hallway. "Get the doctor and the general. Now."

The guard dashes down the hall. I step back until I'm standing next to Wes. His hands are clenched into fists at his side, and I know that being in this room, so close to those children, is killing him. I brush my hand against his, and his fingers unfold, wrapping around mine.

Dean paces the room. Every once in a while he looks at me and shakes his head, like he can't believe what's happening. I gaze at him with sympathy, but I don't know how to make this better for him.

The door opens. The doctor I saw through the vent enters the room, his stocky frame wrapped in a white lab coat. Behind him is a straight-backed, barrel-chested man in uniform. He's older than both Dr. Faust and Dean, with a wide, heavily wrinkled face and a gray mustache. General Lewis.

Dean sees him and salutes automatically.

"At ease," the general says quickly. His voice is gravelly.

The three men look at one another. Dean seems manic, practically vibrating as he faces down the other men. Wes and I stay against the wall, our hands clasped together. Wes is tense, and I wish I could tell what he's thinking.

"What the hell is going on here?" Dean finally asks. He sounds like he's about to start screaming.

"This is not for your eyes," Dr. Faust says. I can place his accent better now that I'm not hearing it through a vent: German, I think. Strange. The upward tilt of his mouth makes him look almost pleasant, but his eyes are tiny and shrewd.

"You both knew." Dean's voice is filled with accusation. "How could you do this?" He stalks to the window and slaps his palm against it hard. The sharp sound makes me flinch, and Wes squeezes my hand in his. "Those are *children* down there. This is not what I built with you."

The general still hasn't spoken. He looks at Dean thoughtfully. Dr. Faust steps forward. "The small children are better equipped for the machine, we think. They will travel more easily and your men won't die anymore. You should be pleased."

Dean's face turns red. "Pleased? You're torturing these helpless children and you think I could be *pleased*? When was the last time they were given food?"

Dr. Faust glances at the window. "Before they are ready, they must be conditioned."

"Jesus." Dean breathes. He turns to General Lewis. "You pulled me out of the field to come work for this project. You said it was close to my home, that I'd be near my family. You told me I would be making a difference. You ordered me to start a Recruitment Initiative, and I built it from the ground up. I thought we were doing something good. I thought you were a good man."

The general's mouth is a narrow line under his heavy mustache. "There's a difference between being a good soldier and good man, Bentley. I'm a decent man, but I'm a great soldier. A soldier does what needs to be done to protect his country, no matter what. I thought maybe you had that in you. I was wrong."

"Protecting one's country doesn't mean taking advantage of its most vulnerable citizens." The fight seems to have gone out of Dean and he slumps forward.

"Sometimes it does." The general steps to the side.

Wes goes still and quickly looks toward the door. He angles his body so that I'm behind him.

"Take them," the general says without emotion. "Take them all."

Guards storm the room. The general and Dr. Faust stand

back, watching passively. Wes moves forward in a blur. He kicks and a guard falls. Dean throws a punch and a guard stumbles against the window. Another guard comes for me, his arms outstretched. I back up, and as soon as I have an opening, I kick him hard in the leg. He grunts and falls to his knees. I kick him again, in the side this time. He curls up, moaning. But as soon as he's down, another guard is there. He wraps his arms around me and I struggle, punching and kicking and biting any part of him I can.

I see Wes trying to reach me, but three guards swarm around him. My attacker yanks me up against him and pulls a knife out of a loop on his belt. He holds it to my neck. "Wes!" I cry out, and the man squeezes me tighter.

Wes and Dean both freeze. There's a pile of fallen guards at their feet, but at least ten more guards pour through the open door. Wes lets himself be grabbed, his eyes on the knife pressed against my skin. Dean lets go of the guard he's been fighting and puts his hands up slowly.

The general steps forward. "Lock them up. We'll figure out what to do with them later."

Wes catches my eyes, a dark flash. It only lasts a second before the guards pull us from the room.

CHAPTER 20

"*What* about the reptoids?"

"What?"

"The reptoids. I just remembered them. Are they real? Can Tesla's Machine connect to distant planets?"

Wes turns to look at me. We're both sitting on the small bed in the shared cell the guards threw us into. They dragged Dean off toward another cell and we haven't seen him since.

Wes smiles but doesn't answer. He's sitting on the edge of the bed with his feet planted on the ground; I have my back pressed to the wall, my legs stretched in front of me.

"What?" I nudge him with my foot. "I really want to know."

"I know you do. It's just funny."

"If I think about everything else, I might lose it," I say quietly.

He touches my leg. "Reptoids are not real. At least not that I've ever seen."

"Thank you."

We're silent for another minute.

"Wes?"

"What?"

"Do you think this is my fault?" I can't keep the anxiety from creeping into my voice.

"No."

"But if I hadn't gotten involved, maybe Dean wouldn't be in a cell right now." Then I voice the fear that has been gnawing at my chest since we were thrown into this cell. I almost don't have the courage to say it. "Maybe the reason he disappears is my fault and it always has been."

"Lydia." Wes shifts, turning to face me. "You are not the reason Dean is in this situation. He made a choice to get involved in the Project. He knew the risks."

"If I had just left it alone . . ."

"Then something else might have happened to him. Maybe he would have found out about the recruits on his own. You can't predict what could have been." He puts his hand on my knee. "There's not some big, preordained plan that says you're meant to kill your great-grandfather. Trust me."

"You don't believe in fate?"

"I believe in choices. You made the choice to help your family. Dean made his choice. Don't blame yourself for that."

I tilt my head against the wall, feeling my hair drag across the uneven cement. "I guess you're right. I just wanted to be able to do this for my grandfather. And for you. I wanted you to be able to get out of the Project."

Wes presses his hand against my knee.

His black jacket is torn at the shoulder, and I can see part of his upper arm—lean muscles and lightly tanned skin. There's a small, circular scar on his bicep. It reminds me of the one I've always had on my shoulder. I open my mouth to ask how he got it, but I'm interrupted by the sound of a man screaming. There's a dull thump, a crack, and a long, low moan that seems to go on and on. Wes and I both tense as we listen to the noise.

Finally it stops, and I shiver in the silence. "What do you think they're going to do with us?" I ask softly.

"I don't know." He keeps his voice carefully blank. "I don't think they'll kill us outright. They might send us through the TM. Maybe to some earlier time so we can't get back."

My stomach drops, but I force myself to smile at him. "At least we'd be together."

Wes sits up straight, an intense expression on his face. Suddenly I can no longer ignore the questions I've been avoiding about Wes and me: What happens once this is all over? How can we ever be together?

"Do you mean that?" He says the words carefully.

"Yes," I say without hesitation.

He stands and faces me. He looks down, then at me, then away again. "There's something I need to tell you."

I pull away from the wall. "What is it?"

"It's about why I followed you here." He picks a spot on the ground and keeps his eyes trained on it as he speaks.

I'm silent, waiting, wondering. A little afraid.

"I've seen you before. I saw you in the woods that night."

"What?"

"The night before you stumbled into the bunker, I was patrolling outside the Facility and I saw the light from the bonfire. I went to investigate, and then I saw you standing by a car."

"It was you. You chased me." My voice is sharp as I remember running through the trees, knowing something was bearing down on me.

He shakes his head, still intent on that one spot. "I didn't. I just watched you. You were thinking so hard about something, it was like nothing else existed. But then you looked at the exact place I was standing. Right at me. It should have been impossible; no one could have known I was there. But you did."

"I felt you watching me," I admit quietly.

He's silent for a moment. "I should have killed you when I saw you in the TM room." His whole body is still. "Those are our orders. We shoot to kill any civilian that somehow finds a way into the Facility. No one can know that the Montauk Project exists. It's the first thing you learn in training."

He pauses, as if he's gathering his courage. "When I first saw you, my instincts kicked in. I was going to kill you. And then I saw your face." His voice gets softer, lower. "I recognized you immediately, and it made me pause—I couldn't believe that you were the same girl from the night before. You had these huge green eyes. I'd never seen a color like your eyes. I could see how scared you were of me, but I also saw how angry and determined you were. I could *see* you thinking, plotting, trying to get out of the situation. I'd never seen anything like you."

"Wes—" I try to catch his eye, but he won't look up.

"I don't see a lot of good in my world. The other recruits are all like me. Empty and hard."

"You're *not* like that," I say harshly. I see his mouth tilt up, but he still won't look at me.

"I don't even have a name. I have a number. I'm Eleven. There were dozens of Elevens before me and there will be dozens of Elevens after me. As soon as I die, the next recruit will inherit the number. Wes was my name before they took me, but you're the first person to call me that in six years. You're the first person I've told."

I want to go to him, to touch him, but I don't want to break the flow of his words. It's as though the dam that started to crack earlier in the jeep has now fully burst, and

Wes can no longer contain what he's feeling. So I stay still, my knuckles turning white as I squeeze my fingers together tightly.

"I saw you in that moment and it was like you were lit up from the inside. Then you fell into the machine, and I didn't think. I just went after you. I've never done anything like that before."

He shakes his head, then lifts it suddenly. Our eyes meet. "Going back for the pocket watch was my first act of defiance. You're the second. If anyone knew I was here, we'd both be killed."

I press my hand to my mouth. I can't believe the risk he took in finding me again. "This whole time you've been—"

"I'm not good . . . at expressing how I feel. What I felt has never mattered before. I've been trying to learn over the past few days." He says it as if feelings are a course you can study up on.

I smile and scoot to the edge of the bed until my feet are touching the floor. "Wes, you're one of the most sensitive people I've ever met. They didn't take that from you. They could never take that from you."

He falls to his knees in front of me. I can smell him, like the deep forest in the rain.

"I don't know what's going to happen tonight," I say. "But if we make it out of here alive . . . then I want you to come home with me."

He makes a noise in the back of his throat and tries to turn his head away. I grab both sides of his face and look into his eyes. "You can get away from this life for good."

When he speaks, his voice is as jagged as broken glass. "They'll find me, Lydia. You and your family would be in danger."

"You've been in the past for almost a week now and no one has come looking for you. How do you explain that?"

"I don't know. I've been waiting for them to come. It's one of the reasons I've been trying to get you out of this time period."

"But no one *has* come, Wes. That's my point."

"It doesn't work like that." He reaches up to take my hands. He gently pulls them away from his face and holds them clasped between us. "They might not even know I'm missing, because to them I never went anywhere. If I travel back to the exact same time I left, then it's like this never happened."

I raise my eyebrows. "Wouldn't that be fate? I thought you didn't believe in it."

He gives me a half smile. "Not fate. It will be my choice to go back; I just haven't done it yet." His smile fades. "But the point is that it's impossible to hide from the Montauk Project. It's an organization that has informants all over the world, across all of time. I can't expose you like that. I won't."

"I just want you to have a chance at a normal life." I

close my eyes, take a breath, and take a chance. "And I want to be with you."

His hands tighten on mine. I open my eyes slowly. He's staring at me, his mouth slightly open.

"I've never felt this way about anyone before. I didn't know I could feel this way. I think . . . I'm falling in love with you, Wes."

His eyes are liquid black. He pulls me against him. My arms wrap around his neck and then his lips are on mine and he's shifting me even closer, one hand hard on my hip, the other curled into my back.

He tears his lips from mine and kisses my cheeks, my chin, my eyelids. I bury my face into his neck. "I can't lose you," I whisper against his skin. "You have to come back with me."

"The guards are coming," he says hoarsely, pulling away. I'm sitting on his lap, not quite sure how I got there. He lifts me to my feet as the door swings open, hitting the opposite wall with a bang.

The guards grab us roughly by the arms and yank us into the hallway, two men escorting us each. We're pushed down a long corridor and through a doorway. It's difficult to see where we're going; the overhead fluorescent lights are dimmer than they were before, as though a dark film has come down over the entire Facility.

Wes and his guards are somewhere behind me. I know

he could easily overpower them and I wonder why he doesn't. Then I realize he's probably trying to protect me from getting hurt in the struggle that would follow.

The guard holding my arm turns a corner and stops so fast that I run into him. He opens a door on the right and shoves me inside. I stumble forward and catch myself on a low desk. I hear a shuffle and turn to see Wes pushed in behind me.

I straighten from the desk. Wes is already beside me, and he wraps an arm low around my waist. I glance around as I lean into him. We're in a small, dark place and I recognize it immediately: the two-way-mirror room looking down onto the time machine. Wes and I are alone in here—the two doors on either end have guards stationed outside of them.

I'm trying to figure out why they brought us here when I see lights flicker through the tinted window in front of us. Guards in black uniforms and scientists in white coats filter into the time machine room. There's a flurry of activity as the monitors are turned on and the guards position themselves strategically. We can't hear what's happening in the opposite room, but we can see everything.

Dr. Faust enters. His white lab coat flaps open as he rushes to one of the desks. A wide, rounded screen is mounted to the back of it, and a large keyboard sits in front. Faust hits a button and the lights dim. The glass top of Tesla's Machine starts to flash and spark. The dull metal body vibrates and hums.

General Lewis enters the room, followed by two guards. They're dragging Dean between them. He looks barely coherent. He's been beaten badly, and I wonder in horror if he's the man we heard screaming in the cell. I jerk forward, and Wes follows, keeping his arm curled around me.

"They're sending him back in time," I whisper.

Wes doesn't respond. He doesn't have to. It's obvious what's going to happen, and we can't do anything to stop it.

Dean lifts his head with visible effort and turns to face the two-way mirror. I freeze. He seems to know that we're behind the glass, though I have no idea how. He bobs his head up and down, and tries to smile. Red blood drips from the corner his mouth, falling to the white floor. He's mouthing a word at us, but I can't see what it is. I lean forward.

"Peter," Wes whispers into my ear. "He's saying Peter."

I press my hand over my mouth. Tears start to fall down my cheeks.

Dr. Faust says something to the guards holding Dean, then points to the machine. The guards drag Dean forward. He can barely move, but he still tries to twist away from their hold. It's no use—they relentlessly push him into the TM. He falls down and collapses on the floor of the machine, no longer struggling.

One of the scientists pushes a button and the silver doors of the TM slide shut. Dean disappears inside. The room quiets as the lights dim again. A low, throbbing light starts shooting out of the glass top. It builds and builds, until it's a continuous swirl of color, hovering just over the machine.

I suck in a breath. Wes tightens his grip and I turn into him, so that my back is to the time machine room. I picture my grandfather as a little boy, telling me about his father, the war hero. My grandfather the man, reading to me from his father's diary. This is the moment it all starts and ends.

Even with my face against Wes's shoulder, I feel it when he goes. The room fades to black, everything seems to freeze, and then there's a pulsing flash of light, bright enough to burn.

I slump down to the floor of the observation room. Every time I close my eyes I see Dean's battered face trying to form the word "Peter."

I hope that means he doesn't blame me for what happened. Maybe, in the end, he was just happy to know that his son would grow up to become a good man.

Wes crouches next to me. "We need a plan to get out of here alive."

I swipe at the tears on my face and sit up. "What are you thinking?"

"They didn't kill Dean, which means they're not going to kill us. They'll take us to the TM." He sits back on his heels and peers over the bottom ledge of the two-way mirror. "There are three scientists in the room, including

Dr. Faust. Then there's the general and five guards. The scientists won't fight. They don't care about us; we're just guinea pigs to them." He looks back at me. "I can take out the guards. The general is the only wild card."

"I'll distract him," I offer.

Wes is silent for a moment, watching me. "Okay. But be careful. I don't know what I would do if something happened to you."

"I will," I say. "But you need to be careful too. Swear it."

He smiles slightly. "I swear."

"So what happens after we take out the guards? Can we both travel in the TM?"

He shakes his head. "Not at the same time. You'll go first. I'll program it to the exact same time and date you went through before—June 15, 2012, at 5:09. I'll make sure I'm programmed to arrive at least ten minutes before that time. With any luck, this older TM won't malfunction."

My heart races. "What happens if it does?"

"Don't think about that," Wes says. He leans down to look me in the eye. "The important thing is that I get to the future before you do. The Facility in twenty twelve isn't like it is in nineteen forty-four. There aren't any air vents to crawl through. There are alarms and cameras everywhere. If you travel back there on your own then they'll kill you the instant you step out of the machine."

I put two and two together. "You're going to create a diversion."

He nods. "I'll cut the power and open the door to the bunker. The TM doesn't need power to run—it uses natural magnetic energy. You'll have exactly four minutes to get through the Facility and out of the bunker."

Wes is creating the diversion to get me out of the Facility on the exact day and time that I discovered the open bunker. Which was only open because he created the diversion in the first place.

I was lured in by a disturbance that was originally created to get me out. A self-fulfilling prophecy.

"Do you remember how to get out of the Facility through the bunker?" Wes asks.

I think of all those identical white walls, and I shake my head.

"Remember this: right, left, door, right, door."

"Right, left, door, right, door."

"Good."

"Wes." I take his hand. "What about us? Are you coming with me?"

He's silent for a beat, then gently pulls away from me. "Someone needs to make sure you get through."

"Then after. Create the diversion and come find me."

But he won't answer. I try to ignore the sinking feeling in the pit of my stomach.

There's a scratching sound at the door and it starts to open. Wes stands quickly.

General Lewis is in the doorway holding a small gun. He

looks at Wes. "I've seen you fight. You know what you're doing. But you have a weakness."

He points the gun at me. "The girl. You don't want her to die. So play nice."

Wes stiffens, his eyes on the gun. The older man gestures us forward. Wes holds out a hand and pulls me to my feet. I press into his side as we approach the doorway. As soon as we're close enough, the general grabs my arm and puts the gun to my head. Wes breathes in sharply.

"Walk," the general says.

We leave and walk to the door leading into the time machine room. Wes opens it and instantly moves to stand by my side. The general tightens his hold on me but doesn't comment.

Wes was right about who's here. Five guards are scattered at different points, and two young male scientists sit in front of the monitors.

Dr. Faust approaches us. "The machine is almost ready," he tells General Lewis.

"What's the date?" The general cocks his head toward the metal tubelike structure.

Faust grins, revealing small, slightly pointed teeth. "Nineteen twenty. Same as Bentley. Did you find out who these two are?" He nods at Wes and me.

"Don't care," the general replies. "They're dead anyway."

The doctor gives us a curious look, but the general is impatiently eyeing the TM in the middle of the room.

"Let's get this going," he says.

Wes is silent and watchful. I look at him. He senses my gaze and turns his head. When he gives me a tiny nod, I know I need to be on alert.

Dr. Faust approaches one of the monitors. General Lewis pushes me forward.

I feel Wes's fingers brush against my side and then he's gone. He chops his hand across the general's forearm and the gun falls away from my temple. It clatters to the floor. But Wes is already flying across the room. He kicks a guard in the chest, jabs another in the neck, and throws a third against the wall. All three slide to the floor. It takes less than a minute.

The general jerks next to me. He lunges for the gun. I kick his right knee and he stumbles. I throw myself onto his back. We both fall, and the general's head hits the floor with a hollow thud. His body goes limp. I sit up cautiously, but he's definitely out cold.

Wes has already incapacitated the final two guards, one of whom had a gun. He picks it up off the floor and spins in a slow circle, stopping when his eyes find me. He scans my body for injuries. Once he sees that I'm all right, he points the gun at the two younger scientists, huddled against the desks. They're both slight of build, and both shaking as they stare at the gun in Wes's hand.

"Leave," he says softly. They scamper from the room. Dr. Faust stays. During the fighting he didn't move at all, but I noticed that his eyes never left Wes.

"I said leave. Now."

"You are one of them," he whispers. "You're one of the trained children. I can see it in your movements." He looks Wes up and down as though Wes is a science experiment he'd like to take apart. "You are what they can all become."

He grins, and I recoil at the sick look in his eyes.

"Leave or I shoot you in the face," Wes says, refusing to react to the doctor.

Faust reluctantly moves to the door, glancing back at Wes one more time before he finally exits.

Wes locks the door behind Faust. The room is filled with the fallen bodies of the guards and the general. Wes ignores them all as he strides over to one of the monitors. "We don't have much time. Faust will get more guards and they'll break the door down. You need to go, now."

He presses several buttons. The lights start to flash and a loud humming noise fills the room. "It's time, Lydia!"

I hesitate. So does Wes. He steps forward until he's standing right in front of me. Grabbing both of my shoulders, he leans down and kisses me hard on the mouth. It only lasts for a moment before he pulls away. I gasp, and his hands rise to trace the edge of my cheeks.

He looks into my eyes, then closes his tightly. He turns away. "Get in." His voice is strained as he points toward the TM.

"Wes, wait." I practically have to shout over the noise of

the machine. It sounds like an industrial fan. "When will I see you again?" I grab his arm.

He frowns. Colored lights from the machine flit across his face in strange patterns. "Lydia, you need to go."

"No. Please." My voice is breaking, cracking. "I don't want to leave you."

"Lydia—" There's an even louder noise and I stop, confused. Wes lifts his hand to his shoulder. It comes away red with blood. I turn to see General Lewis sitting up and holding a gun.

Wes is shot.

I hear Wes shouting as I launch my body at the general. I catch him by surprise, sending us both flying to the floor. I roll over and punch him hard in the face. It hurts my knuckles, but I don't notice. I hit him again and blood starts to trickle from his nose. He grunts and puts up his hands.

I'm pulled off of him. Wes drops me on my feet, leans down, and smashes his gun onto General Lewis's temple. The older man slumps back to the ground.

I scramble to my feet and help Wes peel his black jacket away. I push his undershirt to the side and examine the wound. The bullet passed cleanly through his shoulder, and a small stream of blood flows down his chest. I press the material of his shirt into the hole as I try to stop the bleeding.

"I'll be okay," he whispers. "You need to go now."

"How?" I'm crying, and the tears falling from my eyes make it difficult to see. *"I can't leave you like this!"*

He winces. "You have to. It's the only way you'll be safe."

"What about you?" I grab his waist with both hands. "Tell me you'll come with me. Please. We could go to nineteen twenty. We'd be stuck there, but at least we'll be together. They could never find you. *Please,* Wes!"

"Lydia." His voice is soft. "I won't do that. Think of your family. Think of your life."

I open my mouth, but he shakes his head before I speak. "I could never do that to you."

The bloodstain blossoms on his shoulder.

"So that's it? We never see each other again?"

His eyes are black as he smiles at me. "There's no way it can work, Lydia. Maybe someday . . ." He reaches out and tucks a piece of hair behind my ear. "We'll just have to leave it up to chance."

I choke, trying not to sob. "I thought you said you don't believe in fate."

He looks at me through half-closed eyes. "Maybe I'll start."

He leans down until our foreheads are pressed together. I close my eyes, breathing him in.

"Go," he says softly. I feel him press something into my stomach. I glance down, surprised. It's his gold pocket watch. I didn't even notice him take it off.

"Take it. I want to know that my two moments of defiance are out there somewhere together."

I pry my fingers from his side and close my hand over the metal, still warm from his body. Then I step away, backing up until I reach the machine. I slip inside and turn to face him as I pull the watch over my head. It swings across my chest. I rest my hand against it, pressing it into my heart. "We're fate, Wes. I know we are."

He smiles, deep enough that I can see the dimple in his right cheek. Our eyes meet and hold. We don't break eye contact. Not even as he backs away, not even as he pushes the button.

The door slides shut, and the machine closes around me.

CHAPTER 21

When I can think again, I'm huddled on the floor, panting and clutching my sides. I slowly rise to my feet. I have only four minutes to get out of here.

The door automatically slides open, and I stumble out of Tesla's Machine and into chaos. Red, blinking, throbbing light. A screaming alarm. It's all strangely familiar, as though the last six days never happened, as though I'm still curiously, naively, wandering down into the depths of Camp Hero.

I cross the empty room and enter the hallway. It's deserted, the guards off to address the security meltdown. I run quietly down the hall, following Wes's directions: right, left, door, right, door. Finally I'm back in the dirty hallway with the dark staircase that leads to the camp outside.

I hear a noise above me and I sink into the shadows behind the stairs. Someone is walking down slowly. I watch as the figure emerges, dark red hair blending into the shadows behind her, a black-and-white shirt tucked into jeans, and my mouth falls open. It's *me*. I'm walking into the Facility for the first time, running my fingers along the sticky wall, smelling that odd mixture of bleach and battery acid, and wondering what I'll find at the bottom of these black stairs.

I can stop her. I lean forward as she passes me. As *I* pass me. I'm ready to call out, to warn her. But I pause. This week I was almost killed. I failed to save Dean. I couldn't recover my grandfather's lost childhood. But I also met my great-great-grandparents. I found a sister in Mary. I uncovered the truth of what was really behind my great-grandfather's disappearance.

And I fell in love.

I want to be a journalist because it forces you to face the truth, even if it might not always be easy. I have to believe that the same is true in my life—that the truth is worth knowing no matter what. I can't hide from what happened in the past. Dean is gone. But I refuse to let what I had with Wes disappear—I don't ever want to forget what it feels like to fall in love, even if that love is an impossible one.

So I'm silent, watching as this inquisitive girl, face curious and open and nervous for what she might find, glides past me. She steps through the door at the end of the hallway, and then she's gone.

I emerge from behind the stairs and begin to climb out of the darkness and into the light of the open bunker. I hurry through the split in the concrete. It's raining outside, just as I remember, misty and damp. My sweater is where I left it, a soggy, wet ball on the ground. This day hasn't changed at all, but I know I have.

I turn back to the concrete as it starts to groan, creak, and then slide shut.

I wonder where *I* am, if I'm in the time machine room, if I've run into Wes, if I'm already in Tesla's Machine, or in 1944.

I touch the watch hanging at my chest. Wes is down there somewhere. He'll become a recruit again, a slave, holding on to the memories of the second time he defied the Montauk Project. But I know that it's not over. That *we're* not over. I'll see him again one day.

I walk through the park, down the paved roads, past the buildings that crumble once again. The radar tower is a rusted cage on the skyline. I follow it toward the parking lot near the bluffs.

There's a tall figure leaning against the old Honda, the ragged cliffs of Montauk Point behind him. I start to walk down the hill and then I'm running, ready to fling myself at my grandfather. But I slow when I realize that it's not my grandfather. It's my father.

"Dad." I lean forward to hug him and he puts his arms around me hesitantly, as if he's surprised by my actions. I can see the ocean spread out over his shoulders, the waves breaking against the rocks below, forever seeking the shore. I breathe deep, knowing I'm finally home.

"Lydia. Have you had your fill of exploring the camp? Your mother is expecting us for dinner." He pats me on the back awkwardly before pulling away.

I scan the parking lot. There are a few cars but no other people. "Sure, I'm ready to go. But where's Grandpa?"

Dad pauses with his hand on the door handle and looks at me. "What are you talking about, Lydia?"

"Grandpa!" I smile. "Where did he go? Is he at home?"

My father gives me a strange look, half confused, half smiling. "Your mother's father is upstate, where he lives."

"Dad, stop kidding around." I laugh nervously. "Where's Grandpa? You know, your father, who lives with us?"

"Lydia." I've never heard my father's voice sound so empty. "You know why he's not here."

I shake my head. Dread spreads through my body, numbing every part of me.

"Tell me," I whisper.

"Your grandfather disappeared over twenty years ago."

ACKNOWLEDGMENTS

Thank you to the team at Full Fathom Five, especially James Frey, for believing in me from the beginning, and Jessica Almon, for being a constant source of support. Thanks, too, to Eric Simonoff and Matt Hudson, who represented the series.

Thank you to everyone at HarperCollins, especially my editors Tara Weikum and Sarah Dotts Barley. You both made what could have been a painful process of revisions surprisingly easy and fun, and knowing that you have my back through the next two books is a huge relief.

I couldn't have written a word without the help of my friends: Christina Rumpf, Asher Ellis, Mike Murphy, Jeramey Kraatz, Starre Vartan, Murwarid Abdiani, Michelle Legro, Jessica Hindman, and Jordan Foster. Thanks for listening to all the rants, taking me where I needed to go (in more ways than one), and generally putting up with me! You're the best group of writer-friends a girl could have, and I fully expect to be in the acknowledgments of your books as well.

And most importantly, I need to thank my entire large, loud, crazy family for their unending love and support. To my grandmother, Virginia: Thanks for giving me a firsthand account of life in the forties. This book would not be nearly as detailed without your help. And to the core of it all, Mom, Dad, Mary, and Emma: Thanks for the love, the honesty, and the refuge in the woods.